D1087803

The Ghosts Of Who You Were

Short Stories by

Christopher Golden

Haverhill House Publishing

THE GHOSTS OF WHO YOU WERE

Cover design and setup by Errick Nunnally

ISBN-13: 978-1-949140-28-6 Hardcover
ISBN-10: 978-1-949140-29-3 Quality Paperback

Haverhill House Publishing LLC
643 E Broadway
Haverhill MA 01830-2420

www.haverhillhouse.com

The Ghosts Of
Who You Were

In memory of my mother,
Roberta Ann Pendolari Golden Poulos,
who always said I could.
April 6, 1936 – February 22, 2021

STORIES WITHIN

ACKNOWLEDGEMENTS

I'm grateful as always to Connie, forever my best friend, my light and laughter, and to our children, Nicholas, Daniel, and Lily, who are now all grown and each of whom brings me joy every day. Thanks to my literary agent, Howard Morhaim, for his faith and keen eye, and to my manager, the indefatigable Pete Donaldson. I'm grateful to the editors who originally bought these stories, John Joseph Adams, Douglas Cohen, Ellen Datlow, Jonathan Maberry, Mark Morris, and Ed Schlesinger. Thanks, also, to the great John McIlveen at Haverhill House for publishing this book, to Peter Bergting for the gift of his hauntingly beautiful art for the cover, and to Errick Nunnally for his design expertise. Gratitude is due to my family, by blood and by marriage, especially my sister Erin Golden and my brother Jamie Golden. Finally, thanks to all of the friends who are there when I need a sounding board, a kick in the ass, or a good laugh, and who help keep me sane.

THE GHOSTS OF WHO I WAS
AN INTRODUCTION

Cards on the table—I'm not a short story writer. Yes, the collection you hold in your hands contains a bunch of short stories and a novella that all bear my byline, so technically I am a writer of short fiction. But of all the writing and editorial hats I've worn in my career, it's always been clear to me that I'm a novelist first. If you go back and take a look at my first collection, *The Secret Backs of Things*, you'll certainly read a number of stories that will make you think I should have stuck to novels. But I do love the short story as a narrative form, and it's my sincere hope that you'll agree that I've gotten better at it over the years.

The first inkling I had that maybe I had turned a corner with short stories came when "The Bad Hour" was nominated for a Bram Stoker Award. It woke me up a little. I'd written that story in a blur of depression, anxiety, and insomnia, in the middle of a ten month period during which I took Ambien to sleep every single night. Yes, every night for ten months. But John Joseph Adams had asked me to write a story, and up until then, I honestly didn't think I was the sort of writer John asked for a story. Later, Ellen Datlow would select it for The Year's Best Horror Stories, which shocked me even more deeply.

I wrote "The Bad Hour" in a single day. I polished it up the next day and sent it off to John. He accepted it, which of course made me think he just needed to fill a slot, and then I basically forgot all about it. Remember, I hadn't had an undrugged night's sleep in months by then. Eventually, my wife and I would have dinner at the home of our friends John McIlveen and Roberta Colasanti, and Roberta would give me some advice about how to manage my insomnia with nothing more than calming words and good intentions, and to my intense relief, I slept that night unaided for the first time in nearly a year. I'm still so profoundly grateful to her for that.

When, much later, "The Bad Hour" was nominated for the Stoker, I was shocked yet again. Unsettlingly, I had zero recollection of the time I spent writing the story. I only vaguely recalled what it was about and never imagined it could be good enough to get any real attention, never mind awards consideration. I had to go and read the story to remember more than just the basic gist, and when I did, I thought maybe I had the makings of a decent short story writer.

You'll find "The Bad Hour" in the following pages, along with nine other stories and my southern border vengeance novella PIPERS. In the end, it's up to you to decide if I've learned anything about writing short stories over the years, but I truly hope you enjoy these. Each of them represents a snapshot of the kinds of things haunting my imagination when they were written. I believe an author's short stories always do that, giving a small glimpse into the dreams and nightmares at play in that moment. I was having a conversation with someone months ago, trying to figure out a way to communicate the advice I hoped they would take. "You've got to leave the ghosts of who you were behind," I said. People always joke about having a separate stomach for dessert, so no matter how full they are, they still have room for something sweet. Writers have a separate brain for moments like this, so no matter how focused we're supposed to be, we still have room to make note of something sweet. *Leave the ghosts of who you were behind*. I thought that was pretty good and I wrote it down.

When talking about my second collection (much better than the first), I said something about how an author's collection is sort of a strange map of the writer's life—as I said above, the things we were intrigued by, frightened of, focused on, dreaming about, and the things we thought might make nasty little twists for the reader. *The ghosts of who you were* seemed to echo that. An author's stories are just that, and it's nice when you get to bundle them together like this and put them behind you, like a parent marking the wall to show how tall a child has grown as the years have passed.

Anyway, that's enough philosophizing for now. In the back of this book, you'll find notes about the rest of the stories. For now, come along and help me put my ghosts to rest.

--Christopher Golden
Bradford, Massachusetts
30th May, 2021

THE ABDUCTION DOOR

You've probably seen the abduction door, maybe stood right beside it and never understood the kind of danger you were in. Might be you never even noticed. That's the way it works. You step onto the elevator and it's just there, no explanation, as if there's nothing at all out of the ordinary about a smaller door set into one wall of the elevator. Not at the rear of the box—like in a hospital, where most of them have sets of doors at the front and back. The abduction door always appears on one of the other walls, illogical and even absurd. The door is too small for a person to walk through, roughly three square feet, and about eighteen inches off the floor. Of course, even if one wanted to go through that door, it doesn't make sense, does it? The only thing that could possibly be on the other side is a wall or the open elevator shaft.

That's true, isn't it?

Of course it is.

When I was a boy, my father did his best to teach me to be brave, but to him "bravery" consisted mostly of ignoring fear. My mother disapproved. She taught me to trust my fears, to explore the shuddery intuitions in life. But even my mother had her limits. Even she told me that my fear of the abduction door was silly and childish.

I wonder what she would say now.

Mostly, I suspect, she'd be screaming.

I'm fairly certain that I was nine years old the first time I noticed the abduction door. That would've been 1986. My parents had taken me to New York City for the Macy's Thanksgiving Day Parade. I'm an only child, so they spoiled me rotten in those days, and I loved every minute of it. When I think back on that weekend, so many images cascade through my mind—the crowds of people lining the sidewalks in Times Square, the massive character balloons floating overhead, the marching bands and floats and Santa waving directly at me, the orange scarf my mother wore, my father's cold-reddened cheeks... so many. But the image that remains the most vivid is my second glimpse of the abduction door.

Not the first glimpse, because with the first glimpse I felt only curiosity. It was the second glimpse that etched a lifelong terror into my mind, the way some things can only manage to do when you're nine years old.

My parents always blamed the bellman, a true New Yorker named Cyril. In his red and black uniform, skinny, sixtyish, white-mustached Cyril seemed almost a part of the hotel itself, as if he'd stepped right out of the lobby wallpaper and would slide back into it when his shift ended for the night. We'd gone out for our Thanksgiving dinner and returned to the hotel—I don't remember the name, but it doesn't matter now, does it? The abduction door isn't there. Not in any predictable sense, anyway. The point is that we'd come back from dinner and Cyril had one of those wheeled carts filled with somebody's luggage and we were all waiting for the elevator together.

I'd noticed the abduction door on our way out to dinner—not before that, though we'd been up and down the elevator half a dozen times since checking in.

Cyril looked wise to me. Old and wise, somehow more a part of the place than the younger people behind the registration desk.

"What's the little door for?" I asked him.

"Say again, kid. What's that?"

My parents shared the smile reserved for mothers and fathers who believe fully in the precociousness of their children and assume that everyone will find their offspring charming.

"The little door in the elevator, on the side. Where does it go?"

Cyril didn't smile. It's important for you to understand that. He didn't smile, he didn't wink at my parents, he didn't crouch down with a popping of arthritic knees or smooth his moustache. His brows knitted together and he glanced at the elevator doors. Above the elevator, the numbers were counting down toward L.

"Started working in hotels in Manhattan when I was still in high school," Cyril said. "In those days they still had elevator operators in some places. This one old fella called it 'the abduction door.' Said kids got snatched right in the middle of their elevator rides... sometimes grownups, too."

I stared at him, forgetting to breathe.

"Hey," my dad said. "That's not okay, man. He's only nine. Kids his age, they believe all that stuff. Tell him it's just a story."

Cyril smiled then, but his eyes were dull and glassy, like doll's eyes—like he wanted to do anything but smile. "Course it's just a story. Sorry, little man," he said to me. "Don't mean to scare you. All these old hotels have creepy stories—ghosts and stuff—but that's all they are. Stories."

He smoothed his moustache now. Glanced away from me. I knew he was lying.

"Do they ever come back?" I asked.

"Stop," my mother said, but I wasn't sure if she was talking to me or Cyril.

"Funny you should ask," the bellman said, and now he leaned on the baggage cart, one foot up on it like the stalwart hero in some old movie. Relaxed and confident, and so I knew the next words would be the truth. "About a month ago—no word of a lie—I'm waiting on the elevator and the doors open and this boy runs out. Little kid, couple of years younger than you. He's scared out of his wits and he grabs onto me and won't let go. Says he got away. Someone grabbed him in the elevator but he got away from 'em. Thing is, we got security cameras on every floor, right? None of the footage showed this kid getting on the elevator, not on any floor. He just appeared on the elevator while it was moving, then jumped out when it hit the lobby."

I could hear my heart drumming in my chest. My mother protested and my father got in between me and Cyril, threatening his job. I think maybe dad even grabbed him by the red lapels of his uniform until mom pulled him away. Cyril said he was just trying to erase what he'd told me about the abduction door, figured the story about the little boy escaping would put it right. My father muttered about him being a fucking psycho. When the elevator door dinged, all four of us flinched.

My dad pointed at Cyril. "You can take the next one."

Cyril held up his hands in surrender, but once my parents and I had gotten into the elevator and the doors were closing, I heard the skinny old bellman finish his story.

"Crazy thing was when they tracked the kid's parents down, they found out he'd vanished from a hotel elevator in *Pittsburgh*," Cyril said. "Figure that one out."

The whole ride up to our floor, I stared at my feet. My parents fumed, determined to call the front desk and raise holy hell about Cyril's behaviour, but I barely heard a word that passed between them. Their fury washed over me, but I kept staring at my feet until the elevator reached the tenth floor and juddered and squealed to a stop. For a breathless moment, it seemed the doors would not open, that we would be trapped inside, suspended, waiting to fall.

Something creaked over my left shoulder. I peeked, and I saw it there. Just a glimpse, through the screen of my father's arm and my mother's purse and the shopping bag in dad's hand. The abduction door.

You can imagine how fast I got the fuck off the elevator when the doors finally slid open.

A quarter century later I'm in Los Angeles with my wife and daughter. We don't live here. Nobody lives in

L.A., not really. Tori and I have moved around a lot in the nine years since Grace was born. Some of that nomadic spirit sprang from me being relocated for work, but several of those moves came because Tori couldn't stand to remain living in communities where she'd humiliated herself so badly. Alcoholism and bipolar disorder make hideous bedfellows, but Tori has them both. She fights that two-front war valiantly and most days she wins, but on the other days things get uglier than you can imagine.

Or maybe you can imagine, after all. If so, I'm sorry for you.

At nine years old, Gracie has seen and heard things no child should see or hear. Doubtless she's got a little maelstrom of love and hate churning inside her that she can't even understand, but somehow she's the sweetest, kindest, gentlest kid you'll ever meet.

Even today, when Tori had a schizophrenic break while we were shopping on Third Street Promenade in Santa Monica, and started screaming at a woman busking on a street corner, convinced that the woman was an alien insect creature—one of millions invading our world—and that her song had taken control of our minds. Tori thought she had to get us away from the music, and monitor us for behavioral changes, and kill us if we showed any sign of alien insect control. Out of mercy, you understand.

The doctors at UCLA Medical Center explained this last part. Fortunately, Tori hadn't come right out and told Gracie and me that executing us was her fallback plan. Maybe you're thinking shit like that only happens in Oscar bait movies, and for your sake I hope you keep on believing that, I hope you never have a reason to come to terms with what can really happen during a schizophrenic break.

They put Tori on a 5150 hold at UCLA Med, which basically means they're keeping her for observation against her will, and even if I wanted to get her out of there, I couldn't. I'm told sometimes these episodes are fleeting, easily treated by adjusting medications... and other times they go on for months. Maybe forever.

By the time Gracie and I flee the hospital it's after dark. My eyes are so tired it feels like there's sand in them, and though Gracie has been a trouper, she's flagging. I can see it. The strain of having to pretend that everything's okay, having to nod earnestly and tell me Mommy's going to be all right—because that's the kind of nine-year-old she is—has exhausted her. I drive us back to the Hotel Beaumont—or just "the Beaumont" if you're a local—and let the valet make the car vanish for us. We don't talk to anyone, barely look at anyone, as we trudge through the lobby. The Beaumont has been restored so that it looks precisely the way it did in the early 1940s, in the age of the Hollywood studio system, when producers and directors met for drinks around the swimming pool in the courtyard, when aspiring starlets sunned themselves by day and sat listening to the big band in the dining room, hoping Frank Sinatra or Burt Lancaster might spot them and turn them into the next great leading lady.

Gracie and I keep our heads down. "You hungry, sweetie?"

"I'm okay, Daddy." She's too tired even to push the call

button beside the art deco elevator doors, so I do it for her.

"We could order room service."

The elevator dings and we wait for two elderly women to get off. They're so old they might well have been a pair of those aspiring starlets hoping to catch Burt Lancaster's eye. Gracie and I shuffle onto the elevator as if we're even older and I smile weakly at the thought. I punch the number seven and the doors glide shut.

Head hung, I feel the elevator moving. It shifts and rattles as if it's an actual relic of those ancient days and not just made to look like one. My thoughts are with Tori, then. All I can see in my mind's eye is the fear etched on her face, the lunatic certainty that the world is secretly infiltrated by dark forces and that somehow she can save us by murdering us. I begin to well up with tears, but I can't let that happen. Not now. Gracie needs me. Sweet Gracie, who looks so much like her mother.

"What do you say, kiddo?" I ask. "Room service?"

Nothing. Then a muffled sniffling noise that I figure means my daughter—whose very existence takes my breath away—is finally crying, overwhelmed by the horror of what's become of her mother.

"Oh, hey, Gracie, it's—" I say as I turn toward her.

Just in time to see the long, spindly arms. The filthy hands. The stained fingers. Just in time to see them drag my little girl through the abduction door. It's the matter of a heartbeat as she vanishes. I scream and lunge, reaching out to catch the edge of the little door, but I'm too late and it clicks shut almost silently. It should close with an earth-shaking clang, but that click is so quiet.

I scream her name, but only twice. All my life I've been wary of the abduction door, I've kept my distance, I've been vigilant. It waited until I let down my guard and now...

I pound at the door, dig my fingers into the crease between its halves. The metal is oddly cold and it hums with a vibration completely divorced from the rattle of the elevator. Tears are streaming down my face and my jaw is clenched and I can feel myself snarling savagely and I know that is only right. I'm savage now. My Gracie, my baby girl... she's been taken and the only part of me that's left is the animal part. The most ancient part. This is what it is to be a parent, to love a child. It's ancient and bestial, and I claw at the edges of the abduction door and I crack a fingernail and blood drips but I manage to force the fingers of my left hand into the crease between the halves of the abduction door and I start prying, and hope ignites and my tears now are tears of rage and determination.

The elevator slows. Dings. I hear the real doors, the full-size doors, start to slide open and I turn, thinking *help me, they've got Gracie.* My fingers slide out.

A thirtyish guy with too many muscles for his silk t-shirt to contain gets on. He stares at me for half a second, maybe wondering if he should wait for the next elevator. Maybe he sees my tears and my hunched posture—maybe he sees the animal in me—but it's L.A. and surely he's seen stranger things than me.

"Help," I say, and I turn back to the abduction door.

But it's gone. With the stopping of the elevator, it has

been erased.

"No," I say quietly. As quiet as the click of the horrid little door. I say it again, louder this time, and I run my fingers over the wall of the elevator, over that smoothness where Gracie has gone. I'm about to scream when I hear the clearing of muscle-man's throat and I whip my head around to stare at him.

He's wary, suspicious, but not scared. One fist is clenched. His brow is knitted, and I think he wants to help but he's also ready for trouble. Maybe those muscles aren't just for show.

"You okay, brother?" he asks.

I can't speak. Can't even take my eyes from him now. We stand like that, locked in a moment of tense possibility, until the elevator dings again. The door opens and he steps off with a single backward glance and a shake of his head. I think he mutters something like "this fucking town," but I can't be sure.

Then he's gone, and I'm alone again on the elevator.

Alone. *Oh, Jesus, Gracie.* The tears come hot and fast now and I put myself into the corner of the elevator, staring at the smooth place on the wall, and I settle in for the long haul. Waiting for the abduction door to reappear. I could call the police, but what am I going to say that anyone would believe? They'd put me in the room next to Tori's at UCLA Med, two-for-one, a special on 5150s today.

So I ride the elevator and I wait. I ride all night.

I hear the woman's murmur before I feel her touch. My

eyelids flutter and I see her standing before me, one hand still on her rolling carry-on. Dark and lovely, so neat in her flight attendant uniform, she gazes at me with open and genuine concern, the kind of real humanity that is so absent in our daily lives that it's shocking when you come face to face with it.

"You okay?"

I nod, struggling to stand upright. I'd been propped in the corner of the elevator, more or less asleep on my feet. Now I scrape the grit from my eyes and try not to release the sob rising in my chest. I nearly spill it all, nearly tell her the truth that would surely get the police involved and end up with me dragged off the elevator, but I can't get off. I can't. So I choke back the unshed tears.

"Long night," I manage, realizing how awful I must look. How exhausted and worn, like some barroom drunk who'd stumbled into the wrong hotel.

"We've all had them," she says gently, trying to reassure me with her smile. Instead her kindness only makes me want to scream.

I want to ask the time but I've drawn enough attention to myself. I figure it's early, that she's heading off to an early flight. The elevator slides downward without stopping and dings at the lobby. She gives me one last reassuring glance and steps out, and I miss her painfully, this woman who offered me a moment of comfort. I want to scream after her. I want someone to help me, please God just help me get my baby back.

The elevator closes. Ticks quietly, awaiting its next summons. A minute or so passes and there's a hum, and it's rising again. Someone else is awake besides the flight attendant, someone else headed out into the pre-dawn hours, and I think of Tori in the hospital and I know—*I know*—I can't get Gracie back by myself.

The numbers illuminate as the elevator climbs. Trembling, I exhale and lean back against the wall, and then I see the abduction door out of the corner of my eye. My keys are out of my pocket even as I turn toward it. The elevator rises and the floors pass by and I know that when it reaches its destination the door might vanish again, so I jam my car key into the crease between doors and lever it hard, not caring about the key or the car. I get my fingers in and the metal edge scrapes the skin and blood wells up but after a second the door gives way. No snap or crack or wrenching of metal, it just gives, almost like it wants to.

The elevator starts to slow. I stare at the space yawning on the other side of the abduction door, the impossible space. Where the elevator shaft ought to be is a narrow corridor, both there and not there. It moves with the elevator, disorienting because I can feel myself in motion but the view through that little door makes it appear that I'm not moving at all. The shadows are fluid in that impossible space, shifting and yet solid at the same time, so that it looks like the unfocused mist of a dream but it feels real and *Gracie's in there*, my Gracie, and if the elevator stops...

I take a breath before I hurl myself through, fingers throbbing, scraped raw and now outstretched as I fall hard to the floor on the other side. The way my elbow cracks as it strikes the floor sends jolts of all-too-real pain up my arm, but the blur of my surroundings stays the same. Real and unreal. I hear the ding of the elevator as if it's right next to my ear, so loud, but when I look up the abduction door has closed. A little smear of my blood remains in the crease.

I should be screaming. I stand and the world tilts under me and I should be screaming because none of this is possible, not with any of the mechanics of any universe I've ever been taught to believe in. I should curl into a ball and cry in terror, but that image pricks my heart and I shake off my terror and shock, because I'm not here as the child trapped in a nightmare, I'm here as the father, and it's my job to free her.

"Gracie," I say, her name a prayer, a mantra, a battle cry.

The world is all narrow corridors and strangely angled doors. The shadowed, shifting halls are filled with the smell of roasting meat and my mouth waters. My stomach tightens. It's been a day and a half since I last ate and the mist in the claustrophobic corridors is the smoke from the ovens of this jagged maze.

I nearly trip over the first one, a man in a torn and stained pinstriped suit. He's unshaven and emaciated and I think of a thousand homeless men I've treated like ghosts in my life. I've given money to some of them, bought meals for one or two, but I'm not absolved for all of the times I've passed them by. This one flinches as I stumble and skirt around him.

"Sorry," I mutter, because I can't care about him.

Gracie is here somewhere.

Just as I realize I ought to ask him about her, I see the next one. A woman huddled in an alcove in jeans and a blood-smeared sweatshirt. Beyond her, on his side, is a dirty, naked man whose filthy beard seems much too large for his withered body. A rattling wheeze comes from his chest and it's a half-second before I realize he's crying.

"Go back," says the woman in the alcove. Her eyes are full of the same gentle humanity I saw in the eyes of that flight attendant, back in the world. At least they look that way for a second before I recognize terror in her gaze. Terror and despair. Maybe that's all humanity ever was.

"Go back," she says again. "Just go."

"Whoever you're looking for," the pinstriped suit man says from behind me, "it's not worth it. Go now."

I stare at the alcove woman. At the blood on her sweatshirt and the screaming sorrow in her eyes. "It's my daughter," I tell her.

She only looks at me sadly and then turns her back, shaking, hugging herself. The naked man on the floor begins to wail and she kicks him hard in the side and screams for him to be silent. Pinstriped suit cries out that I should go back, but instead I run past them... I run past a dozen more scarecrow men and women in the coalescing shadows, the twisting narrowness of this place. I find a set of spiral stairs and I descend, forced to duck my head.

When I pause, heart pounding, I hear the whispers of children and I can barely breathe, suffocated by my own hope as I wind down the steps. The smell of roasting meat is so tantalizing that I have one hand over my tight, grumbling belly, as if my hunger is a child growing there.

At the bottom of the stairs is a smoky chamber whose floor is a latticework of glass panes, but the first step I take, my foot catches in the glass and I tumble forward onto my hands and knees, fingers plunging into the soft, warm, malleable membrane I'd imagined to be glass. It's a honeycomb of strange windows, and I peer down through the sticky mucous and I can see that each one of those panes in the latticework of the floor is not a pane but a *pen*, and inside each of those pens is a child. And below the honeycomb of stolen children is another chamber, where horrible, spindly figures move back and forth to wide-mouthed ovens whose fire—when their doors are opened—turns the honeycombed prison a furious red. The smoke wafting from those ovens makes my mouth water like nothing I've ever smelled before and I weep at the hunger and the revulsion as I see what's being placed into those ovens. I retch but I won't take the time to be sick. Instead I crawl on hands and knees above the gelatinous honeycomb prison, using the strong latticework between the pens to keep myself from sinking entirely, and I whisper her name.

Over and over, I whisper for her. "Gracie. Gracie, please. Gracie, can you hear me?"

I don't hear her answer. Instead, I look down through the cloudy honeycomb pane by pane, pen by pen, until I see her face staring back at me. She's talking but I can't hear her voice. She's crying and her beautiful face, my little girl's beautiful face, is contorted with terror, but it's her.

I've plunged my hands down through the honeycomb pane and am dragging her out before I can even ask myself if it's possible. I know it must be, and it is, and she's stinking and covered with that sticky mucous membrane, but she's in my arms. I shush her as she cries against my chest. I shush her as she turns and vomits whatever's in her belly, and I see some of that hideous honeycomb in her puke and I nearly throw up as well.

The smell of cooking flesh chokes me but I gather her into my arms and then I'm rushing back up the spiral stairs and down that corridor. Arms reach for me, those pitiful scarecrows who told me to go back, told me to give up, and I hate them now. Despise them for even suggesting it. Still they reach for me as if to stop me and I knock a dirty, sneering man aside. Others turn their backs, sobbing as if I've committed some atrocity and they can't bear to look at me. Alcove woman sees me coming and shakes her head sadly, but it's the filthy bearded man who snaps his head up, drags himself into the narrow corridor, and screams at me.

"Stop!" he shrieks. "You don't know what you're doing!"

But I know exactly what I'm doing. Gracie's warm against me and I've never been more sure of anything in my life.

"Daddy," she says. "Daddy, I want to wake up!"

My little girl thinks she's dreaming. I won't ever tell her she's been awake all along.

The pinstriped suit man doesn't move as I skirt around him, and a moment later I'm there. Half of me is convinced the abduction door will be gone, but it remains, its solidity sure and unsure, the walls themselves almost opalescent with their uncertainty about their own impossible nature. I cradle Gracie against me and touch the door. When it took her, it was warm and the metal seemed to hum, but now it is cold and silent.

The elevator. It's not moving. I'm certain that's it. If I just wait—

"Daddy, please," Gracie says, and she looks up at me and coughs and I wipe the last remnants of that stinking mucous from her lips and I know I am getting her out of here. I am getting her home.

I wait, one hand on the abduction door, not hopeful. *Certain.*

I hear shuffling and whispers and I glance over my shoulder and see them, those human scarecrows. Pinstriped suit man and filthy naked guy and alcove woman and a dozen others. Gracie catches sight of them and cries out for me again, but all I can do is hold her more tightly against me with one arm while I keep my other hand against the cold, still metal of the abduction door. I want to scream at them to stay away, those poor husks, but they're not coming any closer. They only watch us, doing nothing. Watch us with pity in their eyes.

I feel the hum against my hand as the metal of the abduction door begins to warm and I want to roar my victory at them. Fuck their pity.

With my hand against the metal I can feel the rattle and rumble of the elevator in motion. I try to jam my scraped-up fingers into the crease, to force the door from this side. I'm sure I can hear—

"Voices," Gracie says. "Do you hear—"

"I hear them." And I do, voices on the other side of the abduction door.

The hum subsides and the metal cools just a bit and I feel my hope collapsing within me, feel my certainty die. But only for a moment, because the hum returns and the metal warms and the elevator on the other side of the abduction door is moving again, but this time there are no voices.

I push and it opens so easily that I whimper with relief and tears stream down my face. Our world is there, on the other side. The elevator lights flicker a bit and I hear tinny music playing inside and I wonder if it's the same elevator or another, on the other side of the world, but I know it doesn't matter. Not a bit. The elevator is empty but moving, the numbers above the door are dinging and I don't know how long it'll stay open, so I pry Gracie away from me. She clutches at my jacket but I tear her loose and half-shove half-drop her through the open door. The sound of her thumping to the elevator floor is the greatest sound of my life and she turns, so brave now, and tells me to come on, Daddy. Come on. Hurry.

But I can't.

There's no barrier. The door remains open. Gracie's standing now, eyes wide, calling for me to come through after her but too terrified to get near the abduction door again.

I just can't. My body will not follow her. I'm wailing inside. Raging. I raise my hands but I can't make them move toward the opening again, can't make them reach through. I feel the shuffling presence of the scarecrows around me, these lost humans who told me to go back, who told me I didn't know what I was doing. They say nothing now, just watching me, part of the shadows of this nothing space.

The elevator dings as it slows to a stop, about to open.

I scream my daughter's name. Gracie cries out for me as the abduction door slams shut, and only now are my hands my own again. I pound against the door. I jam my fingers into that crease and a nail cracks down the middle and blood spills out and all I can hear is the echo of my daughter calling for me.

I put my hand against the metal. It is cool and still.

I round on the scarecrows. They've started to wander away, some muttering and shaking their heads. I grab pinstriped suit man by the lapels and slam him against the wall with such force that his skull bounces off it, but all he can do is cry and then he's sliding down the wall and I can't hold him up. I let go of his suit and he curls into a mound of sorrow at my feet.

Alcove woman hasn't wandered away.

"Please," I whisper to her.

"You took one of theirs," she says.

"No, I… I took my daughter back."

"That's not how they'll see it. You took one of theirs and now they won't set you free until you give them thirteen in return."

I stare at her. The words echo strangely in my head, no sense to them. As impossible as this place.

"Give them?" I say at last. "How the hell am I supposed to give them thirteen children?"

Her face crumples and her lips tremble. She reaches up to wipe fresh tears from her eyes. "Don't you see? That's what the door is for."

And then I do see. Her tears are not for me.

Numb, I look up and down the shifting, narrow corridor at the withered husks of people who inhabit this place and I understand. They weep not for me, not for Gracie, not even for the children. They weep for themselves because they've all done precisely what I've just done and now they're trapped here.

Give them thirteen in return.

The filthy, ragged mothers and fathers scattered up and down this corridor are all abductors themselves, now. They're monsters, stealing other people's children until they've given back a tithe of thirteen to pay for their own.

Or they're hopeless, unable to bring themselves to do it, to steal someone else's child, and they know that as a result they are trapped in this hell forever.

I scream my daughter's name.

And I wonder what I will become.

WENDY, DARLING

On a Friday evening at the end of May in the year Nineteen Hundred and Fifteen, Wendy spent her final night in her father's house in a fitful sleep, worried about her wedding the following day and the secrets she had kept from her intended groom.

The room had once been a nursery, but those days were all but forgotten. She had stopped dreaming the dreams of her girlhood years before, such that even the echoes of those dreams had slid into the shadows in the corners of the room. Now it was a proper bedroom with a lovely canopy over the bed and a silver mirror and an enormous wardrobe that still gave off a rich mahogany scent though it had stood against the wall for six years and more.

Some nights, though... some nights the tall French windows would remain open and the curtains would billow and float. On those evenings the moonlight would pour into the room with such earnest warmth it seemed intent upon reminding her of girlhood evenings when she would stay up whispering to her brothers in the dark until all of them drifted off to sleep and dreamt impossible things.

Wendy had lived in the nursery with Michael and John for too long. She ought to have had her own room much sooner, but at first their father had not wanted to give up his study to make another bedroom and later – when he'd changed his mind – the children were no longer interested in splitting up. By then Wendy had begun to see the Lost Boys, and to dream of them, and it seemed altogether safer to stick together.

That day – the day before her wedding – there had been a low, whispery sort of fog all through the afternoon and into the evening. Several times she stirred in her sleep, uneasy as she thought of Jasper, the barrister she was to wed the following afternoon. She quite relished the idea of becoming Mrs. Jasper Gilbert, and yet during the night she felt herself haunted by the prospect. Each time her eyes flickered open, she lay for several moments staring out at the fog until she drifted off again.

Some time later, she woke to see not fog but moonlight. The windows were open and the curtains performed a ghostly undulation, cast in yellow light.

A dream, she thought, for it must have been. She knew it because the fog had gone. Knew it because of the moonlight and the impossibly slow dance of those curtains, and of course because the Lost Boys were there.

She lay on her side, half her face buried in the feather pillow, and gazed at them. At first she saw only three, two by the settee and one almost hidden in the billow of the curtains. The fourth had a dark cast to his features that made him seem grimmer, less ethereal than the others, though he was the youngest of them. She had not seen them in years, not since her parents had gotten a doctor involved, insisting that the Lost Boys were figments of her imagination. She had never forgiven John and Michael for reporting her frequent visits with the Lost Boys to their parents, a grudge she had come to regret in the aftermath of Michael's death in a millinery fire in 1910. How she had loved him.

By the time of the fire it had been years since she had seen the Lost Boys. After the fire, she had often prayed that it would be Michael who visited her in the night.

"Wendy," one of the Boys whispered now, in her moonlit dream.

"Hello, boys," she said, flush beneath her covers, heart racing. She wanted to cry or scream but did not know if it was fear she felt, or merely grief.

As if grief could ever be *merely*.

She recognized all four of them, of course, and knew their names. But she did not allow herself to speak those names, or even to think them. It would have felt as if she welcomed them back to her dreams, and they were not welcome at all.

"You forgot us, Wendy. You promised you never would."

She nestled her cheek deeper into her pillow, feathers poking her skin through the fabric.

"I never did," she whispered, her skin dampening. Too hot beneath the covers. "You were only in my mind, you see. I haven't forgotten, but my parents and Doctor Goss told me I must persuade my eyes not to see you if you should appear again."

"Have you missed us, then?"

Wendy swallowed. A shudder went through her. She had not.

"As I'm dreaming, I suppose it's all right that I'm seeing you now."

The Lost Boys glanced at one another with a shared, humorless sort of laugh. More a sniff than a laugh, really. A disapproving sniff.

The moonlight passed right through them.

The nearest of them – he of the grim eyes – slid closer to her.

"You were meant to be our mother," he said.

Wendy couldn't breathe. She pressed herself backward, away from them. It was their eyes that ignited a terror within her, those pleading eyes. She closed her own.

"Wake up, Wendy," she whispered to herself. "Please wake up."

"Don't you remember?" the grim-eyed one asked, and her lids fluttered open to find herself still dreaming.

"Please remember," said another, a lithe little boy with a pouting mouth and eyes on the verge of tears.

"No," she whispered.

The hook. Soft flesh against her own. The pain. Blood in the water.

Her body trembled as images rushed into her mind and were driven back, shuttered in dark closets, buried in shallow graves.

"Stay away," she whispered. "Please. My life is all ahead of me."

She did not know if she spoke to the Lost Boys or to those images.

"My fiancé is a good man. Perhaps when we are wed,

we can take one or two of you in. He is kind, you see. Not like..."

A door slammed in her mind.

"Like who, Wendy?"

Hook, she thought. *My James.*

"No!" she screamed, hurling back her bedcovers and leaping from the bed, hot tears springing to her eyes. "Leave me, damn you! Leave me to my life!"

Fingers curved into claws, she leaped at the nearest of them. Passing through him, chill gooseflesh rippling across her skin, she fell to the rug and curled up into herself, a mess of sobs.

In the moonlight, she lay just out of reach of the fluttering curtains and cried herself into the sweet oblivious depths of slumber.

When she woke in the early dawn, aching and chilled to the bone, she crept back beneath her bedclothes for warmth and comfort and told herself that there would never be another night when she needed to fear bad dreams. For the rest of her life she would wake in the morning with Jasper beside her and he would hold her and kiss her until the last of sleep's shadows retreated.

The sun rose to a clear blue morning.

No trace of fog.

The world only began to feel completely real to Wendy again when the carriage drew to a halt in front of the church. Flowers had been arranged over the door and on the steps and the beauty of the moment made her breath catch in her throat. A smile spread across her lips and bubbled into laughter and she turned toward her grumpy banker of a father and saw that he was smiling as well – beaming, in fact – and his eyes were damp with love for her, and with pride.

"Never thought you'd see the day, did you, Father?" Wendy teased.

George Darling cleared his throat to compose himself. "There were times," he allowed. "But here we are, my dear. Here. We. Are."

He took a deep breath and stepped out of the carriage, itself also festooned with arrangements donated by friends of Wendy's mother who were part of the committee behind the Chelsea Flower Show. A pair of ushers emerged from the church, but Wendy's father waved them back and offered his own hand to guide her down the carriage steps.

George stepped back. He'd never been sentimental, and now he seemed to fight against whatever emotions welled within him. Amongst those she expected, Wendy saw a flicker of uneasiness.

"You look beautiful," he told her.

Wendy knew it was true. She seldom indulged in outright vanity, but on her wedding day, and in this dress... well, she would forgive herself. Cream-white satin, trimmed in simple lace, it had been one of the very first she had laid eyes upon and she had loved it straight away. Cut low at the neck, with sleeves to the elbows, it had a simple elegance reflected in the simplicity of the veil and the short train. Her father helped gather her train, spread it out behind her, and took her hand as they faced the church.

"Miss Darling," said one of the ushers, whose name she'd suddenly forgotten. She felt horrible, but suddenly it seemed that her thoughts were a jumble.

"I'm about to be married," she said, just to hear the words aloud.

"You are, my dear," George agreed. "Everyone is waiting."

The forgotten usher handed her a wreath of orange blossoms and then the other one opened the church door, and moments later Wendy found herself escorted down the aisle by her grumpy-turned-doting father. A trumpet played and then the organ, and all faces turned toward her, so that she saw all of them and none of them at the same time. She smelled the flowers and her heart thundered and she began to feel dizzy and swayed a bit.

"Wendy," her father whispered to her, his grip tightening on her arm. "Are you all right?"

Ahead, at the end of the aisle, the bridesmaids and ushers had spread out to either side. The vicar stood on the altar, dignified and serious. Her mother sat in the front row, her brother John stood amongst the ushers. And there was Jasper, so dapper in his morning coat, his black hair gleaming, his blue eyes smiling.

She no longer felt dizzy. Only safe and sure.

Until the little boy darted out from behind a column – the little boy with grim eyes.

"Stop this!" he shouted. "You must stop!"

Wendy staggered, a terrible pain in her belly as if she were being torn apart inside. She gasped and then covered her mouth, glancing about through the mesh of her veil, certain her friends and relations would think her mad – *again. They would think her mad again.*

But their eyes were not on her. Those in attendance were staring at the little boy in his ragged clothes, and when the second boy ran in from the door to the sacristy and the vicar shouted at him, furious at the intrusion, Wendy at last understood.

The vicar could see the boys.

They could *all* see.

"Out of here, you little scoundrels!" the vicar shouted. "I won't allow you to ruin the day—"

The grim-eyed boy stood before Jasper, who could only stare in half-amused astonishment. That sweetness was simply Jasper's nature, that indulgence where any other bridegroom would have been furious.

The third boy stepped from the shadows at the back of the altar as if he had been there all along. And, of course, he must have been.

"No, no, no," Wendy said, backing away, tearing her arm from her father's grip. She forced her eyes closed, because they couldn't be here. Couldn't be real.

"Wendy?" her father said, and she opened her eyes to see him looking at her.

He knew. Though he had always told her they were figments and dreams, hadn't he seemed unsettled whenever she talked of them? *Spirits*, he'd said, *do not exist, except in the minds of the mad and the guilty.*

Which am I? she'd asked him then. Which am I?

Jasper clapped his hands twice, drawing all attention

toward him. The unreality of the moment collapsed into tangibility and truth. Wendy breathed. Smelled the flowers. Heard the scuffling and throat-clearing of the stunned members of the wedding.

"All right, lads, you've had your fun," Jasper said. "Off with you!"

"Wendy Darling," one of the boys said, staring at Jasper, tears welling in his eyes. "Only she's not 'darling' at all. You don't know her, sir. She'll be a cruel mother. She'll abandon her children—"

"Rubbish!" shouted Wendy's father. "How dare you speak of my daughter this way!"

Wendy could only stare, not breathing as Jasper strode toward the grim-eyed boy and gripped him by his ragged shirtfront. She saw the way the filthy fabric bunched in his hands and it felt as if the curtain between dream and reality had finally been torn away.

"No," she said, starting toward Jasper... and toward the boys. "Please, don't..."

Her fiancé glanced up, thinking she had been speaking to him, but the boys looked at her as well. They knew better.

"She's had a baby once before," a pale, thin boy said, coming to stand by Jasper, his eyes pleading. "Go on. Ask her."

"Ask her what became of that child," said the grim-eyed boy.

Shaking, Wendy jerked right and left, trapped by all of the eyes that gazed upon her. Jasper frowned, staring at her, and she saw the doubt blooming in him, saw his lips beginning to form a question. Her father still glared angrily at the boys, but even he had a flicker of hesitation. In the front row, Mary Darling stepped from the pew and extended a hand toward her daughter.

"Wendy?"

Shaking her head, Wendy began to back away from those who loved her, retreating down the aisle. She tripped over her silken train and when she fell amongst the soft purity of its folds, she screamed.

"Ask her!" one of the boys shouted. Or perhaps it had been all of them.

Thrusting herself from the ground, whipping her train behind her, she ran. Her whole body felt flushed, but she caught a glimpse of her left hand as she ran and it was pale as marble. Pale as death. At the back of the aisle, a few crimson rose petals had fallen, petals meant to be scattered in the path of husband and wife after the ceremony. To her they were blood from a wound.

She burst from the church, an abyss of unspoken questions gaping behind her, and she fled down the steps in fear that if she did not run, that yawing silence would drag her back. Pain stabbed her belly and her heart slammed inside her chest. Her eyes burned and yet strangely there were no tears. She felt incapable of tears.

At the foot of the steps she tore off the train of her dress. When she glanced up, horses whinnied and chuffed. Her wedding carriage stood waiting. The driver looked at her with kind eyes and his kindness filled her with loathing.

"Wendy!"

Jasper's voice. Behind her. She dared not turn to look at him.

Racing across the street, she darted down a narrow road between a dressmaker's and a baker's shop. At a corner, she nearly collided with two more of the Lost Boys – *names, you know their names* – and she turned right to avoid them, racing downhill now. Another appeared from an alley to her left, but this boy was different from the others. He'd been badly burnt, skin and clothing charred, and unlike the rest he had no substance, flesh so translucent that she could see the stone face of the building behind him.

She wailed, stumbling in anguish, and fell to the street. Her dress tore and her knee bled, so that when she staggered to her feet and ran screaming – grief carving out her insides – a vivid red stain soaked into the satin and spread, the petals of a crimson rose.

"Mother," the burnt boy said behind her.

She did not look back, but glanced once at the windows of a pub as she bolted past. In the glass she saw their reflections, not only the burnt boy but the others as well, one with his head canted too far, neck broken, another beaten so badly his features were ruined.

Moments before she emerged from between two buildings, she realized where she had been going all along. Had she chosen her path or had they driven her here? Did it matter?

Wendy stared at the bank of the Thames, at the deep water rushing by, and all the strength went out of her. Numb and hollow, she shuffled to the riverbank.

Somewhere nearby, a baby cried.

Glancing to her left, she saw the bundle perhaps a dozen feet away, just at the edge of the water. The baby's wailing grew louder and more urgent and she started toward it.

She knew the pattern on its blanket. His blanket.

Kneeling on the riverbank, her bloodstained dress soaking up the damp, she reached out to pull the blanket away from the infant's face. His blue face, bloated and cold, eyes bloodshot and bulging and lifeless.

The sob tore from her chest as she reached for the child, lifted it into her arms and cradled it to her chest. Still she could not weep, but she pressed her eyes tightly closed and prayed for tears.

The bundle in her arms felt too light. Gasping for breath, she opened her eyes.

"No, please," she whispered as she unraveled the empty blanket. The empty, sodden blanket.

"Mother," a voice said, so close, and a hand touched her shoulder.

Wendy froze, breath hitching in her chest. This was not the burnt boy or the grim-eyed child from the church. This was another boy entirely.

Still on her knees, she turned back to see his face. Nine years old, now, his skin still blue, eyes still bloodshot and lifeless. Her boy.

"Peter," she whispered.

He thrust his fingers into her hair and she screamed his name – a name she had never spoken aloud before today. Wendy beat at his arms and clawed at his face as he dragged her to the water and plunged her into the river. She stared up at him through the water and his visage blurred and changed, became the face of his father, James, the butcher's boy. He'd earned his nickname with the bloodstained hook he used in handling the sides of meat in the shop down the street from the Darlings' home.

Her chest burned for air, the urgency of her need forcing her to strike harder at the face above her, which now became her own face, only nine years younger. The hands that held her beneath the water were her own, but she was no longer herself – instead she was a tiny infant, so newly born he still bore streaks of blood from his mother's womb. An infant conceived by a mother and father who were only children themselves, carried and borne in secret – a secret safeguarded by her brothers in the privacy of the room they shared, a secret which destroyed her relationship with them forever. A secret made possible by a father's neglect and a mother's denial.

Peter, she thought.

Starved for air, thoughts and vision dulling, diminishing, slipping away, Wendy opened her mouth and inhaled the river.

Blackness crept in at the corners of her eyes, shadows in her brain, and she realized that she had stopped fighting him. Her arms slipped into the water and her hair pooled around her face. Bloodstained white satin floated in a cloud that enveloped and embraced her.

The hands on her now were larger. A man's hands. They dragged her from the river and for a moment she saw only darkness, a black veil for a cruel mother.

"Wendy," said an urgent voice.

She saw him then. Not the little drowned boy, but Jasper, her intended. He knelt over her, desperate and pleading and calling her name.

Gathered around him on the riverbank were the Lost Boys, those cast aside children, each murdered by his mother. Those dead boys she had met once before, on the night she had drowned her Peter in the Thames, when they had pointed trembling fingers and told her she would carry the black curse of murder all her days, that she might be allowed to approach happiness but never achieve it. They were the stain on her soul. They had been visible to the people in the church, dark dreams come to life, but now they were unseen once more. Jasper wept over her, unaware of their presence...

Wendy could only watch him, standing a short distance away. Her dress felt dry now, but the bloodstain remained.

"No," she whispered, as the darkness retreated from her thoughts and she understood what she saw.

Jasper knelt there, mourning her, grieving for the life they might have had. Wendy saw her own lifeless body from outside, her spirit as invisible to him as the Lost Boys. Others began to run toward the riverbank – her parents and her brother John, the vicar's wife and Jasper's brother, an aunt and uncle. They seemed like ghosts to her, these living people, their grief distant and dull.

The Lost Boys circled around her, dead eyes now contented.

"Mother," Peter whispered, taking her right hand.

Another boy took her left hand. She glanced down and saw the grim eyes that had so unsettled her in her dreams.

"You promised to be a mother to us all, forever," the grim-eyed boy said.

Wendy blinked and turned toward the river. Somehow she could still see the swaddled infant floating on the water, sodden blankets dragging it down, just as it had on that night nine years ago.

"Forever," said Peter.

They guided her gently into the river, where the dark current swept them all away.

IT'S A WONDERFUL KNIFE

Cassie hated Christmas parties in L.A. It wasn't just the weather, though she'd grown up in Wisconsin, where snow days were more plentiful than holidays and ugly sweaters were more than just ironic fashion statements. She remembered building whole kingdoms out of snow, sledding down streets closed off to traffic, and those first romantic snowstorm kisses with her high school boyfriend on a white Christmas Eve.

Still, it wasn't the weather that put her teeth on edge at an L.A. Christmas party. It was the fakery. The festive decorations, the ornamentation, the wreaths and bows and cheery Christmas music, the unneeded scarfs and crystal punch glasses full of eggnog. So fucking fake, like so much of this city, like the smiles on these faces. Even the house they were all meandering through, this mansion in the hills, surrounded by trees and green lawns and enough land that it was hard to imagine she was still in L.A.…even the house seemed like a set on some studio backlot, like they were all extras in some faux 1950s holiday film.

James Massarsky had come up in Hollywood the way few people did these days. He'd quite literally started in the mailroom and worked his way up through the industry to become head of a studio. After a few glory years followed by one catastrophic summer box office season, he'd been bumped out to make room for the next scapegoat, put out to pasture with a producing deal. In time, he had become an independent producer with more power than most of the studio heads he worked with. Massarsky got movies made. He got shit done. But he'd earned his reputation as a ruthless, narcissistic shitbag.

Nobody cared. His reputation, his behavior, his divorces and scandals...they didn't matter. The crowd at his Christmas party laughed and drank and sang along to holiday tunes. They kissed beneath mistletoe and paused to watch curved-screens silently showing scenes from the greatest-hits of both animated and live action Christmas films. On one sitting-room screen, George Bailey stood up to Mr. Potter, and Massarsky's guests watched without a trace of irony.

"Now this is just a crime," his voice said, silky and low, as his hand glided along her back and he smiled down at her, like he knew something she didn't.

"If you mean the Pink Martini version of 'Little Drummer Boy,' I agree."

Massarsky frowned in confusion. When he laughed, she wasn't sure if he'd noticed the song playing over his sound system or if he simply discarded any human dialogue that diverged from the script in his head, as if original thoughts did not compute for him.

"I mean a beautiful girl like you without a drink in her hand," he replied. "I don't have a pink martini, but I'm sure I can get the bartender to make you one." He guided her into the corridor with that hand on her lower back, steering her. "Or anything else you'd like."

Cassie smiled. She had no choice. It was why she'd come, after all. Just like the rest of them. She'd been in L.A. for four years, been to hundreds of auditions, scored a few commercials and sitcom walk-ons, and finally starred in an indie film about lesbian parenting that got her nominated for best actress at OutFest. Massarsky wouldn't have seen it, but it made her feel like a real actress and it nudged her up a few notches on casting sheets.

Still...*Girl.*

The word did not surprise her. Twenty-six years old, but to men like Massarsky, she'd always be a girl.

"Don't you want to put your purse down? I've got someone checking coats and things."

Cassie smiled, slinging the straps of her purse a little higher on her shoulder. "It's part of the ensemble. The designer who loaned it to me made me promise to keep it with me, show it off."

Massarsky chuckled. "Don't you love this town?"

"More than anything."

She let him guide her to the vast living room, where furniture had been rearranged to make room for the bar. The windows were open to let fresh air circulate. Snowflake decorations were everywhere, but it was seventy degrees even up here in the hills. Christmas in Hollywood.

"I'll have—" she began.

"Can I suggest something?" Massarsky interrupted, and he didn't wait for her reply, looking to the bartender. "Pomegranate Martini." He glanced at her. "You'll love it."

Cassie didn't tell him she'd had one before and had not, in fact, loved it. She took the offered glass and sipped from it and smiled, and when he put that guiding hand on her back again and steered her away from the bar and deeper into the house, she went along.

The walls were decorated with decades' worth of photos of Massarsky with actors and politicians, the famous and the powerful. Always just him and those celebrities. In some of the framed photos, it was clear there had been others in the picture, people whose hands or arms or shoulders remained but who had been cropped out because their presence did not contribute to his legend. This was the kind of man Cassie had come to celebrate Christmas with.

"I didn't catch your name."

"Cassandra Ochoa."

"Oooh. Exotic," he said. "I like it."

She wondered if men like James Massarsky could tell a real smile from a fake one, and realized they probably didn't care. As with a woman's orgasm, the pretense of a smile was enough to reassure him.

"You're an actress?"

"Isn't everyone?"

"But are you a real cinephile? A real movie lover?"

"Of course."

"Old movies are my passion. I collect mementoes from my favorites, oddities and props and rare photographs."

Cassie smiled shyly. "Honestly? That's half the reason I came. My agent and her husband were coming and invited me. Normally I like a quieter Christmas with family, but that's hard these days. Kind of grim in this town. I'd read an article in Variety about your collection and it just fascinated me. Is it true you have the tooth DeNiro had knocked out filming *Raging Bull*?"

Massarsky grinned like a schoolboy. "I know, weird and gross."

"No, it's cool," she said, and touched his elbow the way she knew a thousand other actresses must have.

Balding, sweaty upper lip, pot belly, hairs growing inside his ears, Massarsky either didn't see how repulsive he'd be to most young women or he didn't care. When Cassie had arrived, she had assumed the latter, but now that she'd been in his presence for a few minutes, she had changed her mind. He had an air of confidence, a swagger more appropriate for a leading man than an obese producer careening ungracefully toward his sixtieth birthday.

And yet...something about his excitement, the sparkle in his eyes when he thought about his collection, made him seem human, like in that moment Cassie could imagine the little boy he'd once been. If nothing else, his love of movies was sincere.

He looked at his watch—only men his age still wore watches—and gave her a conspiratorial look. Late as it was, people had continued to arrive, and the boisterous laughter and chatter of his guests nearly drowned out the Christmas music pumping from the speakers.

"I keep the room locked up during parties," he confessed, with a boyish shrug. "A lot of one of a kind items in there. But if you'd like a tour..."

Cassie felt a little thrill travel up her spine. "I'd love it." Even her smile was genuine, and tonight, in the Hollywood hills, that was nothing short of a miracle.

"At some of these Christmas parties, I've taken little groups in with me, but then people get pissed that *they* didn't get a tour. Half of them couldn't give a damn about the collection, but they feel slighted or they're trying to curry favor."

Massarsky paused, eyes narrowing with suspicion. "What's your favorite old movie?"

"You mean aside from *It's a Wonderful Life*?"

"You're saying that because it's Christmas."

"I'm not. That movie makes me cry every time I watch it," Cassie said. She wasn't lying. Maybe he saw that in her eyes. "But if you mean something else, I guess I'd say *The Children's Hour* or the Gable version of *Mutiny on the Bounty*."

He smiled. "The Gable version." With a snobbish roll of his eyes, he nudged her back. "Come on. Later on, I'll show you the reel I have from the original version of *Bounty*."

"The Australian thing with Errol Flynn?"

Massarsky beamed. "You really do know your old movies. Most people know nothing about *In the Wake of the Bounty*, but I'm not talking about that. The first version was Australian, but—"

"The silent version?"

Massarsky stared at her. "Wow. That's...I don't know that I've met more than one or two other people who know that movie exists."

"It doesn't. I mean it did," Cassie clarified, "but it's lost. Like thousands of others."

"Correction," Massarsky said, "it *was* lost."

Cassie let her mouth drop open in a little 'o' of wonderment.

"This way," he said.

She hoisted the straps of her purse higher on her shoulder and let him steer her into a darkened side corridor, around a corner, past a pair of French doors that opened into a sunroom, and then up three steps into another corridor. She sipped her pomegranate martini and only grimaced a bit when she swallowed.

Massarsky tapped a code into a keypad beside the door and Cassie heard the lock click. He opened the door and stepped inside. Motion-sensor lights flickered on.

"You wanted to see DeNiro's tooth," he said.

She grinned. "That's so nasty, keeping his tooth."

"It's Hollywood history, honey."

Cassie took his arm and smiled up at him. "Show me."

The lights were low and warm, with individual illumination in most of the cases and small lamps above rare posters and artwork on the walls. The poster for *Revenge of the Jedi*—the original name for the third *Star Wars* film—hung on the wall, and she pretended that she hadn't seen it before. It was very rare. In the condition it was in, she figured it must be worth at least five thousand dollars, but compared to the truly unique props and other items in his collection, the poster was unremarkable.

Massarsky showed her DeNiro's tooth. It had yellowed, but it looked like there might still be a bit of blood on it. When he brought her over to a small case holding the prop gun that had killed Brandon Lee on the set of *The Crow*, Cassie got a chill. There were other unsettling souvenirs as well. The glove that Harold Lloyd had worn to hide his missing fingers in the 1920s, after he'd picked up a bomb he'd thought a prop while shooting publicity photos for *Haunted Spooks*. The dress Virginia Rappe had died in. A portion of the Fokker D-VII that stunt pilot Dick Grace crashed filming 1927's *Wings*.

"Dick Grace. That was a crazy one. The guy broke his neck and crushed four vertebrae, and he was back to work like a month later," Massarsky said, beaming. "They don't make men like that anymore."

"At least he lived," Cassie replied. "Some of these are pretty grim."

"That's half the fun for a collector. The macabre stuff always goes for top dollar. That and the erotic. I had one guy try to sell me a half stick of butter he claimed was from the filming of *Last Tango in Paris*. I've been known to have a kink or two, but that seemed pretty disgusting to me, not to mention impossible to prove."

Cassie wrinkled her nose. "We all have a kink or two. I'm glad you didn't buy that."

Massarsky hadn't missed that fact that she'd agreed with him about people and their kinks. He slid his arm around her and they proceeded through his little Hollywood museum more intimately after that. When they paused in front of a baseball bat from Walter Hill's *The Warriors* and the actual sword from John Boorman's *Excalibur*, he put a hand on her ass and she did not remove it.

"You have another sword. What's that one?"

"Oh, you spotted that?" He turned to look toward the far corner of the room. "You told me you didn't like the gruesome ones."

"I said some of them were pretty grim. I didn't say I wasn't...intrigued."

A shiver went through her, something dark and delicious. He must have seen it in her eyes, because he inhaled deeply and his smile widened.

"Okay. It's a great story. Maybe not the best story I've got, but fucking tragic," he said as he guided her, hand at the small of her back, toward that far corner. "You ever heard of *They Died with Their Boots On*?"

"Of course. Errol Flynn and Olivia de Havilland. God, she was beautiful."

"She was."

"So the sword is from that?" Cassie asked as they stopped in front of the glass case. The light shone up through the case, gleaming on the blade within. She tucked a lock of hair behind her ear and turned toward Massarsky, shifting her purse straps on her shoulder again. "So what's this tragic tale that goes along with it?"

He glanced at his watch, a look of pleasure crossing his face.

"Am I boring you?" she asked, putting just the right touch of petulance into her voice.

"No, no. It's almost midnight. I've got another story for you. The best one. But okay, first...The movie's this bullshit version of General Custer's life, right? Great movie, but they played it like a biopic and it's not that at all. Anyway...do you remember the big cavalry charge?"

"Vaguely, I guess. I saw it years ago."

Massarsky's smile dimmed a bit. "Doesn't matter. Point is, during the charge there were accidents. Horses went over. Three riders were killed, including an extra named Jack Budlong, who was riding right next to Errol Flynn when he fell. The guy's going down and in that split-second, he tosses his sword to have his hands free, try to break his fall."

"Don't tell me."

"The damn sword landed handle first, stuck in the mud, and the poor bastard impaled himself on it. Killed almost instantly."

Cassie put a hand to her mouth in a flutter of scandal and horror. "Oh my God. That's awful."

"I know. Great, right?"

"And that's *not* the best story you've got in this room?"

"Nope. I've got a handful of things in here connected to accidents and famous deaths, but only one actual, real-life murder weapon."

Her mouth went dry. She wetted her lips with her tongue and watched him notice. Her face flushed and she let out a small, nervous laugh. "Show me."

Massarsky reached out and touched her face, moved the same lock of hair she'd shifted before. He pressed himself against her. If he'd been a younger man, she was sure she'd have felt an erection, but there was nothing. Not yet. He bent to kiss her and she let it happen, let his lips brush hers for just a second before she bit him. Just a playful nip.

He drew back, eyes wide as he prodded his lip, then glanced at his fingers. No blood. Not this time. Cassie let him see the danger in her smile and Massarsky nodded in approval.

"I did say we all have our kinks," she reminded him.

He grinned, then glanced at his watch. "We'll get to your kinks. But I promised you this story. I'll keep it short. The clock's ticking."

"What does time have to do with it?" she asked.

Massarsky turned toward another case, two down from the sword that had killed the unlucky horseman. This case was smaller, and empty.

"There's nothing in it," Cassie said.

"That's not strictly true."

She moved closer, and realized he was right. At the back of the case was a small wooden object, some sort of display stand—though there was nothing on display. Flat on the bottom of the case was a photo still from *It's a Wonderful Life*, a shot of a very scruffy, wild-eyed Jimmy Stewart.

"Were you robbed?" she asked, turning toward him. "I mean, I told you it was my favorite, but what am I missing?"

Massarsky's eyes clouded. "I've been robbed, yeah. A few years back. But it wasn't this case. Inside this case is the greatest thing that's ever come into my collection."

"You said a murder weapon. I see a photograph."

He stroked her neck, ran his hand along her back and over her ass. "You'll never believe me." His voice deepened. "Not at first."

Cassie sighed impatiently and glanced toward the door. He saw that, too. For a man with his reputation, James Massarsky seemed to notice a great deal, even if his attentions were mainly focused on his precious collection and wanting to fuck her.

"This is your favorite movie," Massarsky began. "So I know you remember this scene."

"Of course. This is in the alternate reality, where George Bailey was never born. He and Clarence go into the bar, but it's like a nightmare version of what it used to be. Even the bartender's horrible. The angel orders a Flaming Rum Punch. I remember that because I tried it once."

Massarsky looked impatient now, glancing at his watch again. "So here's the story. The girl who played Violet, Gloria Grahame...rumor had it she was sleeping with a guy named Tommy Duggan at the time, and got him a job as an extra on the film. He's in the background in a few scenes, just barely there. No lines, nothing, but if you had a picture of Duggan and you freeze-framed your way through the picture the way I have, you'd find him. They mostly cut him out."

"Cut him out? An extra? Why would they bother?"

Massarsky grinned. A shark's grin. For the first time, she was nervous.

"This scene...they shot it on Christmas Eve. Trying to get it in the can before they broke off for the holidays. They were shooting late. Understand that Duggan had a reputation as a tough guy. Maybe he did some work for organized crime or maybe people just didn't like him. Either way, in the midst of that crowd scene, when they're all jammed around George Bailey and Clarence the Angel, the camera drifted past Duggan and then he was out of the frame. It was midnight when that happened. Exactly."

Cassie felt her throat tighten. Her heart had begun to race. It seemed colder in the room than it had before.

"What happened at midnight?"

"Someone stabbed Duggan in the back, nicked his spine and punctured a kidney and twisted it. Thing is, in a room full of people, everyone was focused on the main actors, so nobody saw who did the deed. There were four or five people close enough to Duggan to have stabbed him and the police had suspects, but they could never prove a thing. Duggan fell on his face with the knife sticking out of his back. A dozen people were staring at him, saw the blood starting to pool. The guy playing Nick the bartender started swearing—Henry Travers, who played Clarence, remembered that. They were staring at that knife...and it just vanished."

Cassie shuddered and stared into the case. She wanted to touch the glass, reached out to do so, but then hesitated. Massarsky kept these things sparkling clean and she didn't want to mark it up.

"That's not possible," she said, though she knew her voice sounded hollow.

"I didn't think so either, but I've shown this case to people on Christmas Eve at least half a dozen times. They all see it. They think it's some kind of trick, some fucking smoke and mirrors David Blaine bullshit, but it's real."

Cassie frowned. "Go on."

"We've got maybe a minute before midnight. When the clock strikes twelve on Christmas Eve, you're going to see that knife appear, right there in the case. For sixty seconds, exactly. One minute. And then it's gone for another year."

Entranced, she stared into the case. "Where did it come from?"

"I've heard a dozen stories, most of them about magic and deals with the devil, but it's all just myth-making as far as I'm concerned. Maybe one of those stories is true, but I'll never know which one. And it doesn't matter. The best part of the story is the murder of Tommy Duggan."

Cassie exhaled. Reached back and took Massarsky's hand. "You show this to people every year? And it's really there?"

"Not every year. Not last year."

"What happened last year?"

He squeezed her hand. "I met someone who...distracted me before midnight."

Cassie grinned at him. "Bad boy, James. You find yourself a distraction every Christmas Eve? Is that all I am?"

He moved closer to her, kissed her neck from behind. "Of course not." This time she thought she did feel something stirring against her back. Maybe his age hadn't completely unmanned him yet, or maybe it was the Viagra talking.

"Actresses, I bet," she said. "You make them promises, right? Isn't that the game?"

Massarsky stopped kissing her neck. "I help people out sometimes. Have a little fun along the way. I can see you're not naïve. You're too pretty not to know the way this town..."

"The way this town what?"

But Massarsky had stiffened, and now he shifted her aside. "What the hell?"

He glanced at his watch, then into the case. He put his hands on either side of the glass, peering inside. "What the hell?" he said again.

Midnight, she thought. "Maybe your watch is wrong."

"I set it just for this," he sniffed. "Down to the fucking second." Baffled, he stared at the glass case. At the little wooden display stand, upon with nothing at all had appeared.

"I expected smoother moves from a guy with your casting couch history," Cassie said. Smirking, she stepped back from him. Reaching into her purse, pushing aside her cell phone.

Massarsky huffed. He scratched his head and stared at the case. "Get the fuck out," he said, without bothering to turn. "You were interesting. Most don't know movies like you do. But now you're just getting on my nerves."

Cassie drove the knife into his back. Stabbed deep and twisted the blade before sliding it out. He cried out and dropped to the floor, reaching around for the wound as if there was anything he could do about it. Flopping, twisting, he started to swear at her, and she stabbed him in the gut. Blood poured onto the floor, pooling around him. Cassie stepped carefully, avoiding the blood, trying to keep as clean as she was able.

He stared at the knife in her hand.

"I stole it last year, since you're wondering," she whispered. "You were fucking my friend Anita over by your precious DeNiro tooth. At midnight. You didn't get to tell your story last year. But I'd heard it before, the year before that, when I was heavier and blonder, and you had half a dozen people in here for your midnight story. You barely noticed me."

"Fucking bitch," he slurred. "Fucking..." Massarsky drew a deep breath, preparing to scream for help.

Cassie stabbed him in the throat. Blood burbled up through his lips and ran down over his chin. She smiled.

"Three years ago, it was my sister Cori in here with you. Oh, the promises you made, just to get her to open her legs. She had stars in her eyes when she came home. She told me about your collection, about this knife, called it magic. Told me you'd promised to do some magic for her career. And you did. The cell phone video you made, the one you showed to all your fucking cronies, it got her all sorts of offers. The kind of offers that made her take all of the pills in her bedside drawer. Your little game killed her. The magic you promised her."

The knife disappeared, right out of her hand, blood and all.

She didn't need it anymore. Massarsky's eyes had already gone glassy. His chest had stopped rising and falling. She went to the little bathroom at the back of the room and washed her hands, then checked her clothes and shoes and legs for blood. Most of Massarsky's friends would know his habits, know not to come looking for a while after he'd taken an actress to see his collection. They all played the game. Still, she had to hurry.

Where the knife had fallen, she had no idea. Next Christmas Eve, it would appear again, likely on the floor. But only for a minute.

She paused on her way out, just beyond the expanding pool of blood, and peered again into the glass case. For the first time, she noticed the little bone-white card set into the nearest corner, just below and to the right of the photo from the movie. She saw what Massarsky had printed there and a quiet laugh crossed her lips, followed swiftly by a whimper, as tears began to spill from her eyes.

Backing away, covering her mouth to keep from screaming, she rushed to the door, peered into the corridor, and slipped out. The words written on that bone-white card stayed with her as she fled, and she knew they always would. Massarsky's sense of humor made her wish she could kill him again. But the words on the card had been accurate, she couldn't deny that.

1946, it had said. The year of the film's release. And then four words.

It's a Wonderful Knife.

And it was. Oh, it was.

She retraced her steps to the sunroom and pushed through the French doors. The room had been decorated with ribbons and Christmas knick-knacks and the largest gingerbread house she'd ever seen. A massive wreath hung on the back door, and when she unlocked the door and yanked it open, the bells on the wreath jangled merrily.

Cassie froze, hung her head, and couldn't stop the smile on her lips as she drew the door silently closed.

Every time a bell rings, she thought.

Then she darted across the lawn, pulling off her shoes as she went, laughing to herself even as she wept for Cori. She could almost hear her sister's voice in her head.

"Attagirl Cassie," she said aloud. "Attagirl."

WHAT HAPPENS WHEN THE HEART JUST STOPS

Kayah Fallon stood in the doorway to her bedroom, eyes wide, frozen to the spot, afraid she was watching her mother die. Details whispered at the edges of her peripheral vision—the open dresser drawer, the tumble of half-folded laundry, the smell of vomit—but she could not tear her gaze away from the pain etched upon her mother's face.

"Kai?" her mother rasped, and the word snapped Kayah from her paralysis.

She rushed across the room and knelt beside her mother. Naira Fallon lay with one leg folded underneath her. Halfway to sitting, she clung tightly to the mess of bedclothes tangled at the foot of her daughter's bed, as though she'd been trying to rise but hadn't quite managed it. Some of the fresh laundry had spilled onto her lap and the rest had tumbled to the floor with the basket.

Naira tried to speak again but only managed a wheeze.

"What happened?" Kayah asked, hating the fear in her own voice. "Come on, lay down." She took her mother's right arm—the one propped on the bed—and found that her fingers were fisted in a knot of blanket. "Let go, Mom. Lay down."

But Naira seemed unable to unclench her fist. She groaned and her breath came in quick, hitching gasps.

"It hurts to breathe," Naira said.

Kayah looked around the room as if some solution—some miracle balm—might suddenly present itself. It did not. The pitiful painkillers in the meds cabinet would do nothing for whatever the hell this was.

"Where does it hurt?" Kayah asked. Stupid question. Automatic.

"My back. My chest...feels like a bear hug that won't...let go."

Again, Kayah tried to get her to lie down. She couldn't think of anything else to do. Naira's skin was clammy with cold sweat, and Kayah's brain started to pull together pieces of a puzzle she hadn't realized needed solving until now. The last couple of afternoons, coming home from her job as a seamstress, Naira had complained about pain in her back and side. She had pulled muscles on the job before, and this had not seemed much different, though a little more painful. The discomfort had made Naira's sleep restless, and this morning she'd been short of breath. Kayah had demanded she stay home and rest, even if Naira missing work might mean a day or two when they wouldn't have enough to eat. The disagreement had turned to a squabble, and the last thing Kayah had said to her mother that morning had been curt and unkind. The memory weighed on her.

Now, Kayah glared at the spilled laundry as if it were her enemy. Her mother had been restless. Washed both the city soot and the dirt and manure of the farm from her daughter's clothes. Tried to clean Kayah's room and get the laundry folded and put away. And she'd been struck down.

Heart attack, Kayah thought. It has to be.

Which meant there wasn't a damn thing she could do for her mother here in their apartment. Like some trigger had been pulled inside her, Kayah tore from her mother's side and raced from the room. The butchers at the Emergency sometimes did more harm than good; everyone knew that. But right now, they were Naira's only hope.

The apartment consisted of five rooms—kitchen, common room, bathroom, and two bedrooms—on the fourth floor of a dingy, half-empty building. Once there had been an elevator, but it had rusted so badly the smell filled the corridors, and it hadn't run since some time before Kayah had been born. Now there were only the stairs, and there was no way that her mother would be able to descend on her own, nor could Kayah carry her. She stood in the common room, a moment of indecision halting her as she glanced at the door and tried to imagine some way to drag her mother down four flights.

Impossible.

Her little sister, Joli, was two floors up, being looked after by Mimi Cheney. The old woman loved taking care of the seven-year-old while Naira and Kayah were at work, and Joli often stayed with Mimi until dinner was ready. But there would be no dinner tonight.

Kayah darted to the corner of the living room, where cracked windows looked down on the street, long unrepaired. The late afternoon sun cast long shadows, throwing much of the road below into darkness. But she heard a whoop of amusement and then a low bark of derisive laughter and she went to the west-facing window.

In the alley below, half a dozen skids were gathered around, encouraging the efforts of a seventh boy, who stood atop a small tower of rusty barrels, spray-painting a design that would've been lovely if the words hadn't been obscene. Even with the afternoon shadows, Kayah recognized most of the kids. Ever since the Cloaks first appeared, people tended to stick to their own neighborhoods. She might not roam the streets with them, but she knew their names.

She had to bang the frame to get the window to give way, and the warped wood shrieked as she dragged it upward. The late summer afternoon had turned cool and the breeze chilled her, despite the blood rushing to her face and the way her heart hammered in her chest. She stuck her head out the window.

"Quinney!" she shouted.

They all turned to look, four boys and three girls, all of them skids. Street kids. Skidmarks. The patch left on the ground when their parents tore out of town. Some of their parents had been taken rather than left, but the effect was the same. They were all orphans in one way or another.

Tynan, the boy atop the rusty barrels, twisted around to glance up at her, lost his balance, and fell back against the spray-painted wall before crashing down amongst the toppling barrels.

The rest of them fell about, laughing at Tynan. All except for Quinney, the tall, ghostly-pale ginger boy they all followed. He wore tattered denim and a ragged brown canvas jacket that had once been waterproof, he looked every inch the scavenger and future thug. And maybe he was both, but right then, Kayah needed him.

"What is it?" he asked, throwing the words at her as a challenge, even as the others kept laughing at Tynan, pointing at the paint smears on his clothes and arms.

"I need you up here, right now!" Kayah called.

The whoops were predictable. One boy patted Quinney on the back and a dark-skinned girl started to swear, obviously staking her claim on her boyfriend.

"Shut up and listen!" Kayah shouted. "I've gotta get my mom to the Emergency. I think she's having a heart attack but I can't get her down the stairs by myself."

"And you expect us to carry her down?" one of the other boys sneered. "It's gonna be dark soon."

Quinney slapped the back of his head hard enough that he went sprawling to the ground, then looked up at Kayah again.

"You know I'm not your friend," Quinney said, looking up at Kayah.

She wanted to scream. Her hands were shaking and the chill of fear made it feel like her blood had turned to ice in her veins. Was this death approaching? Did she even know if her mother was still alive, back in her bedroom?

"She made the blanket your mother wrapped you in when you were born," Kayah pleaded. "Without help—"

"Kid ain't wrong. Nightfall's coming. You want help, and I want a kiss," Quinney said.

No whooping accompanied the words this time. The girl who'd thought Quinney her boyfriend glared at him. The others grinned or stared in surprise. Tynan whistled in appreciation of the bold callousness of it.

"You son of a—" Kayah began.

"One kiss!" Quinney said, grinning, arms spread wide, as if she were the one being unreasonable.

Kayah glanced up at the eastern horizon, where the deep indigo of dusk had already begun to settle in.

"If she lives," she said.

"Done!" Quinney declared.

He turned and started barking orders, grabbed Tynan and practically flung him from the alley, and in moments, all but two of the skids—one boy and one girl—had vanished from sight. Kayah could hear them shouting at each other as they raced around the front of the building, could hear Quinney's voice as he instructed Tynan to find them a vehicle to beg, steal, or borrow.

A dreadful numbness had started to envelop Kayah. Help was coming, but somehow their imminent arrival made it all the more real. She ought to return to her mother's side; she knew that. But it terrified her to think what she might find. Her mother had been in so much pain that she had vomited next to the sprawl of clean laundry; this woman, always so proper, had lost control of her body. And it was killing her.

Kayah stared down at the boy and girl in the alley, him with curly hair and nearly black eyes, her with that dark skin and a knotted ponytail. Quinney's girlfriend. Kayah expected to see hate in her eyes, but instead she saw pity.

Strange that with all of the assaults upon her emotions in the past handful of minutes, this would be what made her cry. But the tears started then.

Shaking, she turned back toward her bedroom, thinking, *Mom.* Thinking, *don't go, please don't die.* Thinking, *she shouldn't be alone.* Then Quinney was banging on the apartment door. He'd made it up the stairs impossibly fast, or so it seemed. Suddenly time was playing tricks on Kayah.

Like ice shattering, she broke. The world sped up around her. She heard the noises of outside her window, the sounds of people hurrying to prepare for nightfall. She felt the cool breeze and heard her name called from out in the hall, and she moved. Her mother would not die tonight.

Kayah sprinted to the door, threw the lock, hauled it open. Quinney's playful swagger had been replaced by an intensity she had never seen in him before, though they'd lived on the same apartment block all their lives.

"Where is she?" he demanded.

Kayah led the way, Quinney keeping pace with her. As she hurried into her bedroom, she saw that her mother had slid to the floor after all. Naira lay on her side, skin paled to gray, beads of sweat on her face. She still breathed in quick gasps, as though each sip of air pained her, and as Kayah knelt by her again, Naira shuddered in despair.

"Stavros, grab the blanket," Quinney said.

Kayah glanced up at the skids moving around her. She knew them all. Delmar lived on nine block, but had been hanging around with Quinney and the dark, silent Stavros for years. The scrawny, tattooed girl who'd come up with them was Priya, but she looked skittish, like she'd bolt the second something went wrong.

"Get it together, Kayah," Quinney said. "We've gotta move fast."

She nodded. Who the hell was he to tell her? It was her mother, gasping and shuddering on the floor. And night was coming.

"Give me that," she said, reaching for the blanket as Stavros tried to find its corner. Kayah snatched it from his hand, snapped it open and spread it on the floor. "Delmar, take her arms."

The burly kid glanced at Quinney, uncomfortable with someone else giving him orders.

"Move it, Del," Quinney snapped. "Lady's dying."

Kayah gripped her mother's ankles, nodded to Delmar, and together she and the skids lifted her onto the blanket. The numbness inside Kayah echoed Quinney's words. *Lady's dying. Oh, spirits, no. The lady's dying.*

"Can I—" Priya began.

"Back up, Pri," Delmar said. "You ain't got the muscle."

The girl scooted backward, moving out of the way so Stavros could move in beside Kayah. Delmar and Quinney each grabbed a top corner, while Kayah and Stavros took the bottom edges. At Quinney's signal they hoisted Naira off the floor. To Kayah, her mother felt impossibly, alarmingly light, as though her life had already begun to ebb, leaving her almost hollow.

"Priya," Kayah said. "My little sister's upstairs at

Mimi's—"

"I'm gone," the girl snapped, and darted back the way she'd come, understanding immediately.

Joli would have to stay with Mimi for tonight. If they got to the hospital before the Cloaks came for them, they would be fools to do anything but spend the night there. In the morning, if all went well, Kayah would come back and take Joli off the old woman's hands.

If things went poorly...Mimi would be looking after Joli for a lot longer than one night.

"Quickly, now," Delmar said, and Kayah wanted to hit him. What a stupid thing to say. Did he honestly think she needed that prodding?

Quinney caught her eye and Kayah saw that he understood. It stilled her frantic heart long enough for her to focus on the moment, and on her mother. Kayah stared down at Naira as they hustled her through the living room, maneuvered her through the apartment door, and started down the stairs. A hundred thoughts flitted through Kayah's mind like bits of shattered crystal, each one jagged with another facet of her fear. Was it too hot, wrapped in that blanket? Would it make it harder for her mother to breathe? Would the pain of being carried down the stairs worsen her condition?

She'd seen a body wrapped in a blanket before, an old man named Antonio from down the hall. His apartment had always reeked of garlic and sickness and the smoke from clove cigarettes. But by the time Antonio had come to be wrapped in a blanket, he'd been a corpse, slung over the shoulder of his huge, slow-witted grandson.

The grandson had left Antonio at the curb with an array of metal trashcans that lined the block on rubbish day, still wrapped in his blanket. The thought made fresh tears spring to Kayah's eyes, but she bit her lip and forced them to cease. Her mother was still alive, and Kayah would die herself before she would let Naira be tossed out and forgotten like garbage. Or kill, if she had to.

As horrible as that had been—that body left at the curb, rolled in a blanket—there were worse ways to die. She refused to think about that. Come nightfall, she would have no choice, but there was still light in the sky.

Soft grunts and whimpers issued from Naira's lips as they bundled her down the stairs, turning at the landings. Stavros seemed not to care, but Quinney and Delmar both wore deep frowns of concern, and more than once Kayah saw them wince when they thought they had hurt Naira.

"Watch it, Stavros," Quinney snapped as they reached the first floor and Stavros backed through the door into the building's dingy lobby.

"I can do fast or I can do gentle," Stavros muttered. "Kinda hard to do both."

Quinney shot him a hard look. "Try harder."

A wave of gratitude flooded through Kayah. It felt ridiculous—Quinney had stuck up for his mother, not saved her life; that was yet to come—but it was something. It said Quinney didn't think her death was a given, that he believed there was a chance to save her. That meant everything.

Priya came rushing down the stairs behind them. "Mimi's got your sister, but we're losing daylight fast!"

Down below, Tynan popped his head through the building's entrance.

"We've got a truck!" he shouted, before turning to bolt out the door again. "Come on!"

A truck. Kayah burned with hope and fear in equal measure, but now she felt a new rush of strength coursing through her. Getting to the hospital before dark would have been a fantasy without transport, but now they had a shot.

She adjusted her grip on her corner of the blanket and moved with the skids toward the front door. She had avoided looking at Naira's face and now she glanced down, watching the pain moving her mother's unconscious features, as if she were asleep in the grip of some endless nightmare.

Then they were outside, the wind blasting the neighborhood's stink—a familiar odor of rust and sewage and cooking grease—full in her face. Far off, a siren blared, but she knew it wasn't coming toward them. It would be too much to hope that someone in authority would come to their aid. As dusk neared, even the police went into lockdown. The Cloaks didn't care much about badges.

"Where the hell is—" Delmar started.

A horn blared and they all turned to see the battered, filthy white delivery truck that sat half on the curb and half in the street. The big door at the back had been rolled up, and Tynan stood behind it with a case of whiskey in his arms. He hurled the case to one side and Kayah heard bottles shatter inside. There were other cases there, dozens of them, and as the wind shifted she smelled the sweet, powerful aroma of alcohol. It ran in the gutter, sluicing into an ancient, cracked sewer grating.

"Let's go!" Tynan said. "Almost ready."

Kayah, Quinney, Delmar, and Stavros practically ran toward the rear of the liquor truck, despite their burden. Naira had ceased to cry out in pain, but Kayah tried to tell herself that her mother had just fallen deeper into unconsciousness.

A tall cinnamon girl called Song stood in the back of the truck. One by one, she chucked cases of vodka and rum and whiskey down to Tynan, who tossed them aside.

"That's it!" Tynan said. "There's enough room."

He gestured, but there was no need. They all understood. Tynan and Song had cleared space in the back. Swift and careful, Kayah and the boys slid her mother into the truck. Naira's face was bathed in sweat and her breath came in shuddering little gasps that did not seem like they would be nearly enough air to keep her lungs working.

"Stop..." a voice groaned from around the other side of the truck. "You can't..."

Kayah tore herself out of the cloud of her anguish long enough to glance around the corner of the truck. The last of Quinney's little tribe—a wiry, cruel-eyed blond girl named Hope—had the heel of her boot pressed down on the skull of a bearded man in stained work clothes who could only have been the truck driver.

When the driver saw Kayah, his eyes lit up, as if he had mistaken her for someone who might rescue him. And another day he might not have been mistaken. She would have stepped in, driven the others away.

"He wouldn't let us take the truck," Hope explained.

"You can't..." the driver said. "It's gonna be dark—"

Hope she kicked him in the back of the head. "So go inside. No one's stopping you."

The man cried out and curled himself into a protective ball. Kayah noticed that one side of his face had begun to swell and his mouth was smeared with blood from the beating he'd already received. But her mother would die without transport, so sympathy and regret would have to wait for another day. And Hope was right—if he banged on doors, somebody would let him in...as long as there was still some light in the sky.

"Kayah!" Quinney called.

Delmar ran for the front of the truck as Quinney, Priya, and Tynan climbed into the back. Quinney and Tynan reached down and each took one of Kayah's hands, hauling her up after them. Stavros stood in the road with Song, watching them as the truck's engine growled to life. Hope had already begun going through the cast aside liquor cases, sorting through shattered glass to find the bottles that were unbroken. The three skids that were staying behind would go back inside, lock the building up, and have themselves a party.

With a final glance outside, Kayah felt hopelessness descend. The sky overhead bled indigo and the sun had already touched the western horizon. They would never make it. She thanked whatever god might be listening that the skids were crazy enough to try, as if running the gauntlet of dusk was an adventure that had always been waiting for them. All it had needed was the trigger, the dare that had come in the form of Naira Fallon's heart attack.

"Stand back," Kayah said, grasping the handle over her head and dragging the door down, even as the truck lurched into gear.

The door bounced upward a few inches, but Kayah forced it down again and this time the latch clanked into place, cutting off all outside light. She thought of Joli, back at Mimi's place, and was just happy that her little sister had someone to look after her from now on.

They rode in darkness, listening to her mother's ragged, shallow breathing and soft moans of agony. Five people, jammed in amongst stacked cases of wine and liquor, forced into a closeness Kayah had never shared with anyone. Touching their skin. Breathing their air. Smelling their scents. Physical intimacy, yes, but something more. Mortal intimacy. The knowledge that death waited just a breath away.

She'd never been so close to anyone, and she had never felt so alone.

Kayah held her mother's hand, searching Naira's face for signs of consciousness. The truck swayed back and forth and when Delmar took a hard turn they all had to brace themselves. Naira lay atop a rumpled mess of unfolded blanket, unmoving except when Delmar's driving made her head loll to one side or the other, her face pale as the moon.

"Is she still breathing?" Quinney asked, his voice

gentler than Kayah had ever heard it.

Kayah gave a single, curt nod, but her mother's breathing was so shallow that she held onto Naira's wrist, feeling for a pulse. It was there, but faint.

"I wouldn't take any bets," Priya muttered.

Quinney hissed at her to be silent, but Kayah paid her no attention. Quinney and his crew watched each other's backs because none of them—not a one—had anyone else to look out for them. Tynan and Quinney had no parents, while Priya had parents who didn't give a shit. Delmar lived with his junkie older sister. Kayah had always felt sorry for the skids. Though she and Naira fought plenty, she knew how fortunate she was to have a mother to go home to, someone who would never shut her out and who would love her no matter what mistakes she made. The rest of them might envy her that love, but they could never understand how much Kayah truly cherished it, or how much she feared losing it.

Tires screeched as Delmar took another sharp turn and the truck canted dangerously to one side.

Tynan banged on the wall, screaming for Delmar to be more careful. "Getting us to the Emergency's no good if you kill us on the way!"

"You want us to slow down?" Priya asked. "You saw the skyline."

"Dead's dead either way," Tynan said. He drew back his jacket to display the gun tucked into the waistband of his jeans. "We get caught outside, we got a chance, but he plows us into a storefront, we don't live to see the sun come up."

Kayah caught his eye and he grinned at her. Tynan had a skittish, manic energy and a talent for saying the wrong thing, but she knew he meant well. She mustered a wan smile, then focused again on her mother. Kayah pushed Naira's hair out of her face. Her clammy skin had turned cool and seemed even paler, now, though that could have been Kayah's imagination.

The stink of gas and chemicals filled the back of the truck, overcoming the stale, sweet smell of old whiskey that had soaked into the floor and the crates. Kayah pulled up her shirt to cover her mouth but kept her other hand firmly on her mother's wrist, feeling the thready flutter of her pulse.

"God, the smell," Tynan groaned.

"Gotta be the refinery," Quinney said. "Means we're only a few blocks from the Emergency."

He glanced at Kayah as he said this last bit, trying to reassure her. But she barely saw him, staring instead at the narrow gap at the bottom of the truck's rear door. There had been a hint of light there before—but now there was only darkness.

Nightfall.

Kayah slumped back against liquor boxes. Hollow, utterly empty inside, she glanced up at Quinney as if this pale, rough-hewn ginger boy might be able to remake the world, the spin it backward to a time before darkness meant death.

The truck rocked to one side, the engine roared as Delmar gunned it, and then just as abruptly they came to a juddering halt. Kayah pushed stray locks of hair away from her mother's face, and then the skids were in motion. Quinney ratcheted the latch back and hauled the door open. Tynan jumped out into the parking lot, shouting for help.

"Quiet, idiot!" Priya barked as she followed him out.

Into the dark.

Time had seemed to flicker past while they drove, but Kayah saw that long minutes had gone by and a blue-gray filter had fallen across the city. In the parking lot, cars shone in the wan yellow light of the rising moon.

"Go," Quinney breathed.

The word snapped her back to reality. Kayah leaped out the back of the truck, dropped to the pavement, and turned to grab the edge of the blanket. Quinney and Priya slid her mother to the edge and Kayah grabbed hold as Priya jumped down to help her. Naira's face had gone slack and her chest seemed to have stilled.

No, Kayah thought, feeling the night around them and fearing they had risked all of this for nothing.

The city air had gone still. Even the breath in her lungs seemed to stop moving as she and Hope held either side of the blanket and Quinney jumped down from the truck to take hold of the fabric with both hands, almost cradling Naira's head. Kayah's mother hung down like a child in a sling but they had no choice now—no better way. Delmar stayed in the truck, behind the wheel, and Tynan ran for the emergency room doors, the soles of his shoes scuffing the pavement.

"Oh, shit..." Priya whispered.

Kayah had been hustling along, arms straight down,

trying to glide her mother as smoothly through the parking lot as possible. Trying not to breathe even as she wondered if her mother had stopped. Now she whipped her head up and stared at Priya...saw where the other girl was looking, and felt herself deflate. Tears sprang to her eyes.

"No," she said.

Quinney shot her a glance meant to silence her.

Sorrow and anger boiling up inside her as the first tears slid down her face.

"No!" she repeated, louder now.

The emergency room entrance had already been shuttered. At dusk, metal doors and grates would be lowered into place on structures all over the city, but hospital emergency rooms were supposed to remain open at least thirty minutes after nightfall, with armed guards at the doors.

Not tonight. The plate glass windows that looked out on the parking lot were shielded, and the doors were closed up tight.

"Tynan," Quinney rasped, "see if you can get them to open up. Be quick, but be damn quiet."

He glanced up. Kayah didn't dare. They were like ghosts out there in the moonlight, all of them pale and unearthly and easily spotted from above.

Tynan slapped an open palm against the metal doors. Kayah could hear him hissing quietly, talking low in hopes that whoever was on the other side would open up. She could barely make out the words, but the phrase "dying woman" floated out across the lot as though they had been spoken right into her ear. In the cab of the truck, Delmar swore. Kayah and Priya and Quinney shuffled toward the blocked E.R. entrance with Naira hammocked in the blanket between them, but there seemed little point.

"This is damn stupid," Delmar said in a low voice. "We're dead out here, man. Get in the truck."

Kayah shot him a murderous look. His eyes were wide with fear so complete he didn't even seem to see her. Something broke inside her.

"Quinney," she said as they reached the metal doors blocking the E.R. "You guys should go."

Tynan jumped back from the doors, nodding with a kind of manic energy, his arms flailing in a kind of pantomime. "That's what I'm saying. Shouldn't be out here to begin with."

Kayah nodded to Priya. A chilly breeze whistled past them, rustling the bushes off to the right of the E.R. entrance as the two girls gently lowered the blanket to the ground. Quinney had no choice but to do the same or risking dumping Naira onto the ground.

She crouched by her mother's side, afraid that all of this had been for nothing, but then she saw the shallow rise and fall of Naira's chest and knew they still had a chance. Kayah kissed her mother's cheek and then jumped up and turned toward the metal doors. She slapped a palm against it, the blow echoing across the parking lot and into the night.

"Don't do that," Tynan said.

Kayah put her mouth to the gap between the metal

doors. "Please?" she begged. "My mother's had a heart attack. Please!"

"Damn it, shut your—" Tynan began.

"Go," she said. "Just go. I understand."

"We're not leaving you here," he said.

"Maybe *you're* not," Priya replied.

Quinney snapped his head around to stare at her.

Priya sighed, bouncing nervously from foot to foot. "We gotta go, Q. You know it."

"Not if the hospital lets us in."

Kayah touched his hand and he froze at the contact. Lifted his gaze slowly and stared at her.

"Thank you," she said. "But they're right."

Quinney hesitated again. "We had a deal."

For half a second, she didn't remember. Then she stared at him in horror. "You're crazy."

He gave her a sad, hopeless sort of smile and for the first time Kayah understood that Quinney had not come with her for a kiss or to save her mother or out of some manic courage. He had helped her because he had grown tired of being afraid all the time.

"Count to ten and decide if you want to put your mom back in the truck," he said. "We're leaving. You stay, it won't just be her heart that stops tonight."

He started to walk away.

"Quinney," Kayah said softly, and when he turned she rushed over and kissed him softly on the cheek. Then she shoved him backward. "Go."

The others urged him on. Delmar started up the truck and it growled loudly to life, the noise rumbling across the lot. Kayah pounded on the E.R. door four times in rapid succession and called out for someone to let her in.

Over the truck's engine she could barely hear the voice from inside telling her to go away.

"Not a chance!" she snapped. "Let me in or you're killing me and my mother both!"

Behind her, Priya called to Quinney.

Once. Then a second time, and the second time her voice was full of despair, almost a moan. Tynan swore and Quinney snapped at them all to get into the truck, hissed at Delmar to roll up the driver's window.

Kayah turned and saw them running for the back of the truck. Tynan had his gun out and now she saw Priya flip up the back of her jacket and slip her own nine-millimeter from a thin holster clipped to her belt. Quinney glanced up at the sky as he ran. A shadow passed through the moonlight and then, even over the rumble of the truck's engine, Kayah heard the sound, like the unfurling of a heavy canvas flag.

She looked up.

The Cloaks circled above, leather wings outstretched and long necks extended. Kayah had seen them from inside, cruising the night skies as if flying itself was enough of a pleasure to keep them contented. They sailed in the moonlight, and for a moment the wind gusted and the updraft off the face of the hospital pushed them higher. But she knew they would not stay aloft.

She twisted around and lifted a hand, ready to pound on the metal doors. Her hand never fell. Whoever stood on the other side had not been willing to open the door before—they would never do it now that the Cloaks had arrived.

Kayah knelt by her mother's side again and took her hand. In the moonlight, Naira's eyes were open and gleaming, staring up at her.

"Momma?" Kayah said.

Naira couldn't speak. Pale and sweating, brow furrowed with pain, she couldn't manage a word, but she was alive.

In her eyes, Kayah could see the reflection of the Cloaks circling overhead.

She saw the first one dive toward the ground.

Delmar put the truck into grinding gear and it lurched and began to roar away. Kayah closed her eyes.

"Damn it, girl, fight!" Quinney shouted as he lunged past her and slammed into the metal barrier. He banged on the E.R. door once, twice, a third time.

The first of the Cloaks arced down toward them, leathery wings fluttering. Kayah covered her mother's body with her own. Quinney swore again and she glanced up in time to see him turn, take aim with his gun, and shoot the Cloak in the head.

It screamed—the sound spiking through her brain—and crashed into the pavement only feet away. For several heartbeats it lay still, but then she heard the wet sounds of the creature peeling itself from the ground and it began to push itself up on hands and feet that were dry black leather, but somehow almost human.

"They left you," Kayah said, numb inside. *You're in shock,* she thought. But still the idea that the others had let Quinney get out of the truck, let him fight to save her, astonished her.

"Or I left them," he said, stepping up and firing at the grounded Cloak again before he turned to her. "Now we're going."

Quinney grabbed her wrist and yanked her away from her mother. Her feet were moving before she even realized it. Thirty yards away, the truck bumped to a stop and the back door rolled up. Tynan and Priya stood in the open back of the liquor truck, outlined in the moonlight, firing at the Cloaks that began to descend as if they had a hope in hell of doing anything but slowing the things down. Bullets weren't enough. They had to take the monster's heads and set them on fire.

Fire, she thought, a sliver of hope rising in her. The liquor would burn all too well. In that moment, she allowed herself to rush toward the truck with Quinney, who continued to yank her along as he fired at two Cloaks who slid down through the moonlight toward them, long hands out and mouths gaping, silver teeth gleaming.

They darted away, avoiding the gunfire, and in that moment Kayah realized her mistake.

"Shoot them!" she screamed, grabbing Quinney's gun hand and trying to force it around.

He did, but too late. Her hands opened and closed emptily and then she grabbed for his gun, tried to wrest it away from him so that she could do the shooting herself. So that she could do something.

The Cloaks alighted around her mother. One of them ripped the blanket away with those long black talons, so like human fingers. Naira flipped onto the ground between them as a third Cloak landed next to the other two and grabbed hold of her mother.

"Come on!" Tynan shouted from the back of the truck.

Gunshots cracked the air, bullets slicing upward toward the Cloaks who dove at the truck. Tynan and Priya were protecting themselves. Kayah fought with Quinney over his gun and finally he just let her take it.

She screamed as she marched toward the creatures crouched around her mother. Tears slid down her face as she pulled the trigger, emptying the magazine. Two of the Cloaks went down, but in the space between breaths they were stirring again.

Quinney shouted her name, but she figured he was running for the truck.

Like Kayah should have been.

Like her mother would have wanted her to.

The last Cloak turned to sneer at her.

A burst of blinding light made her cry out and shield her eyes. The Cloaks began to scream and she heard the ripple of their leathery wings as they jerked backward. They turned their backs to the enormous battery of solar lamps that shone down from above the E.R. entrance and smoke rose from their flesh. The Cloaks stood up straight, wings wrapped around them as they padded away, unable to fly as long as they needed the wings to shield them. Wings furled, they looked like darkly hooded men, sinister figures in Cloaks, lurking in the dark corners of human nightmare.

Just beyond the reach of the lights, the Cloaks began

to shriek at the nighttime sky and spread their wings once more, leaping up into the darkness.

Kayah aimed Quinney's gun at the moon, hoping to shoot them before remembering that she had run out of bullets.

The truck began to roar in reverse, Delmar coming back for them. Or at least for Quinney.

With a loud clanking, the metal doors in front of the E.R. began to roll upward.

Kayah and Quinney spun to see a scowling, white-haired man step out into the glare of the solar lamps with a pair of women in security uniforms behind him. The guards carried assault rifles and hustled out, trying to cover Kayah and Quinney and the rumbling truck and the perilous night sky all at the same time.

"Idiot kids," the scowling man said. "Get inside. You've got about thirty more seconds of this light. We don't have the power to keep the lamps on for longer—that's why the damn doors were closed!"

The skids were already running from the truck, lured by the promise of the open door. They would be safe in the hospital until morning came and they could go back to their lives.

Quinney gave Kayah a push and she started moving, too.

"My mother—" she began, and the two of them turned together. They would take Naira inside and the doctors would see to her.

Except that her mother had begun to writhe on the ground. Smoke rose from her face and seeped out from inside her clothes. Kayah couldn't move. The breath froze in her lungs and the tears dried on her cheeks.

Beside her, Quinney spoke her name, oh so gently. That made it worse. His tenderness made it real.

On the pavement between Kayah and Quinney and the open doors of the E.R., Naira began to howl in anguish. The armed guards and the white-haired man jerked backward, ducking back inside. Beyond them, in the darkened corridor of the E.R., Delmar and Tynan reappeared, trying to get a glimpse of what transpired outside.

Naira's scream cut off.

She bucked against the ground, more smoke rising from her flesh, and then she began to crawl. Kayah moved then, reaching for her, whimpering a word that might have been "mama." Quinney slammed into her, wrapped his arms around her, and yanked her out of the way as Naira scrabbled and slithered past them, dragged herself out beyond the reach of the sun lamps.

The sun lamps, whose battery life was ticking down to nothing.

The doctor and the security guards shouted at them to get inside but Kayah felt as if they spoke to her from some other world, from beyond the wall between day and night. Hollowed out inside, she watched her mother rise from the pavement, there in the shadows at the edge of the pool of light.

Naira rose, shuddering, and the sound was like tearing leather.

The wings ripped out of her back and spread wide,

then wrapped around her in a healing cocoon. A shroud. A cloak.

Quinney grabbed her face, turned her toward him. "Kayah!"

She fought him off, watching as her mother took flight, slipping up into the night sky as if she had been born to the moonlight. Almost beautiful.

"Come on!" Quinney shouted in her ear.

Kayah looked at him, met his gaze and saw his regret.

"They bled her," he said. "You did everything you could, but they're gonna come back, Kai. We've gotta go inside!"

Voices were shouting from the E.R. She glanced over and realized that she had been hearing a grinding noise for several seconds—the sound of the metal barriers rattling back down in their frames. The sun lamps flickered and began to dim, leaving bright after images in her eyes.

"Come inside!" Quinney insisted.

Kayah breathed. She stared at him. "You know I can't."

"Kai—"

"You know where she's going."

Quinney swore. He pressed his eyes shut for a second and then turned to stare out at the black silhouettes of the city at night, the buildings in the distance and all the open space in between.

They both knew where Naira would be flying. When the Cloaks bled someone, when they reproduced like that, the newborn monstrosity rose into the dark with only one objective—to return home and kill everyone they found there.

Joli, Kayah thought.

"Quinney," she said, taking his face in her hands. Turning him toward her, just as he had done a moment ago. "She's all I have left."

The truck still idled, engine growling, not thirty yards away.

Kayah and Quinney stood face to face as the metal doors of the E.R. rattled all the way down and locked into place and the sun lamps flickered out, leaving them in darkness.

They began to run.

THE REVELERS

We've all had a friend like that. You know what I mean.

Jon was mine.

Jonathan Vincent Carver showed up in my class halfway through seventh grade, something to do with his dad's job. Like a military brat, he'd been moved from state to state his whole life and he had the combination of feigned arrogance and desperate yearning that often goes along with that kind of upbringing. Translate that to mean that he lied a lot, said whatever he had to say to be accepted. To be liked. They were little white lies, mostly, so my buddies and I didn't mind much. Jon was usually good company, and by high school, he'd become one of my closest friends.

If you're lucky, you gather a small tribe together when you're young, people you believe will have your back in the dark times. But even the lucky don't usually stay that lucky. College comes and people drift and change. Jon put on a mask of arrogance and faux-charm in his quest to enter the business world, the kind of thing he believed would make him a lot of money after graduation. He recognized the process, pursued it with an admirable single-mindedness, but at the same time, he held on to his high school friends and the tangible truth of our tribe, the people we'd been. It was only later that I'd realize he needed the reminder of who he'd been because he was finding it harder and harder to remember that the grinning salesman face was only a mask.

The first clue came our junior year in college. He'd been going to Fordham down in New York and come back to Boston for a long weekend right at the beginning of baseball season and he wanted to catch up. I was his touchstone, you see. That reminder he needed. He could only do Sunday night—he had no classes on Mondays that semester, but I did, and my political science professor had scheduled a test at 8:50 a.m. The test had me worried, but Jon had always been so persuasive.

We met early for dinner. He told the waitress all about our high school glory days, and then he sprang it on me—he had tickets to the Red Sox game. Could we eat in a hurry and head over to Fenway Park? I insisted that I couldn't, offered to let him out of dinner and he could shanghai someone else into going with him. He let it go…until we'd eaten, and then somehow I let him talk me into it, but only because he promised to drive me back to campus as soon as the game let out. I still needed to study and the clock was ticking, but him driving me back would save me three quarters of an hour or so.

What he hadn't told me was that he had a couple of pals from Fordham meeting us there—guys I'd met before, guys who only saw Jon's mask and who had fashioned their own façades of smug assholery. He hadn't told me, because he knew I'd never have gone along to hang out with these two.

When the game ended, the Fordham boys wanted to go

out drinking. Jon extolled the virtues of this plan, trying to persuade me, but I had an early exam I wasn't ready for, remember, Jon? And you promised to drive me back to campus?

He gave me a sour look, pulled a twenty out of his wallet, and tucked it into the pocket of my jacket like I'd just given him a sloppy back alley blowjob and this was my reward. "Sorry, man. You're right. Take a taxi on me. I owe you."

I couldn't even argue. All of the abuse I wanted to hurl his way just sat in my throat, lodged there like something I'd need the Heimlich to choke up. The Fordham boys went off, having quite a laugh.

Have you ever tried to get a taxi within a mile of Fenway Park right after a Red Sox game?

Yeah. It's like that.

The moment stuck with me. I ran into Jon's father in a restaurant a few months later and I couldn't help myself. I told him that story. The elder Carver seemed disgusted but unsurprised, and that was when I realized that even his parents thought their son was a bit of a prick.

We saw each other less and less. We graduated. He went back to Boston for work, while my fortunes took me to New York, to a magazine publisher where I'd been working for a couple of years by the time I got that phone call from Jon. The phone call that led to meeting Mollie and Leigh and the party in this girl's apartment.

"Tim Donovan," I announced as I answered the phone.

"Timmy! You don't need your dancing shoes, but put

your motherfucking drinking hat on!"

I laughed, sat back in my chair. "What the hell do you want, Carver?"

"What time can you kick off work?"

My cubicle had a great view of Times Square. Rent would drive the company out of there a few years later, but those were halcyon days, so even a little punk like me had a view. I poked my head up to see who might overhear, but the three other staffers who shared the office were all elsewhere—coffee break, cigarette break, or running errands for the higher ups.

"I usually get out of here around seven. The boss is out of town, though, so I figure six o'clock sharp," I said. "From the question, I assume you're in town."

"I have meetings till three-ish," Jon said. "Then I'll hit up my local office for a few hours and meet you at six-thirty. Wherever you want, provided there's a bar with women in it."

We met at Dooley's Tavern, an Irish pub at the corner of 57th Street and 7th Avenue. It was the kind of place we'd always frequented in college, all brass railings and dark wood soaked in decades' worth of spilled ale, so the whole place had the stale-beer stink of fraternity basements. In those days, to me, that was the scent of nostalgia.

I slipped through the door at quarter past six and sat at the bar to wait, ordered a pint of Guinness and chatted up the bartender for half an hour until Jon arrived. The bartender's name was Leigh, a tall brunette with wildly curly hair and mischief sparkling in her dark eyes. Smart and funny, she kept the conversation going, kept the counter clean, kept the drinks coming, managed to take care of everyone without making anyone else feel left out.

"Maybe your friend's not coming," she said at one point.

"Nah," I said, "he'll be here. He's what you call 'mercurial.'"

"Meaning he thinks his time is more important than yours," Leigh observed. She cocked an eyebrow, maybe realizing that had been a little more honest than it was smart for a bartender to be if she wanted decent tips.

I smiled. "Oh, there's no doubt that's what he thinks."

And you let him? She didn't ask the question, but I could see it in her eyes.

Half a second later, Jon pressed himself against my back, reaching around me to start caressing my chest through my shirt. I spilled a couple of ounces of my beer onto my pants and laughed, twisting out of his grasp before he could tweak my nipples.

I swore at him, setting my beer down, but I was laughing as we embraced. We'd had a lot of good times together. Despite the way our friendship had withered, I was happy to see him. His eyes were glassy from the several beers he'd doubtless already had while he spent the afternoon at his "local office," which was a stool at a strip club half a dozen blocks from our present location.

"So this is the infamous Jon," Leigh said, placing a coaster on the bar. "What'll you have?"

Jon grinned, studying her like she was the menu. "Is that an open-ended question, or are we just talking alcohol here?"

Leigh arched an eyebrow. "Why don't we start with alcohol and see where that takes us?"

It might have been a bartender's diplomacy, a way to sidestep the come on, or she might've been flirting with him. I wasn't sure at the time and I'm not really sure now, regardless of where it went. It always astonished me how successful Jon was at seducing women. He wasn't the best-looking guy in a room. Too short, too cynical, too many damn teeth in that shark smile. The pickup lines he used should have been comedy gold. *Sorry about last Christmas; Santa forgot to pick me up*. That shit should not have worked, and yet somehow he'd figured out the formula, the perfect ratio of cockiness to charm, to move things from conversation to copulation.

He flirted with Leigh. As I downed my second Guinness, I did the same. We told stories about our high school and college days, trying to amuse her but mostly just amusing ourselves. It felt good to reminisce.

"This guy and I grew up together," Jon told Leigh, brow furrowed. "Hung out at each other's houses after school, drank in the woods together, did our stupid science project together. Life goes on, right? But if you have a couple of friends you can hang onto from when you were a kid, it means something, y'know? There's always someone who knows who you really are."

Leigh cocked her head, her lips pursed together, pert with attitude. "You're either sweeter than you look, or drunker than you sound."

He laughed. "Maybe both."

I put a hand on his back. "All right, brother. Time to get a table and order something to eat."

He made a pistol out of his thumb and forefinger. "Excellent idea."

Jon picked up the bar bill. I worked in publishing and he worked in sales. The guy could have sold ice to Eskimos, so needless to say he was making a shitload more money that I was. I offered to pay, but he rolled his eyes. He knew my salary.

Leigh waved over a waitress and introduced us. "Sit in Mollie's section. She'll take good care of you."

Mollie looked me up and down the same way Jon had looked at Leigh. Almost elfin, she was a tiny redhead with a spray of freckles across the bridge of her nose, and she wore a black skirt so short it might as well have been called a sash. Mollie started to lead us over to a table.

"Hey," Leigh said as I turned away from the bar.

I glanced at her.

"He's everything you said he was."

"Is that good or bad?"

She smiled. "Probably both, don't you think?"

I returned her smile and carried my third Guinness with me to the table.

In the interest of honest reporting, I must say we were drunk as fuck. We'd had our dinner and talked for hours about old times and new times. Being with Jon had reminded me why we had been such close friends in high school and college. He might have been a bullshitter of the highest order, but he knew me better than almost anyone and I knew him, and one of the first things I'd realized about post-college life was that those kinds of intimacies were hard to come by. I had started to wonder if maybe I still loved him a little more than I hated him.

We had pulled other patrons into our conversation, but most of them had left after a while, and come last call, there were about a dozen customers left in Dooley's. Mollie had closed out her station half an hour before and sat at one of the many empty tables around us, tallying her tips for the night and making sure all of her math had been correct. In the midst of that, she'd said something nice about my eyes, and Jon had taken that as his cue to play matchmaker. He spent some time extolling my virtues, and when Mollie had taken off her apron and grabbed her coat, instead of leaving she took a seat with us and got a beer of her own. We were seven or eight drinks ahead of her.

"You know the drill, amigos," Leigh called from behind the bar. "You don't have to go home—"

"—But you can't stay here!" the chorus of people with nowhere better to go chimed in.

Mollie had just said something funny and I realized I'd smiled a little too long at the joke. Smiling at her was easy. She confessed to being an actress and a dancer and that she had been writing a musical about a cocktail waitress in 1940s Los Angeles who spent her nights serving stars of the silver screen and dreamed of being discovered, but who felt invisible every moment of her life, except when she went to the movies. Sitting in the theater with the lights down, Mollie said, the waitress could always feel like she lived amongst those stars.

I fell in love a little, I think. Drunk as I was.

Jon said he'd produce her show after he made his first million, but only if he got to help with casting, so he could see if all of the stories about hungry young actresses were true. Maybe once I would've laughed, but you couldn't hear Mollie talk about her dreams and think that line was funny. Unless you were Jon.

Mollie laughed politely as she finished her beer. Last call had come and gone, so I offered her the rest of mine. The staff were getting their coats on when Leigh came and stood beside Jon's chair, hands thrust into the pockets of her ratty old pea coat, a bright raspberry scarf around her neck. Out from behind the bar, she seemed taller than ever.

"Where are you guys going from here?" she asked.

I blinked in surprise and glanced at Jon, who grinned. To him, it didn't seem at all unusual that Leigh might want to spend more time with him, no matter that she was stone cold sober and we'd been drinking for hours. We weren't incoherent—we'd been drinking all night, but we'd had a meal and hours had passed—but we were drunk enough to irritate sober people.

"We have no plans," I said.

"We do now," Jon corrected me, sliding back his chair and standing to look up at Leigh. "We're going wherever you're going."

Mollie downed the last of my beer and stood as well. "Leigh and I are headed to a party, if you guys want to come."

"Might be we've partied enough," I found myself saying. Then I saw the disappointment on Mollie's pixie features and wondered what the hell was wrong with me. "You guys don't mind us being so far ahead of you?"

"Mollie's got a little packet of something to help us catch up," Leigh said.

The mischief in her eyes made Jon very happy. Mollie took my hand and guided me away from the table, and suddenly we were leaving the restaurant and walking the streets of New York, and pretty soon I wasn't sure where we were, which was quite a feat when you consider that most of Manhattan is comprised of numbered streets and avenues. It's hard to get lost there. I wondered if I'd lost count of my drinks at some point during the night.

Then Mollie slid her arm through mine and started to sing a wordless tune, softly but beautifully, and I stopped worrying. I worried too much, Jon had always told me. I felt sure, in that moment, that he had been right.

Mollie took a little plastic bag out of her pocket, tapped a couple of pills into her palm and swallowed them dry. She offered them around. Leigh took two, but cautioned Jon and me to start with one each, given we were already slightly hammered. I followed their advice. Always the cautious one. But not so cautious I wouldn't take a pill a pretty girl gave me out of a plastic bag from her pocket.

"Where's the party?" he asked Leigh.

"This girl's apartment."

"That's all you know?" I asked.

Mollie bumped me with her hip. "It's supposed to be a massive bash. Late night party, past the witching hour in

New York City. What else do you really need to know?"

I smiled, recognizing truth when I heard it. *This girl's apartment* really was all I needed to know.

We never met the girl. Or at least, I never did. The party raged on the third floor of an old brownstone jammed between two modern structures, like a piece of an earlier New York had been somehow passed over by the passage of time. Forgotten. I hoped for one of those great, claustrophobic elevators with the accordion gates, but the place was a walk-up. Whatever Mollie had given us had kicked in on the way up the stairs, so as the thump of blaring hip-hop drifted down from above, Jon started bopping to the music. He took Leigh by the hands and danced up the last flight of steps. At the landing there were cases of empty beer bottles, neatly set out for return and redemption.

"Empty!" Leigh said, laughing in frustration, as if she'd really thought they might be full cases of beer. Her pills had kicked in, too, and her eyes were wide and hypnotic. That's mostly what I remember of her from that night, those kaleidoscopic eyes. I might have dreamed them, I don't know. It's been a long time since then.

"Fucking empty!" Jon echoed.

He picked up a case of the empty bottles, turned and hurled it down the steps. The cardboard box dulled the thump and the sound of glass shattering inside, but it was loud enough to make us all flush with guilty amusement.

The drugs racing through me, I shoved the nearest stack of cases over, toppling them onto the stairs.

Jon and Leigh looked at me in shock, then started whooping. Jon patted me on the back and yelled something about getting fucked up. Or maybe that was me doing the yelling.

They led the way out of the stairwell and into the hall. Mollie took my hand again. She cocked her head and even soaring on whatever she'd given me, I could see she was looking at me differently. What I couldn't tell was whether or not it was good differently or bad differently.

She kissed me, and from the hunger in it, I had my answer.

The room thumped with the music. The walls breathed with it. The lights were dim and though all of the windows were wide open, the gyrating bodies were sheened with glistening sweat. Side tables were laden with top shelf booze and clean glasses that seemed to appear without being replenished by anyone I noticed. Coolers full of beer on ice stood in corners. The drugs, though...they were never on display. They manifested in people's hands as if summoned from the ether. I saw one girl, maybe seventeen, pull a small vial of cocaine from the unruly bun of her hair.

"This is fucking amazing," Mollie said, dancing with me. Holding my hands and gazing into my eyes.

The apartment had seemed like one big room with a bathroom and small bedroom off to one side, but as we burned up the small hours of the night and we kept dancing and drinking, I realized we'd moved into a different room, and that the place must be larger than I'd at first imagined. The sweaty little box we'd started in had given way to a much bigger space, and the music kept shifting styles, sometimes improbably as hell. Somebody put on Frank Sinatra, and then something older, a heartbreak ballad from the 1920s or 1930s, followed by a screaming bit of party blues from the Sixties. Whoever had been picking the music had to be on even better drugs than we were. Mixing it up like that only ever worked with a group of people as fucked up as we all had gotten by then.

I had no idea of the time. Once in a while I'd glance out the window, expecting to see the edge of dawn creeping into the sky, but the old building had been swallowed by modern New York, so I wasn't sure if we'd even notice the sun come up.

Whiskey burned my throat. I blinked, coming to my senses for half a second, wondering how much time I'd lost. How much of that whiskey I'd had to drink. Feminine hands caressed my stomach, fingers stroked the front of my pants, nails scratching, stirring the most familiar of all urges. Blond hair whipped around her face as she danced, but Mollie wasn't blond.

Frowning, I stumbled back from her, glancing around in search of her. I spotted Jon and the bartender. *Leigh*, I reminded myself, though I forgot her name again a moment later. So fucked up by that time.

The dancing bodies made strange shadows on the wall, undulating darkness. The music had shifted and I stumbled amongst the dancers, shoved a couple aside. The woman wore flowers in her hair and a gypsy skirt.

Her partner wore a suit with thin stripes and a wide lapel, a long sloped hat. I turned to stare but the hat had vanished. The lights flickered and I turned to glance at the walls, where gaslight burned inside sconces, little flames casting odd shadows of their own.

I spotted Mollie with another guy, tall and dapper. Bow tie undone. They had taken a small mirror off the wall and were snorting lines of something off the silver glass. Coke, maybe. I had no way to know.

"Hey," I said into her ear as I moved up beside her and took her by the hand.

Her eyes were glassy, her pupils dilated so large they were nearly all black. She kissed me, pushed her fingers through my hair and pulled me close so she could deepen that kiss. She ground herself against me and I flushed with the best of hungers. Kissed her back, put a hand on her ass and pressed my hard cock into her so she could feel what she had done to me.

Then she was kissing the other guy. Dapper fucking Dan. His hand slipped down her pants and I saw her shudder with pleasure. She reached for my hand as if she wanted me to stay, but I'd never been good at sharing. I started to back away and she paused Dapper Dan and shot me a disappointed look.

"I should go," I mumbled. Blinking. Unsteady on my feet. I shook my head to clear it but was unsuccessful. "Come with me?"

She seemed to be considering it. Took one step toward me. Then she stopped and swayed, nearly fell over. Dapper Dan caught her.

"I don't think I can," Mollie said, a look of surprise on her face.

Hammered and high, stung by her, I staggered away. In the haze, I tried to focus on the room around me, searching for an exit. I didn't recognize the art on the walls and for a few seconds it seemed to me that the music filling the apartment had strings and horns, some baroque composition that these people would never have chosen as their evening's dance soundtrack. These people, men in black tie and women in elaborate gowns.

Bile burned up the back of my throat and I bent for a second, leaning against the wall, feeling the texture of the wallpaper under my hand. I blinked, trying to breathe, and looked around. What the fuck had Mollie given me? I'd never had hallucinations before, but now...what else could that have been?

I weaved amongst the dancers and the drinkers, all of them just as fucked up as I was by now. Their eyes looked hollow to me, their smiles false masks. Were they all so shallow, or was I just pissed at myself for being lulled by nostalgia into forgetting how much Jon had changed over the years? This wasn't the life I wanted, but should I hold it against these others, who had never been my friends?

I just wanted out. The party around me seemed like it might go on forever, and that was all the revelers wanted. There seemed so many of them now—impossibly many—the room impossibly large, people crushing against me as I tried to find my way out, searching for Jon along the way. Bitter as I was, I needed to tell him I was leaving.

What room was I in? How had I made my way there?

Girls dressed like flappers did the Charleston in the center of the crowd. I spotted them for a second and then they were gone, my view obstructed by human flesh. By a strange masquerade of unfettered joy and depravity in equal measure.

I found myself in another room. Then another. Each seemed new to me. I bumped into a table laden with champagne flutes, spilled several glasses and saw that there was confetti on the floor, as if tonight had been New Year's Eve and I had somehow missed it, though months had passed since then.

A dancing couple collided with me and herded me into a narrow corridor, thick with other human flesh. A doorway presented itself, the door hanging half open, and thus I discovered Jon and Leigh by accident in a bathroom complete with brass fittings and clawfoot tub. She snorted a line of cocaine off the sink while he worked her panties down, reaching for his own zipper.

The temptation to close the door, to just go, dragged at me. Instead I knocked hard, slid into the bathroom, and turned my back so as not to get a glimpse of them. In my peripheral vision I could see their faces in the mirror above the sink.

"Timmy, what the fuck?" Jon barked. "Give us a minute, okay?"

"Take all night, man. I just wanted you to know I was leaving."

Leigh didn't care. She didn't know me. She did another line.

"You fucking pussy!" Jon cried in dismay. "This is the

best party ever! I'm never leaving this goddamn place!"

I hesitated. Wrecked as I was, unable to focus my vision, I still managed to worry about him. I shook my head to clear my thoughts, wondering if he'd be all right.

He sneered at me. "What do you want, *cab money*?"

I went cold. We'd never talked about the night of that Red Sox game, but apparently he remembered it as well as I had.

"Fuck yourself," I spat.

I reeled out of there, stumbled down the corridor and into another room. My vision blurred again and I saw those gaslight sconces flickering on the walls. They couldn't have been there. The building might be old, but surely such things were not legal now. I went to my knees and someone stepped on my hand. My head pounded as dancers swirled past me. Some of them wore masks, as if I had accidentally stepped into some nineteenth century masquerade ball.

Darkness edged in at the corners of my vision and my head lolled forward, dreadfully heavy even as the rest of me seemed to lighten, to drift and float. Someone shoved me and I managed to crawl enough to find a wall. A window. I sucked in the cold air breezing in from outside and then I glanced out at a city that could not have been, a Manhattan without skyscrapers.

I puked out the window, body rigid as vomit poured out of me. I heaved a second time, and then a third before I could catch my breath. The cold air felt good but did not clear my head. With the back of my hand, I swiped a sleeve across my mouth and then the world turned to shadow again.

Someone slapped my face, more than once.

I tried to focus, barely managed, and saw it was Mollie. She hadn't poured all of the beer and whiskey down my throat and she hadn't made me take the damn pill from her little plastic baggie, but she had been the one to give it to me.

My hand closed around her wrist and I dragged her down to the floor with me. "What the hell did you give me?"

I slurred the question, but she understood.

"It was just Ex!" she said, extricating herself from me. "Just Ecstasy. But there's something else...something..."

Mollie took my face in her hands and shook my skull, forced me to meet her terrified gaze. "We have to leave."

Upon that we could agree. But her eyes held something other than urgency. They were full of fear.

"What...what's happened?"

Mollie slapped me hard. "Look around, Tim. Jesus, look!"

She slapped me again and my mind sharpened just a little, the fog clearing. I slid my back up the wall beside the window and blinked, sucking air into my lungs. What I was seeing could not be. I tell myself even now that it had to be the drugs, that there must have been something in that pill, or in the whiskey I'd been drinking at the party. Some of the revelers were as I'd seen them before, wasted shells, club kids or young professionals blind drunk, having the party of their lives. Others were true husks, barely shadows of people. They might have been ghosts, but in that moment, I felt sure they had begun just like the rest...like me and Jon and Mollie and Leigh, young and searching for meaning and identity in a city that denied both, desperate to feel something other than the uncertainty of new adulthood. They'd found this party just like we had, and they'd surrendered themselves to it.

Mollie took my hand. "Come on. I've got to find Leigh."

I flashed on the bathroom. The lines of coke on the sink. The sneer on Jon's face. *What do you want, cab money?* Fuck them.

"We have to go," I said, echoing Mollie's own words.

She'd taken my hand, but now it was me dragging her. Mollie protested, but not much. Fear became her engine. I kept shaking my head, forcing the fog to clear from my thoughts, keeping my vision from fading. And yet it did. Whatever moment of crisp clarity Mollie had given me, I lost it quickly. The husks had their masks on again, looked just like the rest of the revelers, but I had seen them now. All around us were faces from other eras, clothing from decades past. The music shifted with the décor as we shoved through dancers and drinkers and people smoking all manner of things.

Fear suffocated me. It felt like a kind of madness, seizing me, building up in me like steam in a kettle. Just when I thought I might scream, Mollie and I pushed our way through the throng and into the room where we had first entered. I recognized the door. Seeing we meant to leave, several of the dancers reached for us, snagging our clothing. One girl kissed me, her mouth tasting of burnt smoke and herbs. We yanked ourselves free, and I felt so grateful that I could no longer see which of the revelers were new arrivals and which were only shadows.

The door resisted at first, but Mollie put her hand over mine and something about that moment of contact, the warmth of her touch, must have given us both a bit more clarity. The knob turned, the door opened, and we stumbled into the hall. As the door slammed behind us, muffling the thumping hip-hop we'd heard on our arrival, Mollie pulled me into the stairwell and we picked our way carefully past the cases of empty beer bottles we'd knocked over earlier. She'd given up on Leigh, no longer determined to go back for her.

Until we reached the street.

The sky had lightened slightly, deep indigo to the west but to the east I could see the soft glow of impending dawn. I glanced around, grateful that the street seemed the same as the one we'd left behind. The modern buildings dwarfing the ugly brownstone.

"We have to go back in," Mollie said, standing beside me. She'd let go of my hand at some point and I hadn't noticed.

"Are you out of your mind?"

"Tim, we have to. I can't leave Leigh in there. And what about Jon?"

What do you want, cab money?

I shook my head and staggered across the street. Whatever clarity I'd achieved had started to wear off and now the alcohol and drugs crashed back into my system like adrenaline had built a dam and now it had let go.

Sometime later—I don't know how long, but there

were people out jogging and walking their dogs and the yellow edge of the sunrise had just touched the eastern edge of the city—Mollie shook me awake. I'd passed out in a shoe store doorway across from the brownstone.

There were tears on her face.

"She's gone," Mollie said. "I went up and I knew it the second I got to the top of the stairs. The cases were gone, the ones you guys smashed. Just gone. No broken glass, no boxes, nothing. And the music had stopped."

"That's..." I started to say *impossible*, but bit down on the word.

Mollie had knocked on the door, hammered on it, until she heard someone swearing on the other side. She'd pleaded for it to be opened and when at last her pleas were answered, she found herself confronted by an old man holding his stained robe closed with one hand while he cussed her out and threatened to call the police.

"It's over," I said.

"It can't...where have they gone, Tim?" Mollie asked, wiping at her tears, afraid for her friend.

I thought about all of those different rooms, the view from the window, the shifting music and clothing I had seen.

"The party's moved on. Go home, Mollie."

"But Leigh and Jon..."

"They got what they wanted. They moved on, too. So should you."

Mollie stared at me, frowning at first in shock and then in revulsion. She took a step back, moved off the curb and then froze at the blaring horn of a taxi. She waited while it slid by, the cabbie stabbing his middle finger out his window as he passed. Then she hurried off.

I watched her until she reached the end of the block, where she turned a corner, shoulders hunched, and disappeared. I never saw Mollie again, but the memory of her face is vivid in my mind. Her eyes, especially. The disappointment that shaded them in that last instant, when she glanced at me while the taxi drove past. I had not turned out to be the person she thought I was.

As for Jon, I took my own advice. I let him go. The city had claimed him. Changed him. So fuck that guy, y'know?

But.

I'd let him go.

Which meant it had claimed me, too.

Maybe it gets us all, in the end.

A HOLE IN THE WORLD

WITH TIM LEBBON

Vasily Glazkov was warm. He reveled in the feeling because he had not been truly warm for a long time. His fingers and toes tingled with returning circulation, and he could feel a pleasant stinging sensation across his nose and cheeks. Beyond the open doorway, Anna held a steaming mug out to him. She was grinning. Around her was the paraphernalia of their mission—sample cases, laboratory equipment, tools and implements for excavating, survival equipment, and clothing. As he entered the room the door slammed shut behind him, the window shades lowered, and they were alone in the luxurious warmth. Nothing mattered except the two of them. He took the mug and sipped, the coffee's heat coursing through him and reaching even those deepest, coldest parts that he'd believed would never be warm again.

Anna started unclipping her belt and straps, popping her buttons. She dropped her rifle and pistol, her knife, shrugging out of her uniform to reveal her toned, muscled body. He felt the heat of her. He craved her familiar warmth and scent, her safety, but he still took time to finish the coffee. Anticipation was the greatest comforter.

"Vasily!" A hand grasped his arm and turned him around. He frowned, stretching to look back at his almost-naked lover. But however far he turned she remained out of sight.

"Vasily, wake up!"

Glazkov's eyes snapped open. His breath misted the air before him, and he sat up quickly, gasping in shock as his dream froze and shattered beneath gray reality.

"Amanda?"

Amanda Hart stood in his small room, bulked out in her heavy coat. There was ice on her eyelashes and excitement in her eyes.

"Vasily, you've got to come."

"Where?"

"Down into the valley. It's stopped snowing, the sun's out, and you have to come. Hans is getting ready."

Glazkov looked around and tried to deny the sinking feeling in his gut. His room was small and sparse, containing his small supply of grubby clothing, a few books, and a single window heavily iced on the inside.

"You've been out alone again?" he asked. They had all been warned about venturing beyond the camp boundary on their own. It was dangerous and irresponsible and put all of them at risk. But Amanda was headstrong and confident, not a woman used to obeying orders. He wondered if all Americans were like that.

"That doesn't matter!" She waved away his concerns.

"So what's down in the valley?" Glazkov asked. The cold was already creeping across his skin and seeping into his bones. He wondered whether he would ever be warm again, even when he and Anna were together once more. It was only twelve weeks since they'd last seen each other, but the inimical landscape stretched time and distance, and the sense of isolation was intense. In this damned place the cold was a living, breathing thing.

"Come and see," Hart said, and she grinned again. "Something's happened."

Outside, the great white silence was a weight he could almost feel. It always took Glazkov's breath away—not only the cold, but the staggering landscape, and the sense that they might be the only people alive in the whole world. There were no airplane trails to prove otherwise, no other columns of smoke from fires or chimneys. No evidence at all that anyone else had ever been there. Old footprints and snowcat trails were buried beneath the recent blizzard. The three interconnected buildings that formed their camp—living quarters, lab and equipment hall, and garage—were half-buried, roofs and upper windows protruding valiantly above the white snowscape.

"We taking the snowcat?" Hans Brune asked.

"It's only a mile," Amanda replied.

The German tutted and rolled his eyes. His teeth were already clacking, his body shivering, even though he was encased in so much clothing that he was barely identifiable as human.

"Come on, Hans," Amanda said. "I've already been down there once this morning."

"Stupid," Brune said. "You know the rules."

"You going to report me?"

Hans shook his head, then smiled. The expression was hardly visible behind his snow goggles.

"So if we're going to walk, let's walk," he said. "I'm freezing my balls off already."

"You still have balls?" Amanda asked.

"Big. Heavy. Hairy."

"Like a bear's."

They started walking, and Glazkov listened to the banter between his two companions. He knew that there was more than friendship between them—he'd seen creeping shadows in the night, and sometimes he heard their gasps and groans when the wind was calmer and the silence beyond the cabins amplified every noise inside. None of them had mentioned it, and he was grateful to them for that. On their first day here they had all agreed that any relationship beyond the professional or collegial might be detrimental to their situation. While they weren't truly cut off, and their location was less isolated than it usually felt, there were no scheduled visits to their scientific station for the next six months. Hart and Brune probably knew that he knew, but there was comfort in their combined feigned ignorance.

He knew that Amanda had a husband back home in America. Hans, he knew little about. But Glazkov had never been one to judge. At almost fifty he was the most experienced among them, and this was his fifteenth camp, and the fourth in Siberia. He'd been to Alaska, St Georgia, Antarctica, Greenland, and many other remote corners of the world. In such places, ties to home were often strengthened by isolation, but sometimes they were weakened as well. Almost as if such distances, and the effects of desolate and deserted landscapes, made the idea of home seem vague and nebulous. He had seen people strengthened by their sojourns to these places, and he had seen them broken. He knew the signs of both. Most of the time, he knew better than to interfere.

Amanda led them away from the research station and toward the steep descent into the valley. The trees grew close here, hulking evergreens heavy with snow, and beneath their canopy the long days turned to twilight. But once they were into the thick of the forest the snow was not so deep, and the going was easier.

Glazkov, Hart and Brune were here as part of an international coalition pulled together to study the effects of climate change. While politics continued to throw up obstacles to meaningful action, true science knew no politics, and neither did the scientists who practiced it. Sometimes he believed that if left to real people, human relations would settle and improve within a generation. Sport, music, art, science, they all spanned the globe, taking little notice of politics or religions, or the often more dangerous combination of the two. So it was with their studies into climate change. Deniers denied, but Glazkov had seen enough evidence over the past decade to terrify him.

"So what were you doing out here on your own?" Brune asked.

"Couldn't sleep," Hart said. "And I heard a noise. Felt something. Didn't either of you?"

"No," Brune said.

"Not me," Glazkov said. "What was it?"

"A distant rumble. And something like ... a vibration."

"Avalanche," Brune said.

"It's possible," Glazkov agreed. "Temperatures are six degrees higher than average for the time of year. The snowfalls's been less severe, and there's a lot of loose snow up in the mountains."

"No, no, it wasn't that," Hart said. "I've seen what it was."

"What?" Glazkov asked. He was starting to lose his temper with her teasing.

"Best for you to see," she said. They trudged on, passing across a frozen stream and skirting several fallen trees, walking in silence for a while. "I thought it *was* an avalanche," Hart said, quieter now. "Wish it was. But the mountains are ten miles away. This thing ... much closer."

Glazkov frowned. For the first time since she'd woken him, she sounded nervous.

"Should we call this in?" he asked.

"Yeah, soon," she said. "But we need photos."

"We can do that afterward."

"Not if it goes away."

They trudged on through the snow, emerging from the forest into a deeper layer, grateful for their snowshoes. Brune shrugged the rifle higher on his shoulder, and Glazkov glanced around, looking for any signs of bears. There was nothing. In fact...

"It's quiet," he said.

"It's always fucking quiet out here," Brune replied.

"No, I mean ... *too* quiet." He almost laughed at the cliché, but Hart's and Brune's expressions stole his breath. Heads tilted, tugging their hoods aside so they could listen, he could see realization dawning in both of them.

Far out on the desolate Yamal Peninsula, three hundred miles north of the Arctic Circle, there were few people, but they were used to hearing the calls, cries and roars of wildlife. Brown bears were common in the forests, and in more sparsely wooded areas there were elk. Musk deer were hunted by wolves. Bird species were also varied, with the great eagle owl ruling the skies. Some wildlife was dangerous, hence the rifle. Yet after twelve weeks here, not a shot had been fired.

"Nothing," Brune said. He slipped the rifle from his shoulder, as if the silence itself might attack them.

"I didn't notice before," Hart said. "Come on. Not far now, and we'll see it from the ridge."

"See what?" Glazkov demanded. Hart stared at him, all the fun vanished from her expression.

"The hole," she said. "The hole in the world."

Oh my God, she's right, Glazkov thought. It really is a hole in the world. But what's at the bottom?

"I didn't go any further than this," Hart said.

"I don't blame you," Brune said. "Vasily?"

"Sinkhole," Glazkov said.

"Really?" Hart asked. "It's huge!"

"It's inevitable. Come on."

They started down the steep slope into the valley and the new feature it now contained. Glazkov thought it might have been over five hundred feet across. With the sun lying low, the hole was deep and dark, only a small spread of the far wall touched by sunlight. At first glance he'd had doubts, but there was no other explanation for what they were now walking toward.

A melting of the permafrost—an occurrence being seen all around the globe—was releasing vast, stored quantities of methane gas. Not only a consequence of global warming but also a contributing factor. In some places such large quantities were released that these sinkholes formed overnight, dropping millions of tons of rock down into vented caverns hundreds of feet beneath the surface.

"We'll need our instruments," he said. "Methane detectors. Remote camera. Everything."

"So let's go back and get it all," Brune said. "And we need to call this in. We really do."

"Yes," Glazkov said.

"Yeah," Hart said.

But they kept on walking toward the hole, hurrying now, excitement biting at their heels.

It took fifteen minutes to descend to the valley floor. It would take a lot longer to climb back up, but Glazkov didn't care. He could already detect the eggy trace of methane on the air, but it didn't smell too strong for now. It started snowing again, and as they followed a stream across the valley floor toward the amazing new feature, visibility lessened. The stream should have been frozen at this time of year, and much of it still was. But a good portion of the water flowed. Approaching the hole's edge, Glazkov heard the unmistakable sound of water pouring down a rock face.

"What was that?" Brune asked. He was frozen behind them, head tilted.

"Waterfall," Hart said.

"No, not that. Something else."

They listened. Nothing.

"We should head back," Brune said. "We need breathing equipment, cameras."

"Not far now," Glazkov said. He was unsettled to see that Brune had slipped the rifle from his shoulder.

"What are you going to shoot?" Hart asked, laughing. "Monsters from the deep?"

Three minutes later, as they emerged from a copse of trees only a hundred feet from the hole's edge and saw what waited for them there—the crawling, tentacled, slick things pulling themselves up out of the darkness, skin pale from lack of pigment, wet mouths gasping in new air—Amanda Hart was the first to fall.

Captain Anna Demidov and her team were ready. Fully equipped, comprehensively briefed, fired up, she was confident that it would be a straightforward search and retrieval without the need for any aggressive contact. But if the separatists *did* attempt to intervene, Demidov's small Spetsnaz squad was more than ready for a fight. Either way, they would return with the stolen information. In this day and age a printed file seemed almost prehistoric, but the habits of some of Russia's top intelligence operatives never ceased to amaze her.

With her squad milling in the helicopter hangar, she took the opportunity to assess them one last time. Her corporal, Vladimir Zhukov, often teased her about being over-cautious and paranoid about every small detail. Demidov's reply was that she had never lost a soldier in action, nor had she ever failed in a mission. It was something he could not argue with. Yet the banter continued, and she welcomed it. The good relationships between members of her five-person unit was one of the most important factors contributing to success.

"All set, Corporal?" she asked.

Zhukov rolled his eyes. "Yes, Captain. All set, all ready, boots shined and underwear clean, weapons oiled, mission details memorized, just as they all were five minutes ago."

Demidov appraised the corporal from head to toe and up again. A full foot taller than she, and a hundred pounds heavier, some knew him by the nickname *Mountain*. But no one in their unit called him that. He didn't like the name, and none of them would ever want to piss him off.

"A button's undone," she said, pointing to his tunic before moving on. She heard his muttered curse and allowed herself a small smile.

Private Kristina Yelagin was next. Tall, thin, athletic, grim-faced, she was one of the quietest, calmest people Demidov had ever met. She had once seen Yelagin slit a man's throat with a broken metal mug.

"Good?" Demidov asked. The woman nodded once in reply.

"I don't like helicopters," Private Vasnev said. "They make me feel sick."

"And when have you ever been sick during a helicopter trip, Vasnev?" Demidov asked.

"I didn't say they *make* me sick, Captain. I said they make me *feel* sick."

"Feel sick in silence," she said.

"It's okay for you, Captain," Private Budanov said. He was sitting on a supply crate carefully rolling a cigarette. "You don't have to sit next to him. He's always complaining."

"You have my permission to stab him to death if he so much as whispers," Demidov said.

Budanov looked up at her, his scarred face pale as ever, even in the hangar's shadow. "Thank you," he said. "You all heard that? All bore witness?"

"See, now even my friends are against me!" Vasnev said. "I feel sick. I don't want to go on this mission. I think I have mumps."

A movement caught Demidov's eye and she saw the helicopter pilot gesture through the cockpit's open side window.

"That's us," Demidov said. "Let's mount up."

Professional as ever, her four companions ceased their banter for a while as they left the shadow of the hangar, boarded the helicopter, stowed their weapons, and cross-checked each other's safety harnesses. Demidov waited to board last. As she settled herself and clipped on her headset, and the ground crew closed and secured the cabin door, the crackle of a voice came through from the cockpit.

"We've got clearance," the pilot said. "Three minutes

and we'll be away."

"Roger," Demidov acknowledged.

"Sorry to hear about Vasily, Captain," the pilot said.

Demidov froze. The rest of her squad, all wearing headsets, looked at her. Corporal Zhukov raised his eyebrows, and Vasnev shrugged: *Don't know what he's on about.*

Demidov's mind raced. If something had happened to Vasily and she hadn't been informed, there must be a reason for that. Perhaps the general would assume that such a distraction would affect her current mission, and that he'd inform her of any news upon her return in six hours.

But after the pilot's comment, her distraction was even greater.

"What's that about Vasily?" she asked.

The comms remained quiet. A loaded silence, perhaps. Then a whisper, and the helicopter's turbines ramped up, the noise increase, and the green 'prepare for takeoff' light illuminated the cabin.

Demidov hesitated, ready to throw off her straps and slip through to the cockpit. But she felt a hand on her arm. Budanov. He shook his head, then lifted what he held in his other hand.

Without pause, Demidov nodded, giving silent assent.

Private Budanov was their communications and tech guy. Just as heavily armed as the rest of them, he also carried a bewildering array of hi-tech equipment, some of which Demidov barely understood. There were the usual satellite phones and radios, but also web-based communication systems and other gadgetry, all designed to aid their mission and help them in case of trouble. He'd saved their skins more than once, and now he was promising something else.

Sorry to hear about Vasily, Captain.

As the helicopter lifted off and drifted north, Budanov opened a palmtop tablet and started tapping and scrolling. Three minutes later he handed it to Demidov, a map on the screen. He motioned for her to place her lover's last known position on the map, which she did—the scientific research base on the Yamal Peninsula. He took the tablet back, nursing a satellite phone in his other hand, and four minutes later he paused.

None of them had spoken since taking off. When Budanov raised his eyes and looked at his Captain, none of them needed to.

Demidov took the tablet from his lap and looked at what he'd found.

"This is all on me," Captain Demidov said. Her heart was beating fast, and a sickness throbbed heavy in her gut. Part of that was understanding what she was doing––disobeying orders and going AWOL whilst on a highly sensitive mission, as well as hijacking a Russian army helicopter. But most of the sickness came from the dread she felt about Vasily's doom.

Science team missing ... seismic readings from the area ...

"Captain, I can't alter course," the pilot said. She could see his nervousness. He and his co-pilot were sitting tense in their flight seats, and she could sense their doubts, their inner debates. They wore pistols, true. But they also knew who they carried.

"I'm ordering you to," she said.

"Captain, my orders—"

"I'm not pulling rank," Demidov cut in. "This isn't about that. But I *will* pull my gun if you don't do what I say."

"And then what?" the pilot asked. "You'll shoot me?"

... drastic landscape alteration ... entire region quarantined ...

"Let's not discover the answer to that question. Yelagin, here with me." Private Yelagin squeezed through into the cockpit beside Demidov and behind the two pilots. "You know what to do," Demidov said.

Yelagin leaned forward and started flicking switches. She'd been a pilot before being recruited into Spetsnaz, and she knew how to disable tracking devices and transponders, and where any emergency beacons might be.

"Keep an eye on them," Demidov said. "I'm going to speak to the others. And Kristina ... thanks."

Yelagin nodded once, then settled against the bulkhead behind the pilots.

Back in the cabin Demidov looked around at the others. She saw no dissent. She hadn't expected any—they'd been together as a solid core group for over four years, had seen and done many terrible things, and she knew that their trust and sense of kinship went way beyond family. Yet she still felt a burning sensation behind her eyes as she met their gaze.

"You know what we've done," she said, a statement more than a question. Of course they knew.

"We're just following your orders," Zhukov said.

"I can't order you to do this."

"You don't need to," Vasnev said. "Vasily Glazkov is your friend, so he's our friend too. We all help our friends."

"There'll be repercussions."

Vasnev shrugged. Budanov examined his fingernails.

"Right," Demidov said, sighing softly. "It's only an hour's detour. Our original target isn't going anywhere, and we'll finish our mission as soon as possible."

"That's if the Major doesn't send a jet to blow us from the sky," Zhukov said. His voice was matter-of-fact, but none of them dismissed the notion. They were on dangerous, unknown ground now, and no one knew exactly what the future might hold.

We're coming for you, Vasily, Demidov thought.

Anna will come for me, Vasily Glazkov thought. She'll hear about this, put her team together, and come to find out what happened.

He could see nothing around him in the darkness. But he could feel them there, sense them, and whenever they moved he could smell them—rotting meat, and grim intent.

If only I could warn her to stay away.

"Captain, you need to see this." The pilot sounded

scared, and as Demidov pushed through into the cockpit she fully expected to find them facing off against two MI-35s. That would be the end of their brief mutiny.

But the airspace around them was clear, and she saw from Yelagin's shocked expression that this was something worse.

"What is it?" Demidov asked.

"Down there." The co-pilot pointed, and the pilot swung the helicopter in a gentle circle so that they could all see.

There was a hole in the valley. Hundreds of feet across, so deep that it contained only blackness, it had swallowed trees and snow, ground and rocks. Two streams flowed into it, the waters tumbling in spreading sprays before being swallowed into the dark void. It was almost perfectly circular.

It looked so out of place that Demidov had to blink several times to ensure her eyes were not deceiving her.

"What the hell *is* that?" Yelagin said.

"How far's the scientific station?" Demidov asked, ignoring her.

"Just over a mile, north and over the valley ridge," the pilot said.

"Take us there."

She heard his sigh, but beneath that was a groan of fear from the co-pilot.

"Don't worry," Demidov said. "We can take care of ourselves." She knew that was true. She commanded the biggest bad-asses the Russian army could produce, and they'd seen each other through many treacherous and violent situations. They had all killed people. Sometimes the people they killed were unarmed, more often than not it was a case of kill or be killed.

They could definitely look after themselves.

But none of them had ever seen anything like this.

"Get ready," she said back in the cabin. The others were all huddled at the cabin windows, looking down at the strange sight retreating behind them. "We're going in."

Where the hell are you, Vasily?

Demidov stood in the main recreational space of the research base and stared at the half-drunk cup of coffee that sat on the edge of a table. Somebody'd walked away from that cup. Maybe the coffee was shit, or maybe they'd been in a hurry.

“Captain?”

She turned to see Corporal Zhukov filling the doorway. His face told the story, but she asked anyway.

“Any sign?”

“Nothing,” he confirmed. “All three of them. Budanov and Yelagin are checking logs to see if there's any record of what drew them out of here, but there's no question that they're gone. Vasnev found nothing in the lab to give us any clue.”

“They went to the hole,” Demidov said, thinking of Vasily Glazkov. Not her husband, but he might as well have been. Would be, someday, if he hadn't fallen into that fucking hole.

“Would they all have gone?” Zhukov said. “That

doesn't seem logical."

"Scientists. Every discovery's an adventure. They know better, and protocol demands certain procedures, but it's easy to get carried away when something new presents itself. Like ravens seeing something shiny."

Zhukov shifted his massive frame, his shadow withdrawing from the room. "I take it we're going out there."

It wasn't a question. He didn't have to ask, and she didn't have to tell him.

Vasnev moaned about the cold every step of the way. To be fair, it was cold enough to kill, given time. So cold that the snow refused to fall, despite the gray sky stretching out for eternity overhead. It was as if the sun had never existed at all.

"My balls have crawled up inside my body for warmth," Vasnev whined.

"You're confused," Yelagin muttered. "They never dropped to begin with."

Demidov tried to ignore them. The wind slashed across the hard-packed snow and the bare rock and cut right down to the bone. They had heavy jackets on, thick uniforms, balaclavas and gloves. Their mission had been meant to take place an hour's chopper flight from here, where it would still have been damned cold, but they'd never have been this exposed for this long.

"This is idiotic," Vasnev groaned. "They kept this from us for a reason. They've got to be sending a team. And you know damn well the pilots have probably already called it in...probably reported us the second we set off. We should just wait for someone else to arrive, someone with better gear—"

Budanov slapped the back of his head. Vasnev whipped around to glare at him, and for the first time Demidov worried real violence might flare amongst them. They'd had their share of hostilities over the year—any team does, given time—but this moment had venom. It had teeth.

"If we wait," Budanov sneered, "do you really think they'll let us help look for Vasily and his science friends? We'll be hauled out of here, original mission scrubbed and this one along with it. We'll be slammed into a room and made to wait while they decide on our punishment, and meanwhile someone else will be looking for Vasily and we won't know how long they'll take or how much effort they'll go to."

Demidov stared at him. They were about the most words she'd ever heard Budanov say at any one time. His ugly face had twisted into something even uglier, but his eyes glinted with fierce loyalty, and she wanted to hug him. Instead, she trudged onward as if nothing had happened.

Vasnev mumbled something else as they all started walking again. Demidov did not turn when she heard the sound of a rifle being racked, but she knew it had to be Zhukov. The Mountain.

"Don't think I won't shoot you just for the quiet," Zhukov said.

Vasnev kept silent for a whole four minutes after that.

It was a brief but blessed miracle.

They reached the ridge above the valley and took a breather, staring down at the hole. The sky gave no hint as to the time, not up here in the frozen fuck-you end of the world, a place the world knew people had once been sent when they'd screwed up worse than anyone. Yet Vasily had been so excited to come here with his two research partners, to live in a prefabricated base smaller than a Soviet-era city apartment and freeze his ass off, all to prove what the world refused to believe. Yes, the planetary climate was changing. But Siberia was still cold enough to kill you.

They slid and climbed and scrambled their way down into the valley. Demidov checked her radio. "Wolf to Eagle. You still reading me?"

A crackle of static on her comms, but then she heard the pilot's voice. "Eagle here. Still tracking."

"You might need to make a pick up in the valley later."

"At this point, why not?" the pilot said. Just as she'd expected. He might have called in their diversion from the mission already, but until someone came to shut them down, Eagle wasn't going to abandon Wolf. Not a chance.

They started across the hard-packed snow toward the hole. Even from a distance, the darkness of it yawned, as if it had a gravity all its own, drawing them in.

"I'm going to be moaning along with Vasnev in a moment," Yelagin said. "I don't know I've ever been this cold." Her teeth chattered.

"Kristina, you're Spetsnaz," Demidov said curtly. But they both knew she meant something else. It wasn't about their training, their elite status, their special operations. It was about being a woman in a field dominated be testosterone-fueled men who waved their guns around like they were showing off their cocks. They had to be tougher, she and Yelagin did. Especially Demidov, the woman running the show.

"I'll bear your disappointment," Yelagin said. "My nipples are going to snap off like icicles."

That got a laugh, breaking the tension, and suddenly Demidov felt grateful to her. Their closeness had started to fray a little, but now they were a team again.

"Captain," Vasnev said cautiously, lagging behind.

"I swear I will fucking shoot you," Budanov reminded him.

Then Corporal Zhukov echoed Vasnev. "Captain."

His voice gave her pause and made her turn. Vasnev had knelt in the snow. Zhukov stood over him, face as gray as the Siberian sky.

Vasnev looked up. "We've been moving parallel to some markings I couldn't make out, like someone dragged branches through here to obscure animal tracks."

"You didn't mention the tracks themselves," Zhukov said.

"Bear," Vasnev said. "And I saw some wolf tracks, too, up on the ridge. Same weird markings there, brushing the snow. But something happens right here, on this spot."

Demidov didn't like the hesitation in his voice. It sounded a bit like fear. Vasnev might have been a malingerer and a moaner, but he'd never been a coward.

"What 'something?'"

Zhukov answered for him. "The bear tracks stop. Whatever made those brush marks, it picked up the bear. Carried it off."

Vasnev stood, pointed at the hole. "It goes that way."

Demidov stood at the edge of the hole, a few feet back, not trusting the rim to hold her up. Sinkholes had appeared in many places in the area but she didn't think any of those on record had ever been this big. The hole seemed carved down into the permafrost and the rock and earth below. No telling how deep it went without doing a sounding. They had nothing to gauge the depth except two long coils of rope they'd found in the science team's base. That seemed unlikely to help them.

"Do you not just want to shout down, see if you get a response?" Kristina Yelagin said, standing at her shoulder.

Budanov snickered. "Yes, let's do that."

Yelagin shot him a death stare, but he ignored her, wrapped up in his own efforts. He had taken out the comm unit attached to his belt and begun searching through channels for any kind of beacon or signal. On each frequency, he'd broadcast the same message. "Research Unit one-one-three, please come in. Research Unit one-one-three, do you read me?" A few seconds, then again. With no answer, he'd move on.

They were getting nowhere. Vasnev had stopped whinging, but the cold had gotten down into Demidov's bones. *Come here, Anna, I'll warm you,* Vasily would have said. And she'd have let him. As she had so many times before. *Where are you, my darling?* The loving part of her felt lost, but Demidov had spent a lifetime training to charge forward when anyone else would flee.

Zhukov glanced around, nervous and on guard. He'd been more unsettled than any of them, and that concerned Demidov. If the Mountain worried, they all should.

"I don't hear a thing but the wind." Zhukov shifted, boots crunching snow. "Don't see a thing. Not so much as a bird."

"Enough," Demidov said. "Private Yelagin, get those ropes out. There were a few pitons with them."

"We don't have enough climbing gear for all of us," Yelagin said. "Shall I radio Eagle, have them bring more equipment from the base?"

Demidov wanted to tell her to follow orders. Do what she was fucking told. The woman made sense, but the problem was that it would delay their descent, and a delay would be costly if Eagle had really radioed the situation back to command.

"I'll do it," she said. "Meanwhile, get those ropes out and—"

"Captain," Zhukov said.

"Fuck me, what the hell is that?" Vasnev whispered.

Demidov narrowed her eyes. Her balaclava had slipped a bit and she tugged it away from her eyes. The others had begun swearing, lifting their weapons, taking aim. Demidov blinked to clear her vision, thinking somehow in spite of her team's reactions she must just be seeing something. Spots in her eyes. The things moving across the valley toward them couldn't possibly be real.

But they were moving nearer, coming into focus, and in moments she could no longer doubt. They weren't spots in her eyes or her imagination. They moved like some strange combination of tumbleweed and sea anemone, their flesh such a pale nothing hue that they blended almost too well against the snowy ground. Had they only stopped and kept still, they'd have been almost invisible at a distance. But they weren't stopping.

"Holy shit," someone said. Demidov thought she recognized her own voice. Maybe she'd said it.

They weren't stopping at all. They came from all directions, perhaps ten or twelve in all, rolling or slithering or some combination thereof, and they did not come without burden. They seemed nothing but a mass of tendrils, but each of them dragged something else behind them—something more familiar. Animals, some struggling and some limp, some broken, some bleeding. A musk deer, some squirrels, a leopard. One of the things had wrapped itself around a wolf. The beast could not extricate itself but it continued to fight, clawing, attempting to escape. It snarled and howled, as if trapped between the sister urges to fight and to scream in sorrow.

"Captain," Zhukov said, his voice gone cold. That was when the Mountain turned most dangerous. The deader his voice, the more she knew he must be feeling. The Mountain didn't like to be made to feel. "Give me an order please, captain."

In the distance, Demidov saw something big and brown in the midst of a squalling twist of those white tendrils. Three or four of the things had surrounded a moose—a fucking moose—and were dragging it back toward the hole. A knot of dread twisted in her gut as it finally hit Demidov. *Stupid,* she thought. *So goddamn stupid. Should have seen it instantly, should have understood.* If they could drag down a moose, a trio of curious, unarmed scientists would be no problem at all.

Feeling sick and jittery and wanting to roar out her fear for her mate, Demidov clicked off the safety on her Kalashnikov AK-12.

"Weapons free. Don't let these things get anywhere near us."

"Weapons free," Zhukov confirmed.

Instinctively they spread into a defensive circle, edging thirty yards away from the hole and using trees and rocks as cover. Demidov glanced around at her squad, already knowing what she'd see—professionalism, preparedness, calm in the face of these strange, unknown odds. Her senses were alert and alight, sharpened on the fear she felt for Vasily.

Whatever the hell these things were—

"Incoming, my eleven," Yelagin said.

The creature carrying the wolf had diverted from its route towards the hole and now moved towards them. The wolf still whined and howled, snapping at tendrils that seemed to arc easily away from its teeth. The creature seemed almost unaware of its burden.

It paused twenty meters away, half-hidden behind a tree.

Almost as if it was looking at them.

"Another this side," Zhukov said. "They're paused, as if—"

The creature holding the wolf slipped past the tree and came towards them across the snow, leaping rocks, compressing beneath a fallen tree and dragging the wolf through the narrow gap.

Demidov's finger caressed the trigger, and she experienced a moment of doubt.

Then Vasnev opened fire. He shot the struggling, crying wolf from sixty yards out. The wolf's blood spattered the snow and bits of fur and flesh scattered across the stark whiteness. The tumbleweed creature twitched and whipped backward, bullets tearing at its tendrils as it dropped the dead wolf. But then it drew itself up and began to slide toward them once more, skimming the surface of the snow, moving quicker as it came on.

"It's not...the bullets aren't..." Vasnev couldn't get the words out.

"Don't just stand there!" Yelagin moved up next to him and unleashed a barrage from her AK-12, took the tumbler mid-center, and blew it apart. It splashed across the snow a dozen steps from them, insides steaming as they sank into a drift. "Keep shooting till it's dead."

"Center mass!" Demidov said. "Blow them to hell."

Hunkered down behind a rock she braced her AK-12 against her shoulder and zeroed in on the thing dragging the musk deer. Then she opened up. Bullets ripped it up, stitching the dead deer and scattering the tumbler's twisted, pale tendrils across the snow. Several of them slapped against a tree and remained there, held in place by the sticky goo that must have been its blood. The fear that had coiled into her heart calmed itself. They could be stopped. They could be killed.

The feel of the recoil, the stench of gunpowder, the reports smashing into her ears were all familiar to her, and she kept her calm amid the chaos. They all did. That was why they made a good team, and why they had never faced a situation they could not handle.

Not ever.

Budanov and Zhukov were on her immediate right and they were both better marksmen. They twitched their weapons left and right, letting off short bursts and then adjusting their aim, anticipating the creatures' movements. All around them, bullets impacted trees and showers of snow drifted down. Visibility was reduced. The creatures took advantage and rushed them, but the soldiers chose their targets and kept firing.

"Ammo!" Zhukov shouted, and the others covered his field of fire as he reloaded.

"How many?" Yelagin shouted.

"Don't know," Demidov replied. She saw movement ahead of her, a pale shape slinking from cover behind a rock, and she concentrated a burst of fire. The shape thrashed and span, tendrils or tentacles whipping up a snowstorm. One more burst and it grew still. "One less."

For a few more long seconds, the hills all around them threw back brutal gunfire echoes. And then it was done.

Demidov's eardrums throbbed in the silent aftermath. She breathed in, let it out, finger still on the trigger.

"Clear," she breathed, and the others repeated the word in turn. She stood slowly from behind her covering rock and stood in the center of their defensive circle, turning slowly to survey the scene. It can't have been more than a minute, but the area around them had taken on the appearance of a bloody battlefield.

Trees were scarred and splintered from the gunfire. The animals being carried by the tumblers were all dead, their demise signed across the snow in blood, bodies steaming, one or two still twitching their last. The other creatures—*Whatever the fuck they are*, Demidov thought––also lay dead, tendrils splayed across the snow's crispy surface and, here and there, melting down into it where their sickly pale blood had been spilled.

Hot-blooded, she thought. Hot enough to melt snow. But what the fuck has blood that color?

"Holy shit," Vasnev said. "What just happened?"

"Something from down there," Zhukov said. "Subterranean. Pale skin, no eyes..."

"What do we do, Captain?" Budanov said. "You want me to call this in?"

"Call it in," she agreed. "But I'm not waiting. We all know Vasily and the others must be down there. Somebody's got to stay up here and wait, but I'm—"

Zhukov and Yelagin called out that there was movement, the two of them shouting almost in the same voice. Demidov swore and lifted her weapon again, scanning the landscape all around. Between them and the sheer drop into that vast hole she saw motion down close to the ground, a slithering undulation, perfectly camouflaged but moving in.

"How many?" she asked.

"Can't tell," Zhukov said. "They're moving differently."

"Almost like they're under the snow," Yelagin said.

"Watch your ammo!" she shouted, then they opened fire again.

Snow flicked up and bullets ricocheted from scattered rocks. One creature erupted from a deep snowdrift and came apart beneath a sustained burst of fire, innards spattered down, those thin, tendril limbs whipping through the air.

Demidov's weapon clicked on an empty magazine. She ejected the empty, reached inside her jacket to grab another, smashed it into place and raised the AK-12 again—

—just as Budanov screamed to her right.

She turned just in time to see his head jerked hard to one side, tendrils across his face, skin stretching where they touched, tugged by some adhesive on those tendrils, or by octopus-like suckers. Even as she brought her gun to bear, blood sprayed from Budanov's mouth. He fell to the ground and the tumbler flowed onto his back, tendrils wrapping tight around his neck and skull.

"No!" Zhukov shouted, as he and the others opened fire. Their onslaught blew the creature apart. The thick white paste, its blood, splashed down across Budanov's back, mixing with his own in a sickly pink hue.

"Form up!" Demidov shouted. "Close in! We've got to get back to the base."

"Up that hill?" Yelagin asked. And she was right.

They'd descended into the valley down a steep slope, almost climbing at times. To retreat up there with these things on their tail would be suicide.

They had to hold out down here.

"Mark your targets!" she said. The matter of ammunition was already worrying her. They'd come equipped for a simple in-and-out, an extraction that might not even have involved a firefight. As such they'd come light, bringing only the bare minimum of spare ammunition. Four mags each, if that, and she was already on her second. Three more shots and—

She ejected, reloaded, marked a new target and fired.

The chaos of battle had always remained outside for Demidov. Inside, her mind worked quick and calm, always able to place an enemy and work out the various strategies and logistics that would enable their success.

Now, everything was different. This was like no fight she'd ever fought, and already she could see its terrible, eventual conclusion.

"Grenade!" Yelagin said, lobbing a grenade and ducking down. The detonation was dulled by the deep snow, the gray sky made momentarily light by sprayed snow and pale body parts.

More came. More and more, and as she loaded her final magazine, Zhukov was taken down.

Three of them wrapped around the big man's legs, throat and right arm, and a wave of tentacles ripped the weapon from his hands. Demidov twisted around and took aim, but she was thinking the same as the others—*Do I pull the trigger?* They could not fire without hitting

Zhukov.

The decision was snatched from them. Tendrils punched in through Zhukov's eyes, he screamed, a creature leapt onto his back and plunged its limbs around and into his open mouth. His throat bulged with the pressures inside, and as he fell he was already dead.

Demidov felt a surge of unreality wash over her. Zhukov had saved her life several times, and years ago before Vasily, the two of them had enjoyed a brief, passionate affair. It had ended quickly because involvement like that would have put their squad in jeopardy. But the affection for each other had remained.

"No," she whispered, and she started shooting. Her bullets ripped through the fallen man and the thing on his back, tearing them both apart.

"Too many!" Vasnev shouted, turning as his machine-gun ran out of ammo, swinging it like a club, falling beneath a couple of tumblers as they surged from the snow.

Yelagin dashed to Demidov's side and turned back to back with her captain, and both of them continued firing for as long as they can.

When Demidov's weapon ran out she drew her sidearm with her left hand. But too late.

Yelagin was plucked from behind her and thrown against a tree, several of the pale, grotesque creatures surging across her and driving her down into the snow.

By then Demidov understood.

They weren't coming from across the valley anymore. A fresh wave had come up from the sinkhole. Dozens of them.

As they crawled over her, wrapped around her throat, tore the useless Kalashnikov from her hands, she raised her pistol. Too late. Her legs were tugged out from under her. Tendrils covered her mouth, pulled her arms wide, and she thought they might just rip her apart, that she'd be drawn and quartered by these impossible things, these tumbleweeds.

But whatever they intended for her, it wasn't instant death.

She felt herself sliding through the snow as they dragged her back toward the hole. They were warm where they touched her, and they smelled something like cut grass on a summer day. It was a curious, jarring scent. She tried to raise her head to see what was happening and whether she was alone. *Am I the only one left alive?* she wondered. But the tumblers were strong, and for the first time she sensed something in them other than animalistic fury.

There was intelligence. They kept her head back so that she couldn't see, and when she struggled she felt a slick, warm tentacle drape itself across her eyes, then pull tight.

Seconds later she felt the world drop from beneath her. She gasped in a breath and prepared for the fall, but she felt herself jerked up and down as the creatures descended into the hole. They must have been using their strange limbs to grab onto the sheer sides. Maybe they stuck like flies, or crawled like spiders.

Coolness became cold. She didn't notice the gentle kiss

of weak daylight until it vanished entirely. The thing carrying her must have needed all its other limbs to descend, and her eyes were uncovered again. She could look up and see the circle of pale grey sky vanishing above. Around her, a strange luminescence seemed to accompany their descent. To begin with she thought it came from the walls, and that perhaps there was strange algae growing there, issuing a pale light through some chemical process. But then she saw a tumbler's limbs working before her as they rapidly descended into the hole, and they glowed.

A procession of terrors crossed her mind. Poisonous! Acidic! Radioactive! But she suspected she would be long-dead before any of those potential hazards caused her harm.

She caught a glimpse of Yelagin being carried by other things further along the sheer rocky wall, and then she heard Vasnev screaming. Three of them were still alive, but Budanov and Zhukov were dead. Perhaps soon she would have reason to envy them.

Amanda Hart was screaming.

Quiet, Glazkov wanted to say. *Stupid American, keep silent. Can't you hear?* He liked Hart, had no real issue with Americans in general, but they had a tendency toward hysterics. Now was not the time for hysterics. In the dim glow of the creatures' luminescence he could see Hart hanging from the ceiling like a forgotten marionette, but of course that was an illusion. Her limbs were not dangling, they were restricted. She screamed his name—

Vasily, Vasily, Vasily—until he wished his mother had chosen another for him at birth.

Yes, Hans Brune might be dead. Given the way his ears had leaked after his skull had struck the wall, he pretty much had to be dead.

But we're alive, Glazkov wanted to say. *We're alive.*

His eyes blurred. It might have been tears obscuring his vision, or it might've been the blows he himself had taken to the head. He blinked and tried to focus. Glazkov hung upside down, so it might have been the head-rush contributing to his blurry vision.

No, he thought, looking at Hart. *That's not it.*

She cried out his name again.

His vision wasn't blurry after all. There were things moving on her face and body—things much like those that had carried them down into the hole, but so much smaller. Tiny things, like spiny creatures he might've found at the ocean bottom, but they were not underwater now. There must have been hundreds of them on her, perhaps thousands of the little things, moving around her with the industry of an anthill or a beehive, all of them producing that sickly glow. They moved with purpose, as Hart screamed.

As loudly as he could manage, Glazkov shushed her. Screaming wouldn't help anyone.

It occurred to him that it was strange, how calm he was. So strange.

But then he felt a little tug on his right forearm and he tried to crane his neck ever so slightly to get a glimpse of it, to see what might have caused that tug, and he saw that they were all over him as well. The tiny ones. *Babies*, he thought. But something told him that despite the size differential, the tiny ones were not the babies of the larger ones. Not at all. No assumptions ought to be made. Particularly not when the tiny ones were so busy, so full of intent.

He felt that tug again and cocked his head, managed a glimpse. They were there, skittering all over him, but now he understood something else.

He understood why Hart kept screaming.

They weren't just all over him, those little ones. They were *inside him*, too. Under the skin. Moving, and busy. So very busy.

Glazkov blinked, and for the first time he understood one other thing. Perhaps the most important thing. They weren't just moving inside him.

They were also speaking to him.

Budanov's whole world was pain and cold. He could hardly see. His head throbbed, his neck hurt, and his skull felt like something was tied around it so tightly that the slightest movement would cause it to burst. He'd spill his brains across the frozen ground. At least the pain would be gone.

No, Budanov thought. *No, I won't let that happen.* He never had given up in anything, and he wasn't about to start now.

He tried moving his limbs. They seemed to shift without any significant pain. Nothing broken. He rolled onto his right hand side and felt a heavy weight slip from his back, wet and still warm. He ran his hand up his front to his neck, checking for wounds. Nothing split open. He spat blood, and a tooth came out, too. His lip was split, and he'd bitten his tongue.

"Fuck," he whispered. *Good. I can still talk.*

Everything was silent.

Still lying on his side, he scanned his immediate surroundings until he saw his gun. It was down by his feet. He leaned down, head swimming, pulsing, and snagged the weapon with one finger. Straightening, hugging the rifle to his chest and checking that it was undamaged, he felt more in control.

He feared that everyone else was dead. His last memory was of one of those things coming at him, tendrils spread wide like a squid about to attack. He'd felt the impact of its warm, wet body upon him, then the sickly sensation of the limbs tightening around his neck and head ... and then nothing.

He glanced behind him and saw the torn ruin of the creature, limbs split, body holed by bullets. A stinking fluid had leaked and melted into the snow.

Budanov sat up slowly and looked around.

Zhukov was to his right, dead. There was so much blood. Budanov's heart stuttered, then he calmed himself and brought his weapon to bear. His head swam. He'd known Zhukov for almost ten years, and they'd fought well together.

"Sorry, brother," he whispered. The words seemed too loud, as if a whisper could echo across the landscape.

He realized how silent everything was. How still.

Groaning, biting his lip to prevent dizziness spilling him to the ground, Budanov stood and looked around. He staggered a few paces from the mess of Zhukov's body and leaned against a tree.

Nothing moved or spoke, growled or sang. The whole valley was deathly silent, and he wondered whether he was actually dead and this was what came after—desolation and loneliness.

Then he heard something in the distance. A buzzing, far away, so faint that he thought it might be inside his head. He tilted his head left and right, trying to triangulate the sound, but it came from everywhere.

There were many of those alien creatures lying dead all around, and trees and rocks bore scarred testament to the strength of the firefight he'd missed. But other than Zhukov's corpse, there was no sign of his comrades.

Except...

Drag marks in the snow.

"Oh, no," Budanov breathed. They'd seen the animals being gathered by the tumblers and hauled towards the hole, before those things had switched their attention to the Spetsnaz unit.

He checked his weapon, switched magazines for a full one, wiped blood from his face, and started toward the hole. He would not leave his people, not while there was even the smallest chance that they were still alive.

The buzzing grew louder. Close to the edge of the abyss he frowned and hunkered, still stunned by its size but now terrified by what might be down there. He turned left and right, trying to pinpoint the sound, but did not identify it until moments before the first helicopter swept into view.

The big Mi24 attack aircraft and troop carrier appeared above the ridge line across the valley, closely followed by two KA-52s in escort formation. Help had arrived, and he hadn't even had a chance to call it in.

Their helicopter pilots must have reported the forced change of destination the moment his unit left the aircraft back at the scientific station. Budanov didn't know how long had passed—he guessed little more than an hour—but that was plenty of time for this new unit to be scrambled and sent their way.

He knew how much trouble they were all in for disobeying orders and scrapping an important mission, but right then he didn't care. Something amazing and terrible had happened here. But for now his main concern, his *only* concern, was for the surviving members of his unit.

Budanov popped a flare and waved it back and forth several times, then tossed it onto a pile of rocks close by. He was ten meters from the hole's edge.

As the three aircraft circled the valley and hovered for a while above the massive hole in its floor, Budanov edged closer. He kept his weapon ready, convinced that at any moment one of those tentacled things would surge up from the depths and come at him.

If it does I'll blow it apart.

But nothing came. He reached the edge, leaned over and looked down, and saw only darkness in that intimidating pit. The walls seemed sheer, and there was no sign of life. He thought of lighting another flare and dropping it over the edge ... but he was afraid of what he'd see.

"Hold tight," he said, but there was no one to hear his words.

As the helicopters swung around and came in to land in a clearing three hundred meters away, Budanov jogged toward them, ignoring his aches and wounds. He wondered how long it would take to make them believe.

Their descent into the pit seemed to take forever.

Vasnev's screaming faded to a whimper, and Yelagin might well have been dead. Demidov tried to keep tabs on them both, alerted to where they were by the strange, shimmering luminescence emanating from the tumblers bearing them. Their bodies glowed, reminding Demidov of deep sea creatures—just as compelling, equally mysterious and alien. She couldn't help seeing beauty in their flowing movements, even though the tumbler held her with painfully tight tentacles, clasped around her stomach, left arm and both legs. It was pointless struggling or attempting to escape, but as they descended deeper and deeper, she had time to plan.

She could not simply submit to whatever was to come. Vasily and his companions were likely dead, but while there was even the slightest chance that they were still alive, Demidov and the remainder of her unit had to fight.

She had a knife in her boot and a grenade still hanging from her belt.

"Oh, my God," Yelagin said from over to her left. "Look

down."

Demidov was glad to hear her friend's voice, but when she twisted and followed her advice, cold fear slithered through her veins. Down beneath them, far down, a faint glow was growing in size as they continued their descent. To begin with it might have been just one more tumbler, but as they drew closer she could see many separate points of illumination. It wasn't one. It was hundreds.

"Yelagin," Demidov said. "Vasnev. We need to get away."

"Captain, there are tunnels in the walls," Yelagin said.

"You're sure?"

"I just passed one. The glow of this thing lit it, just for a second. I don't know how far it went but..."

"But that's enough," Demidov said. "Vasnev? You alive?"

"I can't..." Vasnev said. "I can't believe..."

"You don't have to believe," Demidov said. "Do you still have your knife?"

A grunt that might have been an affirmative.

"We can't let them get us down there," Demidov said, wondering all the time what these things heard of their voices, what they thought, and whether there was any way they might comprehend. She guessed not. *Hoped* not. They were something that no one had ever seen or heard of before, how in the hell could they know Russian? "If they get us all the way down, we're finished. Look down, scan the rock face, and when you see—"

"There!" Yelagin said. "Just below us. A ledge."

"Right," Demidov said. She'd seen it. A narrow ledge

like a slash across the wall, similar to many they might already have been carried past. But this one was where they would make their stand.

As the creature carrying her flowed down the wall, limbs reaching and grasping, sticking and moving, Demidov slid her hand down her hip and thigh, bending slightly, to reach the knife in her boot.

This is when it stops me, she thought. It'll know what I'm doing, sense the violence, and one wrench of those limbs will tear me in half.

But the creature seemed unaware of the weapon now grasped in Demidov's hand. The ledge was close, they were running out of time. Without trying to make out whether Yelagin and Vasnev were ready, she slashed at the tentacles pulled tight across her throat.

The creature squealed. It sounded like a baby in pain, but Demidov was committed now. She cut again, then grasped the thing's body with her left hand—soft, fleshy, wet—and stabbed with her right. She felt the blade penetrate deep into the thing's hide and the squeal turned into an agonized scream. Working the blade hard to the left and right, she gutted the beast.

From a little further away she heard other screams. She hoped they weren't human.

Demidov fought, slashed, thrashed, cutting limbs and seeing them drop away into the darkness like exclamations of pain. A gush of warm fluid pulsed across her throat and face. She tried to close her mouth but wasn't fast enough. She tasted the dying thing, its rank spice, its hot sour blood, and as it dropped her and she fell, she puked into the darkness.

She slammed onto the ledge and the breath was knocked from her. Spitting, wiping a mess of gore and puke from her face, she rolled back against the wall and looked up.

Glowing like a ghost from the gore covering her, Yelagin was climbing down the rock face just a couple of meters above. She dropped and crouched beside Demidov.

"Captain!"

"I'm fine. Vasnev?"

"Vasnev fell. I saw him go, still fighting the thing that had him."

Demidov rolled again until she could look down ... and wished she hadn't. She guessed they were fifty meters above the hole's base, and it was pulsing with the glowing things, all of them shoving forward to congregate around one place at the foot of the sheer side. Vasnev was plain to see, splayed across rock, broken, splashed with luminous gore. If the fall hadn't killed him, they soon would.

"We should go," Yelagin said.

"Go where?"

"A cavern. Just past the end of the ledge, I think we can make it. I saw it as I watched Vasnev fall."

Demidov stood, the two remaining soldiers holding onto each other to protect themselves from the dark, the fall, and the terrible glowing, monstrous things that lived in the depths. They moved carefully along the ledge, and just where it petered out was a crack in the rock wall. Standing before it, a waft of surprisingly warm air breathed out at them, as if this whole place were a living thing.

"What the hell was that?" Yelagin whispered.

"Doesn't matter," Demidov said. She had already heard the sounds from below, and a quick glance confirmed her fears. The things were climbing again. Coming for them, ready to avenge their dead. "We've got no choice."

Yelagin tucked her pistol into her belt and climbed away from the ledge toward the crack. Demidov followed. She had never been great with heights. Inside an aircraft or tall building was fine, but if she was on the outside, then the great drop below always seemed to lure her with the promise of an endless, painful fall. Knowing what was coming for her up from below only made matters worse.

"Here," Yelagin said. She was braced in the crack, back against one side and feet against the other, and reaching for Demidov with her left hand. Demidov grabbed her gratefully, scrambled, and soon they were inside.

It opened into more of a tunnel, relatively flat and leading directly away from the great hole. The wet, stinking remnants of the things they had killed still provided a low luminescence on their clothing and hair, and Demidov hoped the effect would last. They both carried flares, but they would burn harsh and quick. She couldn't imagine anything worse than being trapped down here in smothering, total darkness.

She tugged the grenade from her belt.

"Are you fucking crazy?" Yelagin asked.

"What choice do we have? They're coming!"

Yelagin drew her sidearm again and put it into Demidov's hand. "With respect, Captain, you blow the mouth of this tunnel, you could kill us quicker than those things out there. You'll trap us in here, if you don't bring the ceiling down on us. Hold them off as long as you can. I'll see if the tunnel leads to something other than a dead end."

Demidov nodded, switched the gun to her right hand and the grenade to her left. The bullets wouldn't last very long.

She heard Yelagin move away behind her, using the luminescence from the tumblers' blood to see. As the footfalls faded, fine tendrils whipped up over the ledge, and the first tumbler spilled into the mouth of the tunnel. Demidov took aim, dead center, and pulled the trigger.

"We're to place you under arrest and take you back to base," the Lieutenant said. He hadn't given Budanov his name. He hadn't even seemed keen to give the private any medical aid, but his medic had come forward and started tending Budanov's wounds anyway. While she bathed and dressed, another man—a civilian—took careful photographs of the injuries. Two others had disappeared into the snowy woodlands, each of them guarded by a heavily armed soldier.

Budanov had warned them, but they didn't seem to believe a thing he said. All but the civilians, who looked terrified and excited at the same time. *More fucking scientists*, Budanov thought. *That's why we're here in the first place.*

"But my captain and the rest of my unit might still be down there," he said. "The things took them down, and perhaps—"

"Your fault," the lieutenant said. He seemed eager to move, shifting from foot to foot and looking around at the snowscape. One of the men had thrown Budanov a thick coat, and he was eager for the medic to finish so that he could cover himself. All he wanted now was somewhere warm.

Demidov and the others aren't warm, he thought. *They're down there. Cold, afraid. Maybe dead. But I have to know for sure.*

"Can't you at least look?" he asked. "Get one of the KA52s to hover over the hole, shine a light down?"

"We're not staying long enough for that," the lieutenant said. He was a tall, brash man, young for his rank, but Budanov sensed a good military mind behind his iciness. He knew what he was doing.

"You were coming here anyway," Budanov said. "Before you heard from our pilots. Isn't that right?"

"Not for long," the lieutenant said again, staring him in the eye for the first time. "Just long enough for these white-coats to get what they want, then we're getting the fuck out. You're lucky we're taking you with us. Your pilots left an hour ago when they heard."

"Heard what?"

The lieutenant glanced aside. Frowned. One of his soldiers ran across and stood close, muttering something into his ear.

"Everyone, back to the chopper!" the lieutenant

shouted.

"But we're—" one of the scientists said. He was hunched closer to the hole, examining something hidden in the snow. *One of them*, Budanov thought, and he wondered whether it was one he'd shot himself.

"Do as I fucking say!" the lieutenant said. He looked rattled.

"What is it?" Budanov asked. Bullets were his only answer.

The KA52 that had been circling the site dropped low over the hole and opened up with its big cannons, tracer rounds flashing into the darkness and impacting the wall. The explosions were so powerful that Budanov felt their vibrations through the solid ground, and snow drifted down from trees as if startled awake.

"But we don't know—" one of the civilians shouted.

"We *do* know," Budanov said. He stood, and just for a moment he fought every instinct that was telling him to flee.

I can't just run, he thought. I have to help. They'd do the same for me.

He turned his back on the helicopter and sprinted into the trees. No one called him back; either they didn't see him going, or they didn't really care. That lieutenant had been scared, and he'd had more on his mind than capturing an AWOL soldier.

Skirting around where Zhukov's body had been marked with a red flag, he saw a heavy white rucksack, dropped by one of the civilians. Coiled around its handles was a thin nylon climbing rope. He ripped it open, and inside were various devices and sample jars, and a radio.

As the cacophony of gunfire from the KA52 ceased, the radio hissed into life.

"...leaving in three minutes!" It was the lieutenant's voice. "Ground Cleanse commencing eight minutes after that. You do *not* want to be here when the MiGs arrive."

Oh Jesus, they're going to blast the hole to hell!

Budanov crouched and ran closer to the wound in the land, tied the rope around a sturdy tree, and wondered just what the fuck he was doing as he threw the coiled mass over the edge and started to abseil into the darkness.

He descended nearly a hundred feet before he paused on a ledge, taking advantage of the glow from far below. From his pack he drew a couple of pitons and hammered one into the rock face as quickly as possible. Tying it off, he set his heels at the corner of the ledge and prepared to drop deeper. The seconds were ticking by in his head. How long since he'd heard the transmission? How many minutes remaining before MiGs started bombing the shit out of this hole in the frozen heart of the world?

The smell of methane lingered and he wondered if he was being slowly poisoned to death. Funny way to go, with bombs on the way.

To hell with it, he thought, and kicked off the ledge, shooting downward at reckless speed.

As he swung toward the wall again, boots shoving off for another rapid descent, he heard gunshots echoing up to him from below. He kicked off again, glanced down into the darkness...only it wasn't *truly* dark at all. Far below, a pale white glow rippled and undulated like a strange ocean. Closer, on the opposite wall, the same glow shifted and crawled and slid along the rock, and now he saw them on his side as well. Slowing his descent, Budanov's breath caught in his throat.

He hung on the rope and saw the glowing, many tendriled-creatures coming for him, racing up the rock wall of the hole. He shot a single glance skyward, calculated how long it would take him to reach the top from here, and realized he would be dead soon. In reality, Budanov had known this from the moment he had snatched the coils of rope and run for the methane-cored hole, but now he truly understood what he had done.

Down was his only chance.

"Captain!" he screamed. "Kristina! Vasnev!"

Budanov kicked away from the wall and let the rope slide through his hands, nearly in free-fall. He rocketed downward, and the tumblers raced up at him. All of his choices had been made, now. From this point onward, there were only consequences.

Demidov slid backward, jagged rock floor of the tunnel snagging at her pants. The blood of two tumblers cast a ghostly pale illumination in the tunnel mouth. The pistol was warm in her hand as she waited, heart pounding. One of the tumblers she'd killed had fallen backward off the ledge but the other way lay twitching just a few feet from the soles of her boots. She dug her heel into the rock and shoved backward again, gaining a few more inches of distance from the dead thing and the ledge beyond it.

It hissed as it bled. That might've been the sound of it dying or just the noise of its warm blood staining the cool rock floor of the tunnel, like the ticking of a car engine after it's been shut down. She whispered small prayers, her voice echoing in that cramped space, and she listened for Yelagin's return. How would they get back to the surface? If they kept themselves alive long enough, help might come, but what about Vasily and his science team? The hard little bitch she thought of as her conscience told her the man she loved had to be dead, but Demidov wouldn't listen. She told herself Vasily had to be alive.

Though maybe it would have been better if she could imagine him dead. If she could imagine that he no longer needed her, that she could simply surrender to fate, give herself over to the death that even now crawled toward her.

The dead tumbler twitched and Demidov jerked backward, taking aim. She blinked, staring as she realized it was not the dead thing that moved but a new arrival. Behind the cooling, dimming corpse, another tumbler had crept over the ledge and slithered toward her, camouflaged behind its dead brother. They were getting sneaky now, and that terrified her more than anything.

They weren't just cruel, they were clever.

"I see you," she whispered.

It froze, as if it understood.

Demidov lifted the gun, still clutching the grenade in her left hand. The tumbler whipped to the right, raced along the wall and then onto the ceiling, clinging to the bare rock. Tendrils whipped toward her face and Demidov back-pedaled hard, sliding backward along the tunnel as she pulled the trigger. Bullets pinged and cracked and ricocheted off the walls, sending shards of rock flying. Two caught the tumbler at its core, splashing luminescent blood across the tunnel floor. Tendrils snagged her ankles from above, others tangled in her hair, and she screamed as one of them curled around her left hand—where she held the grenade.

Should have pulled the pin. Should have just thrown it. Should have—

She shot it again, center mass. Three more bullets and the gun clicked empty.

The tumbler dangled from the ceiling, its tendrils still sticking to the rock overhead. Demidov tried to catch her breath, to calm her thundering heart. Setting the grenade into the cloth nest of the crotch of her pants, she patted her pockets and checked her belt. Still had her knife, but she needed ammunition…and found it. One magazine. She ejected the spent one and jammed the fresh magazine home.

Something moved out on the ledge, slithering, rolling.

Demidov didn't even look up at it. She knew. They weren't coming one a time anymore.

Gun still in her right hand, she snatched up the grenade again, pulled the pin with her teeth and held on tightly. The second she let it go, the countdown would begin.

Taking a breath, she looked up.

The tumbler dangling from the ceiling dropped to the

floor of the tunnel, dead, just as the others rushed in. She saw two, then realized there were three, maybe even four, their glowing tendrils churning together and filling the tunnel mouth. Demidov fired half a dozen shots, bullets punching through the roiling mass, but she knew her time had come.

She dropped the grenade, turned, and bolted to her feet.

Bent over, she hurtled down the tunnel, firing blindly back the way she'd come. The countdown ticked by in her head as she ran. In the dimming light offered by the blood soaked into her clothing, she saw the tunnel turning and followed it around a corner. The ceiling dropped and the walls closed in and she feared that she'd found a dead end, except there was no sign of—

"Kristina!" she screamed. "Take cover, if you're here! Take—"

The grenade blew, the sound funneling toward her, pounding her eardrums as the blast threw her forward. She crashed to the floor, skidding along rough stone as bits of the ceiling showered down onto her, dust and rock chips. A crack splintered across the stone overhead and she stared up at it, lying there bruised and bloody, and waited for it to fall.

Nothing.

She took a dust-laden breath and realized she was alive. She'd dropped the gun when the grenade blew her off her feet. She looked around, ears pounding, but in that near darkness the weapon was lost.

She heard footfalls coming her way, reached for her

knife, realized that the tumblers had no feet. The narrow beam of Yelagin's flashlight appeared, along with the remaining glow of the tumblers' blood on the woman's uniform.

"You're alive!" Yelagin said, more in relief than surprise. She didn't want to be alone, and Demidov didn't blame her.

"Seems we both are," Demidov said, sitting up and brushing dust off her clothes. "For all the good it will do us. We'll starve to death in here, if we don't suffocate first."

Yelagin knelt beside her. "We may die yet," she said, "but it won't be in this tunnel."

Demidov frowned, glancing at her, refusing to hope.

"Come on," Yelagin said, helping her to stand. "There's a way out."

"A way up?" Demidov asked.

Yelagin would not meet her gaze. "A way *out*," she repeated. "That's all I can promise for now."

A fresh spark of hope ignited inside Demidov and once again she allowed herself to think of Vasily. Maybe it wasn't too late. Maybe he was still alive.

All she and Yelagin had were knives, but for the moment they were still alive. They would fight to stay that way.

The tunnel sloped downward. Demidov's ears were still ringing, all sounds muffled thanks to her proximity to the grenade's explosion. Her head pounded but she took deep breaths and kept her arms outstretched, tracing her fingers along the tunnels walls as she tried to keep her wits about her. There were ridges and striations along the rock that were quite different from what she'd been able to make out on the side of the massive hole. If that sinkhole had been bored up from below by an enormous methane explosion, as Vasily and his team believed, then this side tunnel had been created by some other means.

Something had carved it out.

Several minutes passed in relative silence, with Demidov following Yelagin, the two women doing their best not to slip. The twists in the tunnel often led to a sudden steep section, and a wrong step might have led to a broken neck.

The luminescent blood they'd been splashed with faded with each passing minute, and soon Yelagin's flashlight was their primary source of illumination. The air moved gently around them, not so much a breeze as a kind of subterranean respiration, the tunnels breathing, evidence that there were openings somewhere ahead and below.

Noises came to them, quiet whispers of motion followed by what sounded like thousands of tons of rock and earth shifting, but they remained very much alone in the tunnel. Demidov exhaled in relief when the tunnel flattened out and she found she could stand fully upright. Yelagin picked up their pace, and soon they were hustling along in a quick jog. The thumping of her heart, the familiar cadence of their steps, lent Demidov calm and confidence that allowed her to gather her thoughts. *Find the source of the air flow*, she told herself. *See if we can climb. Track down the tumblers and try to ascertain the status of the science team—dead or alive?*

"There's a glow—" Yelagin started to say.

Then she swore, stumbled, and hurled herself forward in the tunnel. Demidov pulled back, reaching for her knife, ready for a fight. Her backpedaling saved her. Just in front of her, Yelagin scrabbled her hands to get a grip to keep from falling into a hole in the tunnel floor, an opening that seemed to drop away into nothing. Air flowed steadily up from the hole.

"Kristina!" Demidov called, glancing around, trying to figure out how she could help.

Yelagin had already managed to drag one leg up, prop her knee on the edge of the abyss, and now she hauled herself to safety on the other side of the five-foot gap. She'd seen the glow, but had been moving too fast to stop, so instead she'd jumped. And almost not made it at all.

They stared at each other across the gap, neither of them wanting to be left alone. Yelagin used her torch to search the edges of the hole, and it looked to Demidov as if she would be able to get around it—if she was extremely careful—without falling to her death. She lay flat on her belly and dragged herself to the edge to stare down into the depths, drawn by the soft glow that emanated from within. On the other side, Yelagin did the same.

Demidov went numb.

It was Yelagin who spoke first. "Is that...? Is it a kind of ... *city*, do you think?"

Far below, perhaps hundreds of feet, were loops and whorls of stone, a kind of labyrinth of strange tracks and bowls and twisting towers. From those strange spires of rock hung innumerable tendriled things, either asleep or simply static, dreaming their subterranean dreams or contemplating the labyrinth of their underground world, and perhaps the new world they had discovered above them.

"Oh, my God," Demidov whispered.

"Captain," Yelagin said quietly.

Demidov looked up and saw that Private Yelagin had risen to her knees. Now the woman took to her feet, braced herself against the wall, and reached out across the gap. The message did not require words—*get up, don't look, don't think, and let's get the hell out of here.* Demidov ought to have been the one in command, but in that moment she was quite happy to let Yelagin guide her.

She glanced one more time at the sprawling, glowing city-nest below and then she stood, never wanting to see it again. Taking a deep breath, she put one foot on the bit of stone jutting out from one side of the hole, and then she shook her head.

"No," she told Yelagin. "Back up."

"Captain..."

"Back up, Private."

Yelagin withdrew her hand, hesitated a moment, and then backed away, giving her plenty of room to make the leap. Demidov got a running start and flung herself across the gap. She landed on the ball of her left foot, arms flailing, and then stumbled straight into Yelagin, who caught her with open arms.

For a moment they stood like that, then Demidov took

a single breath and nodded. "Lead the way."

They followed the beam of Yelagin's light, passing several places where the tunnel branched off in various directions, until they found one that sloped up. Demidov paused to feel the flow of air and then gestured for Yelagin to continue upward. They'd been moving for only a minute or two, Demidov staring over Yelagin's shoulder, when she realized she could see more details of the tunnel ahead than ought to have been possible. Her breath caught in her throat and she reached out, grabbing a fistful of Yelagin's jacket.

"Stop," she hissed into the other woman's ear. "Quietly."

For long seconds they stood in the tunnel, just listening. Demidov felt her heard thumping hard in her chest as she stared ahead. Sensing the trouble, Yelagin clicked off her flashlight, confirming what Demidov had feared. Not only did the tunnel ahead gleam with the weird photoluminescence of the tumblers, but the glow was becoming steadily brighter. They could hear the slither of tendrils against rock.

Part of Demidov wanted to just forge ahead. But she remembered all too well the glimpse she'd had of the tumblers killing Zhukov, and she thought perhaps they ought to retreat, find a side tunnel, and wait for this wave of creatures to pass them by.

Demidov took Yelagin's arm and turned to retrace their steps.

The same glow lit the tunnel behind them.

"No," Yelagin said quietly.

Demidov slipped out her knife. They had no other weapons and nowhere to run. A numb resignation spread through her, but her fingers opened and closed on the hilt of the knife, ready to fight no matter what the odds.

The tumblers sprawled and rolled and slunk along the tunnel, arriving first from one direction and then the other. Some slipped along the ceiling or walls, filling the tube of the tunnel with their undulating tendrils and their unearthly glow until it looked like some kind of undersea nightmare.

"Captain," Yelagin whispered. "Look at the little ones."

Demidov had seen them, miniature tumblers about the size of her thumb, maybe even smaller. They clung to the others and moved swiftly amongst them. The little ones seemed to cleave more to the ceiling, creating a kind of mossy mat of shifting, impossible life. The tumblers flowed in until the only bare rock was the small circle where Demidov and Yelagin stood.

And then the smothering carpet of creatures parted and a pair of dark silhouettes emerged, like ghosts against the creatures' strange light.

Demidov could not breathe. For a moment, she could not speak, and then she managed only to rasp out a single word.

"Vasily?"

As Yelagin swore, frozen in shock, Demidov lowered her knife. Vasily Glazkov—her lover and best friend—came to a halt just a few feet away, with Amanda Hart behind him. The small tumblers clung to their clothes and flesh. Hart's face seemed to bulge around her left eye, as if something shifted beneath the skin, near the orbit. Demidov wanted to look at Vasily, but that bulbous pulsing thing in Hart's face made her stare.

"Hello, Anna," Vasily said. His voice seemed different, somehow both muffled and echoing. The tunnel turned it into a dozen voices. He looked sad, and sounded sadder.

"Vasily, you're..." She didn't know *what* he was.

"It's such a shame," he said. "So many dead."

"We're all that's left," she said. But when he next spoke, she thought perhaps Vasily wasn't talking about the soldiers who had died.

"You must understand that they are no different from us."

"What?" Yelagin said, shaking her head in confusion. "They're nothing *but* different from us."

Vasily did not so much as glance at her. He focused on Demidov. "There's beauty here. A whole world of wonder. When the shaft opened above them, they went up to explore, just as we came down. They're studying us, beginning to learn about our world. Already they have touched us deeply. Amanda suffered a terrible injury and they have repaired her, strengthened her."

Things moved beneath the skin of Hart's neck, and something twitched under her scalp, her hair waving on its own. Demidov stared at Vasily, gorge rising in her throat, hoping she would not see the thing she feared more than anything. Was that his cheek bulging, just a bit? Where his temple pulsed, was that merely blood rushing through a vein or did something else curl stretch his skin?

"Who's speaking now?" she asked.

Vasily frowned. "Anna, my love, you must listen. There's so much we can learn."

She could not find her voice, did not dare ask who Vasily meant by *we.*

"Dr. Glazkov," Yelagin said, shifting nervously as the small tumblers skittered above her head. "Whatever there is to learn, we'll find time for that. But some of our team has died and I don't see Professor Brune with you. Captain Demidov and I have to report in. You know this. Can you get us to the surface? Whatever these things are, whatever you've discovered, our superiors will want to know. We need to—"

"Stop, Kristina," Demidov said.

Yelagin flinched, stared at her as if she'd lost her mind.

"This isn't Vasily talking," Demidov said. "Not anymore."

Vasily smiled. Tiny tendrils emerged from the corners of his mouth, like cracks across his lips. "The truth is the truth, regardless of who speaks it."

Demidov raised her knife.

They swept over her.

Yelagin screamed and they both fought, but there were simply too many of the creatures, binding them, twisting them like puppets.

Dragging them down, deeper than ever before.

It made her think of what drowning must be like.

Tendrils gripped and caressed her, surging forward, one creature passing her to another like the ebb and flow of ocean currents. Sometimes tendrils covered her eyes and other times she could see, but the eerie phosphorescence of their limbs—so bright and so near—cast the subterranean labyrinth into deeper shadow. It was difficult to make out anything but crenellations in the wall or the silhouettes of Vasily and Hart. The sea of tumblers brought her up on a wave and then dragged her under again, carrying her onward. Demidov caught a glimpse of Yelagin, and felt some measure of relief knowing that whatever might happen now, they were together.

She tried not to think about Vasily, tried to focus just on her own beating heart and the desperate gasping of her lungs. Had it been Vasily speaking, lit up with the epiphanies of discovery? Or had these things been masquerading as her man, recruiting for their cause, attempting to find the proper mouthpiece through which to communicate with the hostiles they'd encounter aboveground?

The image of the things twisting beneath the skin of Hart's face made her want to scream. Only her focus on surviving gave her the strength to remain silent. Every moment she still lived was another moment in which she might figure out how to *stay* alive.

The ocean of tumblers surged in one last wave, dumped her on an uneven stone floor, and withdrew. She blinked, trying to get her bearings. Glancing upward, she saw that they had brought her to the bottom of the original vast sinkhole. Demidov stared up the shaft, the gray daylight a small circle far overhead, just as beautiful and unreachable as the full moon on a winter's night.

Not unreachable, she told herself. You could climb it if you had to.

But she'd never make it. For fifty feet in every direction, the glowing tumblers shifted and churned, rolling on top of one another, piled as high as her shoulders. Demidov didn't know what they wanted of her, but she had no doubt she was their prisoner. The tumblers parted to allow Vasily and Hart to approach her once more.

"Anna," Vasily began. "They need an emissary. There is so much—"

"Where's Kristina?" Demidov demanded. "Private Yelagin. Where is she?"

With a ripple, the ocean of tumblers disgorged Yelagin onto the ground beside Demidov, choking and spitting, tears staining her face. Demidov took her arm, helped her to stand. In the weird phosphorescence she looked like a ghost.

Yelagin whipped around to face her, madness in her eyes. "I saw Budanov! He's down here with us!"

"Budanov is dead."

"No!" Yelagin shook her head. "I swear to you, I saw him clearly, just a few feet away." She swept her arm toward the mass of writhing tumblers. "He's in there somewhere. They've got him!"

Demidov stared at Vasily, or whatever sentience spoke through him. "Give him to me."

Vasily and Hart exchanged a silent look. Things shifted beneath Hart's skin, bulging from her left cheek. A tiny bunch of tendrils sprouted from her ear for a moment, before drawing back in like the legs of a hermit crab.

"He is injured," Vasily said. "They can help him. Heal him."

Demidov heard the hesitation in his voice, the momentary lag between thought and speech, and she knew this wasn't Vasily speaking. Not really. Not by choice.

"Give him to me," she demanded, "and I'll carry your message to the surface."

The things pulling Hart's strings used her face to smile.

Vasily nodded once and the mass of tumblers churned. Like some hideous birth, Budanov spilled from their pulsing mass. One of his arms had been shattered and twisted behind him at an impossible angle. Broken bone jutted from his lower leg, torn right through the fabric of his uniform. His face had been bloodied and gashed, but it was his eyes that drew Demidov's focus. The fear in those eyes.

"Private—" she began.

"No, listen!" Budanov said, lying on the stone floor, full of madness and lunatic desperation as he glared up at Demidov and Yelagin. "There's an airstrike coming! Any minute now...Fuck, any *second* now! They're going to—"

Demidov stared up at that pale circle so high above.

She could hear them now, the MiGs arriving, the

familiar moaning whistle of their approach. They had seconds. A terrible sadness gripped her, a sorrow she had never known. She looked at Vasily, feeling a hole opening up inside her where the rest of their lives ought to have been. He gazed back at her, mirroring her grief. Then she saw the twitch beneath her right eye.

"All the things we could have taught them," he said, and she wasn't sure whether it was her Vasily talking about them, or them talking about everyone else.

The scream of bombs falling. The roar of an explosion high above—a miss. A shower of rock cracking off the walls of the shaft.

The sea of tumblers closed around Demidov and she shouted, reaching for Yelagin. They covered her, lifted her, hurtled her along as the MiGs roared and she felt the first explosion, the impact, the flash of searing heat as the tumblers rocketed her into their tunnels. They burned, and her skin burned along with them, and then she felt nothing at all.

Just a pinch, at first. That's all it was.

Then a scrape.

Demidov flinched, surprised that she was still alive, but in pain. Searing pain, scraping pain that made her moan and wince and whisper to God, in whom she had never believed.

Her eyes fluttered open and for a moment all the pain faded, just a little. The city around her—city was the only word—could not have been real, and yet she was certain it was no dream. For a moment she let her head loll from side to side, gazing at the beauty and wonder of its whorls and curves and waves, and the strange spires that looked more like trees, towering things whose trunks and branches were hung with thousands of tendriled creatures, all glowing with that pale, ghostly light. She and Yelagin had glimpsed it from far above, but now she was here in the midst of it. She was in their home.

Another scrape and the pain roared back in.

Groaning, Demidov looked down and saw them on her naked skin, a hundred of the tiny things, their tendrils caressing and scrubbing her raw, burned flesh.

"No!" she cried, trying to shake them off and then whimpering with the agony of movement, lying still as her thoughts caught fire with the horror of their touch.

She remembered the bombing, the blast that scoured the tunnel even as they rushed her away.

"They saved your life," a voice said.

Demidov recognized the voice without turning toward him. She steeled herself, because she knew that when she let herself see Vasily it would look like him, but it wouldn't be him. He surprised her by not speaking again.

Swallowing hard, feeling the gently painful ministrations of the tumblers, she looked to her right and saw him standing nearby, watching over her. They clung to his clothes and skin and hair. When he spoke again, she might have glimpsed one inside his mouth, but it might have been a trick of the light.

"Yelagin?" she asked. "Budanov?"

"I'm sorry."

Demidov sighed, squeezing her eyes shut. "Why save

me?"

Vasily's reply came from just beside her. "I told you. They need an emissary."

She opened her eyes and he was right there, kneeling by her head, studying her with kindly, almost parental concern.

"There are other shafts. Other holes. They've been opening up all over this area. Some will be destroyed, as this one was. But not all."

Her burnt skin throbbed, but she could feel that the stroking of those tendrils had begun to soothe her.

Demidov exhaled. "Vasily..."

He ignored her, forging ahead. "They'll share some of their gifts with you," he said. "Teach you wonderful things, including how it is possible for them to heal the damage to your flesh—"

"Vasily?"

"—and then you will carry their message to the surface."

"Vasily!"

Blinking as if coming awake, he looked at her. Vasily had stubble on his face and his dark hair was an unruly mess, just as it always had been. For that moment, he looked so much like himself.

"What is it, Anna?" he asked, eyes narrowing, as if daring her to ask the question.

She almost didn't. Just getting the words out cost her everything.

"Who am I speaking to?" she said.

Vasily did not look away, but neither did he give her

an answer. Several seconds passed before he continued to describe the mission the tumblers intended for her to undertake.

Demidov tasted the salt of her tears as they slid down her scorched cheeks and touched her lips. She hung her head, Vasily's words turning into nothing but a low drone.

Her right arm had not been burnt. That was something, at least. She stared at the smooth, unmarked flesh.

A shape moved beneath her skin.

THE CURIOUS ALLURE OF THE SEA

So stunning was the view from the deck of her new house that Jenny thought it might be worth the loneliness. Late afternoon sunlight made monstrous shadows of the pine trees on either side of the property, but straight back from the deck where the ground dropped away toward the rocks, she had the perfect vista—nothing but the indigo sweep of the Atlantic Ocean, the cold wind off the water, the white froth of the chop around the island, the circling gulls, and the occasional seal basking on the rocks. The romance of it plucked at her heart. She stood on the deck, tugged her thick wool sweater more tightly around her, and thought there might not be a more beautiful place on Earth. The house was hers. The deck was hers. But she couldn't share it with anyone.

Not ever.

It started months earlier, on the rainy autumn morning when they found her father's boat. Tom Leary had gone missing two days earlier after a lifetime at sea. Jenny had spent the time praying for him to radio in, praying the Coast Guard would find some trace of his fishing boat, the *Black Rose*. Praying for it, and dreading it as well.

Matt Finn knocked on her door at just past seven that

morning. She opened the door of her rented cottage in pajama pants and a threadbare Patriots shirt, an arm placed self-consciously across her chest, eyes narrowed because she was too sleepy to open them all the way just yet. Officer Finn normally cut a fine figure in his uniform—Matt had been proud of his badge since his first day on the job, back when they'd still been dating—but that morning he just stood in the rain looking tired and sad, blues soaked almost black, and Jenny took one glance at him and knew.

He hesitated as he tried to muster up the words.

Jenny just shook her head. "I'll get some clothes on and be right out."

She shut the door and let him stand out there in the cold September rain. It never occurred to her until much later that she should have let him in. By then, she'd wish that she had. If she'd known how things would turn out, she'd have savored every moment of contact she could get. But wisdom always came too late.

In the car, Matt shut off the crackling voices on the radio. She was pretty sure he wasn't supposed to do that, but the silence helped.

"They found the *Rose*?" she asked.

Hands tight on the wheel, Matt nodded. The wipers swished the rain off the glass and the engine hummed, and it took him a moment or two before he spoke.

"He wasn't on it."

"No sign of him at all?"

In answer, Matt reached out and took her hand, holding it there on the seat between them as the police car carried her out to the dock. When they'd parked and gotten out and were walking the rest of the way, and she saw the dark figures milling about in the gray storm light, and the Coast Guard ship, and the *Black Rose* bobbing against the dock beyond it, she wished Matt could take her hand again, almost reached for him but thought better of it. He was married now, and didn't belong to her anymore.

Cops murmured words she barely heard. Three strutting seagulls had landed on the boat's bow railing and were squawking at each other in some kind of territorial dispute. When a fourth tried to land, they banded together to chase it off.

A Coastie put a hand on Jenny's shoulder, trying to prevent her from boarding the *Rose*, but a cop intervened and the hand vanished. Her heart broke with the force of her gratitude. She had to see for herself. Her father had always known the sea would take his life, but he'd always said it gave him life, too, so that would only be fair.

It didn't feel fair.

The boat creaked under foot as she stepped down onto the deck. She glanced around, saw an abandoned life vest and some long black Guinness cans, empty of course. This was the debris of her daddy's idea of fishing. His catch would be in the coolers, no doubt, though one would have several more of those black cans. The life vest made her brow furrow, though. Why had he dragged that out from its usual resting place? There hadn't even been a storm.

A couple of the gulls hopped to the deck and started making their way back toward her, angry at her intrusion. Lost in the worst of dreams, Jenny noticed the oddness of their behavior, but only barely. Ignoring the birds, she stepped into the wheelhouse.

It felt haunted, but it took a moment for her to realize it was [illegible] that [illegible] ghostly atmosphere. The bo[illegible]

A creak [illegible] ly Matt and another co[illegible] to

“The engine?” she asked.

“Dead.”

“How does that happen?”

The cops shifted uncomfortably. “It’s being investigated.”

“He still had his cell phone, Matt. Radio or not, he could’ve called. And he would have, unless he thought he didn’t need to. Could he have flagged down another boat? Maybe someone...”

She didn’t want to think about it. About violence toward her father.

“Anything’s possible,” the other cop said. “The weird thing is there’s no damn fish.”

Jenny frowned, glanced past the cops toward the deck. “He drank at least three beers, which meant he was out for a while before...whatever happened. No way did he spend that kind of time and not catch anything. This is Tom Leary we’re talking about.”

Matt shot a dark look at the other officer, then shrugged. “No fish. No sign he’d even been fishing. Equipment all put away, nice and neat.”

Her frown deepened. She hung her head, pondering

what her father had been up to on that morning two days' past. The emptiness of the wheelhouse began to feel suffocating, th[illegible] air too clo[illegible] despite the side windows being open. S[illegible] took a deep [illegible] and felt a tingle at her back, as if someone might [illegible] there with t[illegible] tching from a shadow[illegible] [illegible] no one. [illegible] to the right of the throttle, where her dad had often hung his hat. In its place was a grimy silver necklace upon which dangled a flat, rectangular stone about two inches in height.

Jenny bent to study that stone, reached out to lift it into her palm, chain still looped around the hook. The stone had been carved with three spirals, all connected at the center so they seemed to flow one toward the other, around in a never-ending circle.

Waves, she thought. They look like—

"Hey, Jen, don't do that," Matt said, taking a step toward her. "You know you're not supposed to touch anything."

Jenny let the stone talisman slip from her fingers and it swung for a moment below that hook. She took out her cell phone, opened the camera, made sure the flash was on and snapped a shot. Her fingers felt warm where she'd touched the stone and the urge to reach out for it again grew powerful. An unfamiliar regret ignited inside her, and for just a moment the loss of that stone, the wish to return it to her grasp, seemed more important than the mystery of what had happened to her father.

"Looks pretty old," the other cop said, crouching to peer at the stone. Jenny fought the urge to keep it from him.

"Your father's," Matt asked.

Jenny pulled herself away, skin crawling with unease at the way the presence of that stone tugged at her insides. "I guess it might've been. I don't remember seeing it before."

Matt bagged it for evidence while she stood out on the deck in the rain. Jenny felt the eyes on her as she waited for him to drive her home, knew they were wondering just as she was what happened to Tom Leary, whether he'd gotten drunk and fallen overboard or if there'd been some kind of foul play, or if—as happened from time to time with those men who spent most of their lives alone out on the water—he had just given himself over to the sea.

"The Coast Guard'll keep looking," Matt promised later, as he was driving her home, the shush of the windshield wipers and the drum of the rain on the cruiser's roof making her sleepy. The words sounded hollow coming out of his mouth. Jenny barely heard them and certainly didn't believe them. "We'll find him."

But of course they didn't.

Someone stole the spiral-carved stone out of evidence on that first night. Jenny couldn't stop thinking about it, couldn't stop looking at the photo she'd taken with her phone.

The morning after the Coast Guard called off the search, she had that ocean symbol tattooed on the inside of her right forearm. Three days later, she went back to the same shop and had the friendly, bearded artist tattoo her father's name in the same spot on the opposite arm.

She mourned, of course. Grief cut into her in moments quiet and loud, sometimes out of nowhere. Sorrow welled up like blood in a wound, spilling over and staining whatever it touched. And yet there were good moments as well, and anytime she looked at the tattoo, the ocean rolling on forever in that circle of waves, the infinite sea, a kind of peace filled her. Healed her. Though she'd never been much for fishing, Jenny had inherited her father's love for the sea, felt its allure just as he always had. With that tattoo, it felt like the sea remained with her wherever she went.

And her father, of course. Tom was with her as well.

As much as it hurt to lose him, she felt as if somehow they were still together, out on the water, sharing that serenity. But it was the skin on the inside of her right arm that drew her gaze most often. Sometimes she would trace the three spirals with her fingertip. It relaxed her completely, made her feel as if she might float away. The thought did not trouble her at all.

All would be well. She felt sure of it.

On the third day after her second tattoo, she noticed the behavior of the gulls. In the aftermath of her father's death, Jenny had put off her real estate clients the best she could and spent her time cleaning up after him. The funeral had brought with it a maelstrom of emotions. She'd listened to a hundred stories about her dad, some of them new to her and others comfortingly familiar. There'd been tears and laughter, and the unwelcome presence of her aunt Eleanor, who'd spent the wake and funeral with her lips in a constant twist of disapproval. She'd come with her son Forrest, this woman who'd never understood the way the sea had called to her brother and always believed it had been laziness that caused him not to make "more" of himself, as if a man who earned his living out on the water could ever be conceived of as lazy.

Jenny had wanted to be polite but only barely stopped herself from telling Aunt Eleanor and her tax attorney son to go fuck themselves. Maybe down the line, when Jenny could clear her head, she'd realize she ought to dig through her father's things and mail some keepsake or other to Eleanor, but as she began to go through the old man's belongings, she found nothing her aunt deserved. Not that there was much to choose from. The boat still had a loan and would need to be sold. The house, though—she'd grown up in it, and so had her father. The taxes were nothing to sneeze at, but it had no mortgage, and she was grateful for that. Over the years he'd gone through very lean times, but Tom Leary had never given in to the temptation to take the money out of the house. There'd be an official reading of his will and it would have to go through probate, but she knew what was in it. Whatever he'd had would come to her.

All of these things were swirling in her mind as she parked her car outside the Whale's Tale, a pub that looked over the harbor. As she climbed out, her shoes crunching in the gravel, the tattoo on her right arm felt strangely cold, as if it were winter instead of early fall. She slammed the car door and shivered despite the sweater she wore. She turned her wrist to stare at the tattoo on the inside of her forearm. It looked just as it had before and she felt foolish, wondering what she had expected.

Jenny took the walkway next to the restaurant—the main entrance opened onto a wooden boardwalk facing the harbor. She scanned the handful of people seated on the outside deck in spite of the chill and wondered if her lunch date would have opted for inside. It was comfortable for September, but the sky hung low and the clouds promised rain. She wished Matt had been her lunch date—he'd been so kind and attentive since her father's death that she wondered if they might start over—but instead she was meeting with Rudy Harbard, who'd been one of her dad's competitors and wanted to buy the *Black Rose*. They'd never liked each other much, dad and Rudy, but Tom Leary had always respected the man.

As she stepped onto the boardwalk, Jenny inhaled deeply. The smell of the ocean, the sound of it, filled her heart. She glanced out at the water, at the boats bobbing out there, at the men working on their decks, and she longed to be with them. For a moment the idea of selling the fishing boat felt so wrong that she couldn't take another step. She had always loved the sea, but now she felt a yearning so deep her bones sang with it. If she sold the boat—

A flash of white and gray whipped past her face. The gull cried out as it struck her right arm. She felt its claws but its momentum carried it past her and she twisted away from it. The bird alighted on the boardwalk, sending several people scurrying out of its path. Jenny glanced down at her arm, saw the small trickle of blood there, and then stared at the bird.

"You little shit," she said. "You're in for a kicking."

She marched toward the bird, expecting it to hop backward or fly away, but instead it came toward her. A shiver went through her. Jenny heard another cry and looked up to see other gulls alighting on the little fence outside the restaurant's porch and on top of a trashcan on the boardwalk.

A man touched her back. Startled, she jerked away from him, feeling as if she were under attack. The gull hopped closer.

"Let me help you," he said, so calmly that he almost seemed to be sleepwalking. Maybe fifty years old, handsome and tan but leathery from a lifetime in the sun, he stared at Jenny as if he'd never seen another human being before, studying her as if to decipher some puzzle she represented to him.

"If you want to help—" she started.

The first gull cawed and took flight, right toward her. The leathery man dragged Jenny into a protective embrace. The bird might have struck him, she wasn't sure, but then he turned and shooed it away. A toddler carrying an ice cream cone shrieked as the bird zipped over her head. Two other gulls jumped down to the boardwalk, and the leathery man shooed them away as well.

Over a dozen passersby had paused to become spectators, not including the people on the deck of the Whale's Tale who were observing the show. Several of them, Jenny saw, were focused on her instead of the weirdness going down. One woman had her head tilted, her mouth slightly open, as if she'd taken the world's best drugs. Jenny felt her skin crawling with the attention.

The man with the toddler—her father, she assumed—abandoned his child and walked toward her, scrutinizing her in a way that reminded her of a hundred showing-up-naked-at-school nightmares.

"Hey," he said softly as he approached. "You. I need...I want..." He blinked and crinkled his brow like a flicker of common sense had tried to push into his forebrain. Then he shook his head. "What *are* you? Why do I want to—"

Leathery guy grabbed him from behind and slung him away. The quiet man almost tripped over his own toddler, startling the girl into letting her ice cream drop from the cone. She stared down at the strawberry glob on the boardwalk and her lip trembled, and then she started to cry.

The little girl's sobs drew everyone's attention. Even those who'd seemed somehow mesmerized were distracted long enough for Jenny to rush to the hostess stand. The fiftyish brunette had been watching the whole thing unfold and she frowned with maternal worry as she escorted Jenny straight to the restaurant's entrance.

"Come inside, honey," the brunette said. "We can call the cops—"

The tattoo on her right forearm prickled with the cold, as if the ink had turned to ice on her skin, and Jenny rubbed at it to try to drive that chill away.

"It's okay. I don't need...it was just—"

"Fuckin' peculiar is what it was," the hostess said with

a glance over her shoulder. She dragged open the door, put her free hand on the small of Jenny's back, and gently guided her inside. "Have yourself a drink, at least. Take a breath. I'll let you know when those guys are gone."

"I'm supposed to meet someone," Jenny started to say, as the door swung closed behind them.

The crack of impact made her cry out as she and the hostess grabbed hold of one another. Jenny spun, backing away, staring at the spider-web pattern splintered into the door and the smear of blood streaking the glass. Through the clear, unbroken glass toward the bottom of the door, they could see the seagull that had just killed itself trying to reach her.

"What the hell?" the hostess whispered.

She glanced at Jenny and for the first time that maternal concern vanished. Instead, the woman took a step away, as if to move out of the line of fire, in case of whatever came next. Resentment kindled in Jenny's chest, mingling with anger and wonder and a kind of helplessness she'd never felt before. She stared at the hostess, infuriated by the idea that the woman was afraid to come near her.

Later, she would remember that moment and wish that she could make everyone as hesitant to approach her as the hostess had been.

Over the following days, it escalated quickly. Everywhere she went there were men and women who looked at her too long, watched her too closely. Not everyone—whatever the allure, it wasn't universal—but enough to make her increasingly uncomfortable. Even small children rushed to invade her personal space. Out for a morning run, Jenny encountered Emma Brill, a friend from high school, who'd been walking her infant son in one of those fancy jogger-strollers. The moment the boy saw Jenny, he'd begun to cry, stretching his arms toward her as if desperate to be held. As if Jenny were his mother instead of Emma. For a few minutes, Jenny complied, just so she and Emma could continue their conversation—though it consisted of the same beats as most of her recent conversations, full of condolences and shared memories.

When she'd given the baby back, the infant had loosed a piercing wail, shrieking as he tried to hold on, his face turning purplish-red. Emma apologized, trying to soothe the baby. Jenny whispered her own apology, promised to talk to Emma soon, and started off again on her run, sneakers crunching on the sand and grit in the road. The baby shrieked on, inconsolable, and even when Jenny had outrun the sound, the wind would gust and carry it to her in small, lonely snatches, as if the baby would scream forever.

Gulls cawed and circled in the sky. As she ran along a narrow path just a few hundred yards from the ocean, small crabs scuttled out from the high grass and scrub. At first she ran over them, careful not to step on and crush them, but after half a minute she noticed they all seemed to be moving in the same direction—toward her—and she paused to look back the way she'd come. There were dozens of the little things, and more emerging from the grass. All of them were moving in her direction. The ones she'd passed had changed course to follow her.

A tremor of fear went through her. Jenny sneered at the emotion, angry with herself, and she started running again, part of her convinced she could still hear Emma Brill's baby screaming for the loss of her. Her heart pounded and the tattoo on her right forearm went colder than ever before, as if the ice had slid deeper inside her, right along the tracks of her veins. She put a hand on it as she ran, taking peace from the contact, drawing comfort from the symbol there. For a little while it seemed like her thoughts became softer, and her feet carried her forward in a sort of trance.

The path branched to the right, toward the street that led to her neighborhood. A dozen steps toward home, gulls cawing above, twenty of them circling now, she staggered to a halt.

Three people waited along the path, the high sea grass waving on either side of them. One she didn't know, but the other two were fisherman. Men who'd spent their lives at sea, who felt the call of it in their hearts the same way Tom Leary did.

Jenny backed away. At the split in the path, she took the other fork, picking up her pace. A gull darted past her head close enough that she had to duck, but she only ran faster, kept running without really thinking about where she might go, although in the back of her mind she'd known all along. She fled to the place she'd always run to when she was in trouble.

Home.

The cottage she'd been renting was only a few miles from the old Federal Colonial where she'd grown up, and now her run brought her onto a path that emerged two houses down from her childhood home. All the houses along Dunphy Road sat on a bluff, facing the ocean, with nothing but the street and a pile of enormous rocks separating them from the steep drop off the bluff into the water. Jenny sprinted along the road toward the front steps, heart already lightening.

A car rolled up beside her, slowing to match her speed, and then the tires skidded to a halt. Jenny turned, startled, to see Matt climbing out in that familiar uniform. She saw the pain and regret on his face as he walked up to her and her only thought was of her father.

"Did they…did they find his body?" she asked.

Tears welled in Matt's eyes. One slid down his left cheek, and others followed.

"I'm sorry," he said.

Seagulls fluttered down to alight on his police car and on the front porch of her house. Across the street, a woman had been photographing the ocean. A professional, with a camera strapped around her neck that looked as if it cost more than Jenny made in the average home sale commission. Now the photographer turned and gazed at her like Dorothy at the gates of the Emerald City.

"Where did you find him?" Jenny asked. Horror swept through her as she imagined having to identify her dad after his body had been in the water for weeks.

Matt grabbed her by the arms, held her tightly, and

leaned in to breathe in the scent of her hair. “I’m sorry,” he said again.

She started to protest and he nuzzled her throat, pressed his cheek against hers, kissed her forehead lightly.

“I can’t…” Matt said. “I can’t keep away. I just needed to come to you. Get lost in you.”

The words might have been romantic if not for his grip on her arms. If not for the hopeless look in his eyes and the fearful, desperate tone of his voice.

“Matt, no.” She tried to extricate herself from his grip. Took a step back, drawing him with her instead.

She saw the expectant look in his eyes, as if he felt certain she would understand. And the truth was that she did. Jenny said his name, looked down in frustration at the grip he had on her arms and saw that his hand covered half of the triple spiral tattoo.

“No!”

She twisted her arms down and outward, breaking his grip, then stepped in and shoved him with both hands. Matt staggered backward, arms pinwheeling, and fell on his ass at the edge of the road. The gulls on his car took flight, darting toward her. Jenny spun and raced for the porch, took the stairs two at a time, lifted her arms to protect her face as the gulls there flapped up from the railing and came at her. She batted at them, heart pounding, fighting the scream that had been building inside of her.

Tom Leary’s wicker chair sat on the porch. Jenny picked it up with both hands and used it to shield herself, keeping it aloft with one hand while she plucked the spare key from on top of the lantern to the right of the door. Gulls cawed and pecked at the wicker.

Matt cried out her name and the plaintive tone in his voice made her own tears begin to fall.

The key scratched around the lock and she wanted to scream, but then it slipped in. She turned it, then grabbed the knob and gave it a twist. The door swung inward but the wicker chair caught on the frame and she released it. The gulls scrabbled away from the chair as it fell, just long enough for her to spin around and slam the door, locking it from the inside.

Trying to catch her breath, she glanced at the tattoo inside her left forearm, taking comfort from her father's name inked there. But she felt her gaze pulled toward that other tattoo, and only when she let her eyes shift to it did she find real peace.

A sound broke through her reverie, gulls clawing at the door. She looked up at the peeling paint, and the door shook in its frame.

"Jenny, please!" Matt called.

"Go away!"

"I can't. God help me, I can't."

She turned and bolted up the stairs to the second story, then all the way to the third. At the front of the house, a bay window looked out at the sea, but Jenny had more interest in the yard below. With her left hand, she covered the spiral tattoo, soothing herself. From the vantage point at the window she couldn't see the front porch, where Matt still pounded on the wood and gulls still roosted.

But she could see the road. She could see the cars and pickups that had pulled up there, and the men and women who had begun to gather, gazing up at her home with the sad eyes and heartfelt longing of people who knew the thing that so fascinated them would be forever out of their reach, that the thing they most loved could never love them back. Fishermen and tourists, the photographer and several small children who seemed to belong to no one, who seemed to have wandered away from their parents to follow the allure of something they would never understand, whether as children or as adults…they all wore that same look.

Jenny had her hand on the tattoo, knew she could take that peace with her wherever she went, but there would always be those who felt the same allure. She wondered about the talisman, where her father had acquired it, how deeply it had affected him. If it had killed him.

Though she knew the answer. Of course she knew.

She could remove the tattoo, of course, but she felt it just as others did. It called to her, soothed her, satisfied a yearning in her, and Jenny couldn't surrender that. Not for anyone or anything.

Yet even as she understood that, she also understood they would never stop being drawn to her. She had to get out of there, could make it down the steps and out the back of the house. Her father's old Harley was there, in the shed he'd used as a workshop forever. She knew where he hung the keys. She'd go. She'd do it right now, leave all these people behind, escape whatever drew them to her.

But she knew what drew them. Knew she'd never leave it behind, even if it weren't inked into her skin.

Still, she couldn't stay here.

She bolted. The Harley waited for her.

Beyond that, she didn't know. Not at first.

The current of her life swept her out to sea.

Jenny had given up her rented house, put a For Sale sign in front of her childhood home, and entered a lease-to-own agreement on this starkly isolated spot on Comeau Island. There were twenty-seven other year-round residences on the island, but the nearest was half a mile through the piney woods from Jenny's place. They weren't the drop-by-for-a-welcome sort of neighbors. Nobody came to borrow a cup of tea. People didn't live on a remote island off the coast of Maine because they felt like being neighborly. The best she could hope for would be that someone would come to check on her if they saw smoke rising from her property that couldn't just be the chimney.

These were the only neighbors she could allow herself.

Questions lingered. How long she could last out here? How long would the proceeds from the sale of the family home allow her to live without a real job? The money would be substantial, at least four times what this island cottage would cost to purchase, but it wouldn't last forever. To many people she'd known, it would be paradise—nothing to do but read, watch movies, and gaze at one of the most beautiful views imaginable. But even heaven could become hell if you were a prisoner there.

The questions haunted her, but not as much as they

might have. The tattoo on her right arm would turn cold as ice and she would cover it with her left hand and be suffused with that sense of peace for which she'd yearned her entire life. It soothed her, made the questions withdraw into the recesses of her mind. In those moments, her doubts and regrets seemed small and unimportant. When the gulls landed on the railing of her deck or came too close and she had to chase them off, even fight them off, even kill them when it came to that...she found solace in the infinite ocean inked on her arm.

Four days into her exile, Jenny stood on the deck again in a thick blue sweater she'd owned for years, the sleeves pushed up, her hair tied back in a ponytail. Coffee steamed from the same mug she'd used the previous three days and she cupped her hands around it, enjoying the warmth on that chilly morning. She glanced warily at the sky, watching for the gulls. By now she was familiar with their patterns, the way they would begin to diverge from their natural flight, circling closer and closer until they descended. She had fifteen or twenty minutes to enjoy the deck and the breeze, so she took a deep breath, sipped her coffee, and reminded herself how many people would trade anything to wake to this view every day.

The triple spiral on her arm sent the chill down to her bones and she smiled. Somehow that icy cold made the rest of her warmer.

Her view through the pines had a golden, early morning glow. She'd walked down to the water the first and second day, but yesterday she had not ventured out. It wasn't worth the trouble to bring the baseball bat to deal with the gulls, and the crabs had proliferated between the first and second day. Several sharks had begun to patrol the end of her creaky little dock and though she knew they could not come after her, still it gave her a shudder to seem them gathering like that.

Jenny breathed in the aroma of her coffee, let it fill her head a moment before she took another sip. Gulls circled out over the dock, but there were more of them now, and several looped nearer to the house.

Another sip of coffee. Another pulse of ice from the ink on her arm.

She pressed her eyes closed and inhaled the smell of the ocean. When she opened them, she noticed something moving down by the dock. The rocks and sand seemed to be shifting, but it was too far away to see in detail. Jenny placed her coffee mug on the railing and slid her phone out of the band of her sweatpants, opened the camera function, and zoomed the picture.

The tiniest of sounds escaped her lips. Her hand shook and she almost dropped the phone, but she managed to steady her right arm—left hand over that tattoo, calming her.

The rocks and sand were moving, all right. Shifting and scuttling, covered with crabs large and small. Even horseshoe crabs. There were a few lobsters, dying on the rocks. A small octopus slithered across the sand toward the path, moving almost without moving, as if it glided in her direction by will alone. Down at the water's edge, fish flopped in the surf like they had tried to come ashore.

Staring through the zoomed camera image, breath

caught in her throat, Jenny scanned the path and the water's edge again, but something at the upper edge of the image drew her attention and she tilted the camera up to see pale hands gripping the weathered boards, and then a dead woman hauled herself up onto the dock.

Jenny cried out. Dropped the phone. Heard it crack but reached for it anyway. Bumped it with her fingers so it skittered out of her reach and she had to follow it and pick it up, opening the camera again. Zooming again.

The woman on the dock wasn't alone. A bald man in sodden, salt-bleached tatters crawled and rolled in the surf, managed to get onto his knees, and then stood. He turned and looked through the opening in the pines, straight up at Jenny's house. Or he would have, if he'd had eyes. At this distance, even with the zoom on the phone, it was hard to tell, but they looked like nothing but black pits to her.

Out in the water, something moved. Not a shark fin this time. The top of a head, another man, walking toward shore, his white hair and beard tangled with seaweed.

Three so far, moving in like the crabs. Moving in like the gulls. People who'd been called by the sea and whose lives had ended in its depths, one way or another. Pale things, drawn back by an allure they'd never understood while alive.

Strangely calm, Jenny placed her cracked phone on the railing beside her coffee mug. She closed her eyes, breathing deeply. She traced her fingers over the triple spiral tattoo, that infinite wave, then clamped her hand down over it. The ink turned so cold it felt like teeth biting deep.

Tears welled in her eyes as that familiar floating calm lifted her and she took several breaths. If only she could have kept her eyes closed and floated in that peace forever.

Instead, she opened them. The gulls had begun to circle closer. The blanket of crabs scuttled up the path between the pines. The small octopus would be down there, gliding along with them, although she couldn't make it out. The people, though...she didn't need the camera zoom to see those figures stumbling in the shadows of the pines.

She wanted to give herself over to the ink. To the infinite sea. But she had been a fool to think that she could stay in one place and not have the lure intensify.

Jenny turned in a slow circle, looking past the pine trees and her new house, imagining what lay beyond it all, trying to think of someplace, anyplace, she might run. A flutter of wings made her spin around and she stared at the single gull that alighted on the railing between her coffee mug and her cracked phone. It stared at her, black eyes yearning.

She left the gull there on the deck, left her coffee and her phone and went inside, drawing the sliding glass door closed behind her. The house breathed, quiet except for the crackling in the fireplace. The wood smoke gave the whole place the scent of autumn, reminding her of better days.

The metal screen curtain on the fireplace slid back

easily. Jenny took the little iron ash shovel that hung with the tongs and poker, and she rested it on top of the burning logs. Crouched there, she waited while the iron grew hot, waited as her knees began to ache. When the first gull hit the slider, she didn't flinch. It happened many times a day and she'd learned to ignore the sound. Her gaze shifted to her left forearm. Her sweater sleeve had slid down to cover the tattoo there and she slid it back up so that she could look at her father's name and wonder how it had come to this. Had he been searching for the talisman or had he brought it up from the sea bottom with his net or a hook? Had he cut open a fish and found it inside?

It didn't matter now, but still Jenny wondered.

The little hairs on her arm stood up and she shivered. Despite her nearness to the fire, or perhaps because of it, the ink on her right forearm felt icier than ever. The cold seemed almost to cut her, but she didn't look at that triple spiral now, refused to glance at that symbol of the infinite sea despite the yearning in her.

Long minutes passed.

Another thump against the glass. Something scratched against it but she didn't look. Jenny told herself it was just a gull, or maybe the first of the crabs to arrive.

She took the iron shovel from the fire with her left hand, stretched out her right and placed the flame-heated metal against the spiral tattoo. Hissing through her teeth, shuddering, she squeezed her eyes shut and kept the metal pressed there, as tightly as she could. The smell of searing flesh nearly made her retch and she went down on both knees, weeping silently as she fought the urge to take the shovel away.

At last she slumped to her side and let it fall from her hand. Breathing fast, almost hyperventilating, Jenny forced herself to look at the ruined skin. The tattoo had been cracked and blistered and reddened, but the ink showed through.

The cool solace of the sea slid up her arm, soothing the burn.

Jenny sat up and reached her left hand into the fireplace. She screamed as she grabbed the top log, cried out in agony as she dragged it out and pressed it to the spiral tattoo. Body rigid, she held it until her vision went dark and she slumped again to the floor.

The heat on her face brought her around. Her eyelids fluttered and she found herself staring at the still burning log, bright embers glowing in the wood. It had landed on the tile between her body and the fireplace, and she knew the whole house could have gone up in flames. The idea did not terrify her the way it should have.

Her left hand sang with pain. Her right forearm screamed with it. Awkwardly, she shifted into a sitting position, cradling that left hand in her lap and the right arm across her knee. Full of dread, she began to glance down at the tattoo she'd worked so hard to destroy.

Even before she saw the wreckage there, saw the hideous, blackened, oozing flesh that would bear the scars of this day forever, she shuddered with relief. That peace she'd found had left her. The symbol had been burned away. No cool solace touched her skin.

Slumping, crying softly out of pain and gratitude, she found herself staring at the other tattoo. The one on the inside of her left arm. The one with her father's name and the dates of his birth and death.

A terrible thought occurred to her.

The most terrible thought.

"No," she whispered, launching shakily to her feet. "Oh, no."

In agony from her burns, Jenny stumbled to the sliding glass door. With her good hand she dragged it open, then ran out onto the deck and down the stairs, ignoring her cracked phone and her coffee mug, noticing only that the gulls were gone.

"No," she whispered as she turned at the bottom of the steps and ran down along the path between the pines.

If only she'd waited.

Heart thundering, left hand still cradled against her, she picked up speed, stumbled and nearly fell but managed to catch herself as she ran in the shadows of those trees. There were still crabs there, dozens of them, but they scurried away from her as she ran past them, disturbed by her presence. Searching for some comfort she could no longer provide.

At the dock, she paused a moment, staring out at the waves. Her burns throbbed, the pain only growing, and she felt as if they were still on fire.

Jenny strode out onto the dock, scanning the water for any sign.

"Daddy?" she called, quietly at first. Then again, louder, almost screaming.

She fell to her knees on the warped and weathered boards and stared out at the open sea.

It gave her no peace.

THE FACE IS A MASK

"What do you mean you're going to burn it?" Massarsky asked. "It's a lot of money to shell out for something you're planning to set on fire."

The younger man, Timothy Ridley, perched on the edge of the worn, burgundy leather sofa as if he might make a run for it. He swirled the ice in his glass of pomegranate juice but never seemed to take so much as a sip.

"You know the story behind the mask?" Ridley asked.

Massarsky leaned back in his chair, its matching leather crinkling loudly. "You think I'd have bought the thing if I didn't know the story? Its 'provenance,' as collectors say?"

Ridley nodded. "I've heard about your collection."

"You say that like you've got something sour in your mouth, Mr. Ridley. You come here and tell me you want to buy an item from my collection, tell me you intend to burn it, and then you talk to me like you feel dirty even being in my house."

This last part troubled him most deeply. James Massarsky had worked tirelessly with designers and contractors to get this house built. He had spent decades in the film business, first kissing ass and then making sure everyone else had to kiss *his*, and goddamn if he didn't deserve this house. A man's home was his castle and he had built one worthy of its king. Seven bedrooms, sprawling lawns, central house with two wings and two cottages on the property. Now here comes Ridley, wanting to buy the mask from *Chapel of Darkness* but acting like Massarsky is somehow beneath him.

"I'm sorry," Ridley said. "I just...this isn't a pleasant errand for me."

Massarsky wanted to punch him in the throat. "I've tried to make you comfortable because you're a guest in my home. If you find it so unpleasant--"

"No, wait," Ridley said, as Massarsky began to rise. "I'm not explaining this well."

"That's for sure." Massarsky settled back into his chair. "Tell me again how you ended up calling me. How did you even know I owned the mask?"

"A friend of my family's came to your Christmas party last year--"

"This friend have a name?"

"I'd rather not say. Particularly as you don't seem very happy about it," Ridley admitted. "But apparently she told my mother that the mask was in your collection, and that you said it gave you the creeps and you were thinking you might sell it one day. My mother asked me to track down your number. I called you, and here I am."

Massarsky sipped his scotch. "You an actor? Writer?"

"I'm a history teacher in San Diego," Ridley said. "My mother was an actress. Her name is Athena Ridley."

"Doesn't ring a bell."

This was a lie. Massarsky had a fairly encyclopedic

knowledge of cinema, both the great films and the trash, but Ridley had been rude, and so he wasn't going to give the guy the satisfaction.

Over his career as a studio executive and then as a producer, Massarsky had been involved in dozens of hugely successful films, including several that had earned Oscar nominations and one that had won Best Picture. The walls of his home were festooned with framed photos of himself with some of the great actors and directors of the past forty years, everyone from Robert DeNiro to Denzel Washington to Meryl Streep and Jennifer Lawrence. In most of those photos, he had cropped out everyone who wasn't either famous or his own family. His collection of Hollywood memorabilia--Hollywood ephemera--was a motley selection of rarities and one of a kind items, many with particular significance to him. *Chapel of Darkness* was neither. The film had never been completed, but he knew the name Athena Ridley.

"You've seen the unfinished reels of the film, I assume," Ridley said.

Massarsky sipped his scotch. "Of course. They showed up on YouTube years ago."

"My mother is the woman strapped to the table in the ritual scene at the end of act two. I was born the same night. They hired her because she was nearly full-term in her pregnancy and they wouldn't have to use makeup effects to make her look pregnant. I guess they didn't expect her to go into labor in the middle of shooting, three weeks early."

"No. I guess they didn't." Massarsky hesitated. "Did

they really try to kill her on camera?"

Ridley had been warned about Massarsky. His legend painted him as a ruthless snake, drunk on power he hadn't yet realized had begun to fade. Ridley didn't care--all he knew was that he couldn't leave here without the mask, and that meant pretending the question hadn't made him want to knock Massarsky on his ass.

"This stuff is all fairly personal, Mr. Massarsky--"

"Call me 'James.'"

"James. You can imagine that it's painful to talk about," Ridley went on. "I've never really known my mother, not the woman she was before she gave birth to me. The woman who filmed *Chapel of Darkness*. She's been in and out of mental health facilities since 1961, the year they shot the film. All I know about the original Athena Ridley are things I've learned from relatives and family friends."

He paused. How much could he share? How much, without making a man like Massarsky decide to double the price for the mask? Ridley saw a strange glint in the other man's eyes and wondered how much he might already know.

"My mother had a psychotic break while filming that scene," he went on. "You must know part of this. An actor named George Sumner was one of the masked cultists in the ritual scene. My mother went into labor, probably set a world record, gave birth to me in just over an hour. They kept shooting while she was screaming, sweating. Filming as if it was all part of the ritual. Later, she said they were really going to sacrifice her. That the ritual had been real, that the cult of Belial was real."

"But George Sumner interfered," Massarsky said.

Ridley paused. How much did he really know? He said he had investigated the provenance of the mask, and it seemed he really had.

"Yes, Sumner interfered. He fled the set and called the police. A camera operator named Olmos helped him get away and he was stabbed to death on set for his trouble. With Sumner gone, they didn't have enough people to complete the ritual--the requisite number, according to my mother's ravings, is thirteen. By the time the police arrived, the whole set was in flames. Several people died in the fire, including the director, but most escaped, my mother among them. Sumner did not die in the fire, but several months later he was struck by a car on Pico Boulevard and killed instantly."

Massarsky tapped a finger against his chin in contemplation. "This is all fascinating, Tim. You mind me calling you 'Tim?'"

"Of course not."

"Good. Tim. It's all fascinating, but it doesn't tell me why your mother wants the mask."

"It doesn't matter, does it? I heard you were interested in selling."

"Oh, I am. The thing gives me the fucking creeps. At first, I liked that, but I've owned it for eighteen months and every week it gets under my skin a little more. But satisfy my curiosity, if you don't mind."

"I told you--"

"Your mother wants to burn it. Yes. Now tell me why."

Massarsky tossed back the rest of his scotch. Ridley's mouth felt parched but he didn't want to drink any more of this asshole's pomegranate juice. He could taste only resentment now.

"You know all the other masks were destroyed in the fire."

"Yes. That's what makes this one valuable. According to police reports, it was the one George Sumner had been wearing."

Ridley nodded. "So I've been told. Blythewood was a small U.K. company. They financed a ton of these trashy B-movies in those days, but they worked on a lean budget. Shutting down *Chapel of Darkness* and never releasing it caused a financial burden that nearly ruined them. Some of the footage was used in other films, but most of it vanished into the vaults until the company was sold to Warner Brothers in 1992. Nobody knows what became of the surviving reels of *Chapel of Darkness* after that. I can't show my mother any of that film, nothing to convince her that--"

"Convince her what? That it wasn't real?" Massarsky asked.

"She's an old woman. Forgotten by everyone but her family and diagnosed with schizophrenia. She wanted me to bring her the mask but she wouldn't say why. I guess she thinks somehow it'll prove to everyone she's not as unstable as she seems. Athena's not the one who wants to burn it, Mr. Massarsky. That's my idea. I figure if I burn it in front of her maybe she'll finally be able to put some of those old fears behind her. Even if the cult of Belial was real, they can't hurt her anymore."

Massarsky sat back in his chair, nodding slowly. "Wow. That's just...Tim, that's really sad. I'm honestly sorry."

Ridley blinked in surprise. "Thank you. I do appreciate that. And I appreciate you letting me come here."

They sat together in silence until Massarsky seemed to remember that the next move belonged to him.

"Right. Okay, well, let's have a look at it," he said, lumbering his awkward bulk up from the chair and ambling toward the door. "I should warn you, though, that there's part of the story you don't seem to know."

Ridley followed him into the hall and down the corridor. "What do you mean?"

Massarsky stopped at a thick wooden door and tugged a key ring out of his pocket. "I'll explain in a minute."

He selected a key and slid it into the lock.

As they walked into the vast room, motion sensitive lights flickered on. The illumination had a softness to it that could not have been accidental, and as Ridley glanced around, he realized just how seriously Massarsky took his collection. There were museum quality displays inside clear cubes and behind locked glass cabinets. Some items were individually lit from within. Ridley spotted the rare poster for *Revenge of the Jedi,* the original name for the third *Star Wars* film, but based on what he saw displayed, he figured that was the least unique item in Massarsky's collection.

"This is impressive," he said, barely aware he'd spoken

aloud.

"It's my passion. Almost as much as making films. Sometimes even more so."

Ridley glanced around, spotting a red balloon floating atop its string inside one case and a blood-encrusted sword inside another. He saw a car steering wheel mounted beside a photo of James Dean and didn't dare ask. Rumor suggested Massarsky's collection tended toward the morbid, and Ridley preferred not to know.

"Would you like a tour?" Massarsky asked.

"Maybe another time. For now, I'd just like to see the mask."

"I understand. You must be anxious to try this experiment with your mother."

"I think of it as therapy."

Massarsky nodded as he led Ridley up one aisle and then turned into a short, wide hallway that housed part of the collection. Overhead lights flickered on in this little annex. There were masks, pieces of costume wardrobe, and even a full-size head of the actor who had played a cyborg in the first *Alien* film. Oh, what was his name? Ridley couldn't bring it to mind.

"Here it is," Massarsky said, gesturing toward a glass case about waist-high. Inside, stretched over a plastic mannequin head, George Sumner's cult of Belial mask gazed out at them, eyeless but still somehow ominous.

For a second, Ridley thought it had seen him, and he shuddered.

"You're sure this is it?" he asked.

Massarsky scowled as he used another key to open the

glass case. "I can show you the paperwork. It's been verified by the top Blythewood Studios scholar. More than that, it matches some of the still photos I've acquired from the shoot."

The thing seemed dreadfully ordinary, reminiscent of one of those Carnival masks sold in Venice, but with a lovely simplicity. Its bone white hue had been inscribed with black and red symbols that might have been runes or some kind of occult sigils.

"It doesn't look like much."

"And yet," Massarsky said, "it's what you came for. Now, please, Tim, I have work to do. If you don't want a tour, that's fine, but let's wrap this up."

Ridley approached the case. His breath froze in his chest as he reached out with both hands to retrieve the mask.

"The price we discussed?" he asked.

"Yes. Let's just get it done," Massarsky said, practically barking the words.

Ridley narrowed his eyes and studied the man. For the first time he realized that Massarsky hadn't been lying. The mask really did unsettle him.

"What's the matter?" he asked. "What the hell are you afraid of?"

Massarsky smiled thinly. "Just don't put it on. I've let several people put it on, and it's been a mistake every time. They've ended up with nightmares."

"From a mask?" Ridley asked. "That's ridiculous."

But as he drew the mask from its case and felt the rough, dry leather texture of the thing, he felt his pulse quicken. His heart thumped a bit harder. Unbidden, his hands lifted the mask toward his face and he bent his neck slightly.

"Ridley, wait," Massarsky said, reaching for his arm. "I know how it sounds, but several people have had odd experiences. Said they'd seen--"

Somehow, Ridley managed to pause with the mask only inches from his face. He could see through the eyeholes, could make out a display case containing the derby hat Peter Lorre had worn as Moriarty in the ill-fated, never-completed 1933 German language version of *The Adventures of Sherlock Holmes*. The hat had caught Ridley's attention in the instant before Massarsky had shown him the mask.

"What did they see?" Ridley asked.

"I don't know. It's hard to explain."

"Have you ever put the mask on?"

"Once," Massarsky admitted.

"And what did you see?"

"Nothing," he said, but Ridley thought he might be lying.

The urge to don the mask felt so strong that his hands trembled until he surrendered. With a breath of relief, Ridley placed the mask over his face, tying its silk ribbons at the back of his head.

Massarsky and his collection were gone.

Ridley's hands fell to his sides. His breathing sounded impossibly loud behind the mask. He felt the urge to turn and run, but his body would not obey. Instead he froze, a whispered profanity slithering inside the mask, and slowly scanned the darkened space around him. He had never been on the set of a movie before, but he saw the camera operator and the people swinging microphone booms around and adjusting lighting rigs and knew this couldn't be anything but that.

Not just any movie, either.

The world seemed to tilt beneath him. Ridley nearly collapsed when he allowed his gaze to focus on the stone altar. A much younger version of his mother lay there, head thrown back in a silent cry of agony. A hooded man knelt between her splayed legs as a woman stood over her, an officiant with her arms lifted in mock ecstasy, chanting some guttural gibberish. The woman wore the mask of the cult of Belial, as did the robed extras gathered around the set. The young and beautiful Athena Ridley let out a roar, a kind of battle cry, and her face turned bright red beneath her cinema makeup. She was an actress, but this could not be a performance.

The whole cast took up the chant.

Even Ridley found himself chanting, his mouth moving of its own volition. His mind did not know these words or this language, yet he spoke all the same. A rare exultation soared in his heart, his skin felt flush, and if there had been any doubt that this ritual must be genuine, that joy erased it. The camera kept rolling.

The hooded man received the infant into his arms. Timothy Ridley stared at the newborn, its pink skin smeared with blood and birth fluids. When the hooded man turned, Ridley saw his

mask, and the glint of silver from the blade of the

ceremonial dagger in his hand. He wanted to scream.

Thoughts collided, fear battling reason. Here he stood, impossibly and yet inarguably viewing the past through the mask of a dead man.

The blade severed the umbilical cord. Robed figures moved into a circle around mother and child. Ridley found himself moving, too. From the corner of his eye, he saw the camera operator shift position--saw the director signaling with his hands, saw the boom microphone swing lower.

The officiant behind the altar reached into her robe and produced a dagger identical to the first. One by one, the cultists drew their blades and raised them high. Ridley's own fingers slithered inside the folds of his robe and found a sheathed dagger. He felt the unaccountably icy cold of its handle, and he drew the blade out, against his will.

His eyes welled with tears.

"No," he managed to whisper, even as this body stepped toward the altar. Toward his mother, and toward the newborn that already had his brown eyes, already had the little furrow of the brow that would mark his every adult expression.

Within the vault of his thoughts, Ridley fought back. Mustering his will, he forced his eyes closed. For a moment he felt torn between worlds, times, realities. He could hear, as if from the bottom of a well, Massarsky's voice speaking his name. "Mr. Ridley. Mr. Ridley, are you all right?" Even the temperature of the room shifted, turning into the cool of Massarsky's air-conditioned palace in the Hollywood hills instead of the warm, close, nearly suffocating air on that long forgotten film set, with its choreographed spotlights and strategic shadows.

Wake up, he thought, even though he knew this was no dream.

Steeling himself, he forced his hands to rise. If he could untie the mask, tear it from his face, he could step away from this. George Sumner had been the actor wearing this mask, all those years ago, and he'd found the courage and strength to break away from the scene, to flee the ritual. Ridley had to do the same. Then Olmos, the man behind the camera, would step in to protect the infant.

His left hand touched the silk ribbons tied behind his head, but then he felt a sharp pain on the right side of his neck...the tip of the ceremonial dagger puncturing the skin, drawing his blood. His hand clenched around the hilt and he opened his eyes.

Opened George Sumner's eyes.

"No!" he shouted again, but his time he stumbled forward, and his heartbeat was his own. It thrummed, the wings of a caged bird, and he shoved two of the cultists aside.

A woman pointed her dagger at his sternum and he knocked her hand away, then tore off her mask. Beneath the painted sigils of the cult of Belial was a familiar face, some starlet or other, but with her identity bared she drew away from him--from the altar--as if she could not proceed with what came next without the mask.

By this time, in reality--in history--George Sumner had run. What did it mean that Ridley wore George

Sumner's mask, wore his body, and had not run?

"Cut!" the director barked.

In the scrum of people, Ridley saw and felt everything at once.

The infant in the arms of the hooded man--the bloody, smeared infant with his brow furrowed, about to launch his first plaintive wail in this world.

The strange, sickly glint of light in the eyes of the crew all around them in the dark, beyond the booms and the camera, their silhouettes strangely misshapen, hunched and crooked and waiting like predators full of anticipation.

The actors in their masks, these actors who were not acting, closing in around the altar ever tighter, suffocating.

The hooded man who had delivered baby Timothy Ridley, the man who now held him up as an offering.

The raised daggers.

"Cut!" the director shouted again.

The officiant chanted louder to drown the director out, and the others followed suit.

But it was Ridley's own mother, the young ingenue, half-naked and draped in silk, belly partly deflated, who raised her head and sneered across the set at the director.

"Don't you fucking dare stop shooting," Athena Ridley snarled.

The first dagger swept down, but it did not plunge into her flesh. Instead, the officiant dragged the blade across Athena's belly, splitting the skin so that blood began to seep and run and stain white silk.

"The blood of the mother!" the officiant cried.

The chant was echoed from behind a dozen masks...including Ridley's own. He was himself, but he was also George Sumner. A George Sumner whose moment to flee had passed.

Another blade rose, and Ridley could not let it fall. He bent low and drove his shoulder into a cultist, knocked the actor aside, and threw himself to the stone floor beside the altar. On his knees, he found himself eye to eye with Athena.

"Mom, please," he said quietly. "What do I do?"

"Speak the words," his mother said. "Summon him."

The circle erupted with chanting. Ridley joined them. He felt the name Belial on his lips but could not understand the rest, only watch as the hooded man set the infant back between its mother's legs, still smeared in blood and birth fluids. Again voices called out to Belial.

Ridley couldn't breathe. The room darkened, as if the whole world had dimmed. The film crew were truly only shadows now, shadows and gleaming eyes. Time had frozen between one heartbeat and the next. He felt a loss that cut to the bone, grief pouring into him. Another dagger swept down, this one in the grip of the hooded man, and sliced across the infant's chest, just above his heart, only deep enough to draw blood.

The burn of that cut sliced across Ridley's own chest. He could feel the wicked bite of the blade and the trickle of blood down his skin, though no blade had touched him.

He screamed and lunged for the baby, but an enormous man struck him in the temple and hurled him against the stone base of the altar. A booted foot crunched down on his throat, pinning him to the floor. Inside George Sumner's mask, Ridley began to suffocate.

He still clutched Sumner's dagger, but as he raised his hand, another cultist dropped upon him, a blonde woman whose mask seemed partly askew. He glimpsed the corner of her smile under the mask as she trapped his arm against the floor with her knees.

Her dagger was the first to cut him. She lifted it with both hands and rammed it through the meat of his shoulder, cleaving muscle. Blood sprayed and he screamed with the voices of two men, decades apart. Another blade bit into his thigh. The third plunged into his abdomen, the fourth into his side, the fifth into his right arm, scraping bone as it jammed between ulna and radius. After that, Ridley could no longer scream. Numbness flooded into his veins to replace the blood that spilled out. The blade that thrust into the side of his face, shattering teeth, might have been the tenth or eleventh. He felt that one, though he was no longer capable of screaming. He could weep, though, and he did.

When they were finished, there had been twelve wounds. Twelve daggers. Twelve murderers in their Belial masks on the set of *Chapel of Darkness*, every moment preserved on celluloid.

His mother, Athena, slipped off the altar. Had the afterbirth come? He wasn't sure, but she was there beside him nevertheless, kneeling with the infant Timothy in her arms, still smeared with their shared fluids. The baby suckled at her breast in quiet contentment as Ridley's blood pooled on the stone floor. The officiant raised her arms and began a prayer to gods of pain and cruelty.

Athena bent to whisper in his ear. “He is close. So near to us now. But only you can complete the ritual. Only you can bring him into our midst.”

One hand cradling the babe, she reached the other to touch his arm. She took his right wrist and lifted it, and his fingers began to open but she clasped hers around them, making sure he kept his grip on the dagger. The last dagger. The thirteenth.

As the baby nursed quietly, she helped him bring the dagger to his own throat and she kissed his temple.

“This part must be yours,” she said.

Ridley would have laughed if he could have. Lunacy. It was lunacy. He would never…

But in the shadows overhead, something breathed. The shadows themselves had form and awareness and they waited impatiently, urgent with desire. The chanting rose into a sensual crescendo and it seemed to caress him. This body knew what it had to do.

He drew the blade across his throat and a wave of blissful relief swept over him. It lasted only a moment before a chill seized him, icy needles of pain. Ridley inhaled sharply and his eyes went wide. The shadows roiled and coalesced around him, enveloping him, and as he sipped his last breath, he drew the shadows into George Sumner’s lungs.

As his life ebbed, he heard the baby crying, and the voice was his own.

Massarsky felt the room go cold. He always had the air-conditioning up too high, but this was something else. A rime of frost settled on Ridley's skin. At one point the man had been talking behind the mask, a quiet chant in some language Massarsky could not make out. He'd even reached up to untie the mask, but something had stopped him. Ridley had dropped his hands to his sides again and hadn't moved since. Massarsky had moved, though, backing first a few steps and then a good eight or nine feet away. He hadn't lied about the three people he had allowed to try on the mask before. All of them had seen something when they'd put the mask on, something that had given them hideous dreams, but none had reacted the way Ridley had.

"Jesus," he muttered. He could see his own breath. With a shiver, he crossed his arms, trying to keep warm.

Frost had formed on the mask now, and somehow it no longer really looked like a mask. Instead, Ridley appeared to have a caul over his face, a thin membrane with blue veins just below the surface, veins whose patterns matched the symbols that had been drawn there before.

Ridley turned to look at him, the movement so abrupt that Massarsky let out a tiny squeak of fear. Behind that mask, that caul, Ridley's eyes glittered with flecks like embers, as if they reflected some celestial hell.

"The circle is complete," a woman's voice said, making Massarsky squeak once more.

He exhaled, watching his breath mist in front of him. Massarsky did not turn around. He did not know how she had gotten into the room, though he had known she would come. She had promised, after all, that she would be there.

"You brought payment?" he asked.

Athena Ridley, aged and riddled with cancer, had a rough, rasping laugh. "You are bold," she said. "I've always liked that in a man. And yes, of course. I've left the money on your pillow, the way men like you have always done for whores."

She walked to her son. Or whatever now lived behind that mask, inside those glittering eyes.

"Come, my love," the dying woman whispered, taking the silent thing by its hand. "At last, we may begin."

When they'd left, Massarsky locked the door behind them.

Then he wept.

And then he counted his money.

THE OPEN WINDOW

At first, Tyler thought he'd imagined the voice outside his window. Half-asleep, drifting in that space where thoughts blurred and peace fell over his body as he surrendered to slumber, he jerked awake. He blinked in the darkness of his room, stared at the orange glow of the nightlight he told his friends was only there in case he had to get up to use the bathroom in the middle of the night.

The voice came again.

"Tyler," it said. "Wake up, Tyler. Come out of there."

A shiver went through him. He tried to tell himself he was dreaming, but he could feel the softness of his flannel sheets and they felt so real. He had his back to the window and the voice seemed to slither through the screen and over the sill to reach him.

"Tyler," it said, more urgently. "Please, son, you've gotta come out here."

Come out?

He glanced at his hands. His friend Sarah had told him that if you were in a dream, you could never see your hands, which sounded weird but also true. Tyler could see his hands just fine, which meant the icy fear that trickled along his spine didn't come from a nightmare. This was real.

Fully awake now, his breath caught in his throat. He

stared at that orange nightlight for a second or two, and then slid out of his bed, knelt beside it, and turned to look out the window. The moonlight had turned the night a deep blue. He could see the trees outside his window, the ash and the maple in the back yard, and the pines at the edge of the property. The house was a split-level, with his room upstairs, so the window was too high for him to see much of the yard from a spot kneeling beside the bed.

"Damn it, Tyler!" the voice rasped, frustrated now, more urgent than ever. Hushed, trying not to make too much noise...trying to stay secret. "Please, you're in danger."

Blinking, he stared at the screen. "No way," he whispered, because now that fear had burned all traces of sleep from his mind, he recognized that voice.

Tyler crept onto his bed and looked out into the yard. "Dad?"

Looking down at his father's face in the moonlight, he almost thought he must be dreaming again. He glanced at his hands. Nothing made sense. The hushed fear and rasping desperation in his father's voice had prevented him from recognizing it at first, and now he saw those same emotions on his dad's face.

"Ty, thank God," his dad said, moving closer to the window, lowering his voice to a barely audible whisper. "Listen to me, son. Don't make any noise. Don't ask any questions."

Tyler's fear grew and shifted focus. "What?" he whispered. "Dad, what are you—"

Outside in the moonlight, face etched with emotion,

his dad shushed him. "Just listen. Push out your window screen. There are latches. It's easy. Just unlatch it, push it out, and drop it down to me. I'll catch it, but we can't make any noise. Then you've gotta jump."

Jump? Was he crazy?

Tyler glanced at his bedroom door. The last he'd seen his father had been in the living room. Mom had been working a double shift at the hospital, so it had just been her two men, as she called them. They'd grilled burgers and made salads and then watched a monster movie while they'd demolished what was left of the bag of Oreos mom had bought the day before.

From downstairs, there came a thump.

Tyler flinched. His heart had already been racing but now it thundered so hard his chest hurt. If Dad was outside and Mom was at work, who was inside the house with him?

"Damn it, Ty!" his father rasped.

He heard a creak on the stairs. Someone coming up.

It snapped him into motion. Tyler knelt on his bed and stared at the bottom of the screen. In the moonlight he saw the latches clearly. He flipped the one on the left, but the other one stuck. He could hear himself breathing, quick sips of air, in rhythm with the pounding in his chest.

Another creak, halfway up the stairs now. He knew those stairs so well, but they had a stranger on them now. A stranger in his house.

"That's it," his father said, outside the window. In the yard. Safe.

He'd be safe out there, with his dad.

Tyler forced the other latch. It snapped open and he scratched his finger, drew a little blood but what was a little blood right now?

He popped the screen open, shoved it out, and it sailed down toward the yard. His father lumbered a few awkward steps to try to catch it, but failed, and that felt more real than anything. Dad was a big guy, never the most graceful. Tyler had never loved or needed him more.

"Jump, Ty," his dad said.

Tyler looked down at the bushes in the mulch bed behind the house. It wasn't that high. He'd get scratched up something fierce, might twist an ankle, but if he was careful—

Someone knocked on his bedroom door and whispered his name.

No, no, no, no. His heart hammered even harder and he stared at the bedroom door, watching the knob, waiting for it to turn. His throat closed up, so dry he couldn't even put voice to a terrified squeak.

The bushes didn't matter. The scratches didn't matter. A twisted ankle didn't matter.

He slid the window up as high as it would go, took one more glance at his father's pleading face, and thrust one leg out the window. Then the other leg. He reached back and held onto the window frame and started to inch himself out.

His bedroom door swung open and Tyler snapped his head up.

The man standing on the threshold of his bedroom was his father. Same face as the man in the yard. Same faded blue jeans. Same paint-spattered Boston Bruins sweatshirt. Same graying beard.

Tyler froze, staring at the man. "Dad?"

"What the hell do you think you're doing?" his father barked, in the same tone he'd always used whenever Tyler did something dumb. Like climbing out his window in the middle of the night.

The world seemed to skid sideways. Nothing made sense. If this wasn't a dream...if this wasn't a dream, what was it?

Then, from behind him, below him in the yard, he heard his father's voice again.

Whispering, and so afraid.

"Tyler, listen to me, buddy. It's not me up there. I know it looks like me and it sounds like me, but I swear to you that's not me, and if you don't jump right now, it's going to get you. I'll never reach you in time. Please, Ty...I love you so much. I can't lose you. Oh, God, please believe me. That's not your dad in there. I'm out here. God, please..."

The man standing in the open doorway stepped into the room. "Get your butt inside right now, Tyler. I'm not kidding. I'd say you'd better have a good explanation for this, but I sure can't think of one."

He acted like he hadn't even heard the other voice. The Other Dad.

How could that be?

The Inside Dad walked toward him, brows knitted in anger, teeth bared in frustration—or maybe cruelty. Was that cruelty?

"Ty, please!" Outside Dad called, no longer whispering,

voice full of terror.

Inside Dad reached for him, and Tyler shoved himself backward out the window. As he fell, he caught a glimpse of Inside Dad thrusting a hand out after him, a panicked look on his face, as though he feared Tyler might be hurt. As if he cared.

Tyler crashed into the bushes, felt every scratch and scrape, and then rolled out onto the back lawn. He groaned as he staggered to his feet, stumbled a couple of steps away from Outside Dad.

"Ty?" Inside Dad called from the open window. "Are you okay? Oh, man, why would you...why did you..."

His voice trailed off.

Tyler turned and saw them staring at one another, Outside Dad in the back yard. Inside Dad in the upstairs window. Both speechless, frightened, mirror images of one another.

"Ty," Inside Dad said quietly. "Run around the front. Right now, I'll race you to the door. Run right now!"

Frozen, confused now, Tyler glanced back and forth between them.

Outside Dad began to edge toward him, watching Inside Dad as though fearful of any move he might make. "Don't listen to it, Ty. We've gotta go right now."

As Outside Dad reached for him, Tyler shied away. Took a step back. Anger furrowed Outside Dad's brow.

"Ty," Inside Dad said. "Please, listen to me. I'm right here. Whoever that is...whatever it is, I swear it's not me. You've gotta run around the front. You'll be faster. You're so much faster than I am. Please, run. Mom and I...you're all we have."

From the shadows behind the ash tree, there came another voice.

"He's all you had," the voice said, as a third Dad stepped out from behind the tree.

From the corner of the house, a fourth peered around the edge of the tall bush there. "He's our Tyler now," it said. "You'll have to get another."

Outside Dad began to laugh in that familiar Dad way that had always lightened Tyler's heart.

Now the sound made him scream.

He backed away, stumbled and nearly fell, and then at last he ran.

From the upstairs window, his father cried out his name, promised to meet him at the front door, but even as Tyler put on speed he saw another step out of the pine trees at the back of the yard, and another emerge from the shadows at the far corner of the house.

He ran. He tried, really he did.

But there were just too many of them.

THE BAD HOUR

The hiss of the hydraulic doors dragged Kat Nellis from an uneasy sleep and she came awake with a thin gasp of hope. Her neck ached from the way she'd been huddled in the corner of the bus seat, her skull canted against the window, but at least the dream had come to an end.

The same fucking dream.

It wasn't an every night sort of thing, but frequent enough that whenever she went a few days without having that dream she began to feel not relief but a creeping sort of dread. Ironic, because what made the dream verge on a nightmare was that same feeling, the inescapable knowledge that something terrible was about to happen.

The dreams were always of Iraq, of the time she'd spent escorting convoys along the worst stretch of highway in the world. In the dream she would hold her breath as the truck rumbled over ruined pavement, waiting for a tire to smash down on top of a mine or for a broken down car to explode with a planted IED, or for an old woman or a child on the side of the road to step aside to reveal a suicide bomber. Kat had done hideous things in the war—things that would haunt her waking hours for the rest of her life—but when she slept, it was the dread of the unknown, of *waiting*, that plagued her dreams.

"Come on, honey," the bus driver called back to her. "If you're gettin' off, this is the place. Wish I could get you closer."

Kat stretched her stiff muscles and felt her joints pop as she stood. She'd kept fit in the years since she had left the army, but there were some wounds the human body could heal but never forget. Down in your bones, you would remember. Blown fifteen feet by a roadside explosion, she had survived with little more than some scrapes and bruises and a wrenched back. Kat felt grateful that she still had all of her working parts, that she hadn't been closer to the explosion, but her back had never been the same. She had no shrapnel, no bullets lodged in her body, but her spine always ached and in warm weather she had a tinny buzz in her brain that kept her company everywhere she went.

It was autumn now, though. No more buzzing in her head.

She slipped on her backpack and walked to the front of the bus. Passengers studied her curiously, wondering why she would be getting off in the middle of nowhere. A seventyish woman in a head scarf squinted at her and Kat smiled in response, unoffended by the scrutiny.

"How far is it from here?" she asked when she reached the front of the bus.

The October morning breeze blew in through the open door and a man in the first row muttered something, half asleep, and tugged his jacket tighter around his throat as he nestled back in his seat.

"Gotta be eight or ten miles," said the driver. He took out a handkerchief and blew his big red nose, then sniffled as he tucked the rag away. "Sorry I can't run you down there."

"No worries. I could do with the walk."

Slipping her pack onto her shoulders, she stepped down onto the road. The door closed and the bus rumbled away, the morning sun hitting the windows at an angle that turned them black. Kat inhaled deeply, calming herself. The bus was on its way to Montreal, but she had gotten off about twenty miles south of the Canadian border. She stood on the side of Route 118 and glanced around at mountains covered in evergreens and patches of orange and red fall foliage. Most of the leaves that were going to fall this far north had already fallen.

October, Kat thought. She'd grown up in Montana and though the landscape looked different, the chilly breeze and the slant of autumn light made Vermont feel like home.

Across from the spot where the bus had dropped her, a narrow, road led through the trees. The morning sky might be blue, but the trees cast that street into dusky shadow. No sign identified this as King's Hollow Road, and the bus had already pulled away. No way to confirm her location with the driver. A quick check of her phone confirmed her expectation of crappy cell service out here in the middle of mountainous nowhere.

Kat pushed her fingers through her short blond hair, rubbed the sleep from her eyes, and set off into the shadows.

For the first few miles she doubted she had found King's Hollow Road at all. She passed several farms and spotted a handful of people collecting pumpkins from a field. No cars went by, but she did pass two narrow roads heading off to the southwest. If the bus driver had left her in the right place, this road should take her right into Chesbro, Vermont, if the town still existed.

Not a town, she reminded herself. Chesbro was officially a village, or it had been the last time anyone had noticed there had been a village at the end of King's Hollow Road. She'd had no trouble finding its location on the internet, confirming its existence on Google Earth and studying three-year-old satellite photos of its small village center. But her internet searching had turned up virtually nothing else—no local newspaper, no listing of obituaries. Nothing of note had transpired there in the past forty years.

At the bus station in St. Johnsbury she had found only one person who could tell her anything about the town, an old man who ran the kiosk that sold candy and magazines. The skinny fellow had stroked his beard and told her that there'd been a mill in Chesbro once upon a time, but it had been closed for ages and most of the locals had drifted away. That sort of thing happened more often than people knew. Kat understood that, but the only address she had for Ray Lambeau was in Chesbro. If she intended to find him, that was where she had to begin.

An hour after she'd set out from where the bus has dropped her, Kat rounded a corner and came to a stop on the leaf-strewn pavement. Half a dozen massive concrete blocks had been laid across the road and onto the soft shoulder. The blocks on the left and right had steel hooks set into the concrete and heavy chains looped from the hooks to enormous pine trees on either side of the road. A dirty signpost reading STOP HERE FOR DELIVERIES had been plinked with bullets, some of which had punched right through the metal. There was no other hint that Chesbro lay ahead. Only the certainty that whatever might be down that road, outsiders weren't welcome.

"Fuck it," Kat said, moving between two of the concrete blocks.

She had spent her life going places she wasn't welcome.

The pavement over the next five miles was broken and rutted, weeds growing up from the cracks. Nobody had cut back the trees in years and they had spread into a canopy over the road. Most of the people in the region seemed to have forgotten Chesbro, and the story she'd heard of the whole town being abandoned seemed more plausible with every step. Then she crested a rise in the road and paused to stare at the little village that lay before her.

A white church sat on one end of an idyllic village green with a bandstand at the center. On the other end of the green was a main street with brick buildings, little shops, City Hall, and a little diner on a corner. There was even a little theater with a marquee overhanging the sidewalk, the sort of place she had only ever seen in old movies. If not for the large gray building that sat on the edge of a narrow river on the other side of town, it would have looked like a New Englander's idea of Heaven. In contrast to what her expectations, the village seemed well cared for, certainly not abandoned.

As she walked toward the green, Kat felt her pulse quicken. Chesbro might not look empty, but it certainly felt that way. She passed several large houses and a brick building that might once have been a bank. Unsettled by the silence, Kat had begun holding her breath, but now she heard the squeak of hinges and saw motion in her peripheral vision. She swung around to see a bearded man in green flannel and blue jeans exiting Chesbro Hardware with a small plastic bag in one hand. The other held a can of paint.

The man's eyes went wide and he dropped the can, which plunked to the ground. His reaction—as if *she* were the ghost—struck her as odd, but not nearly as odd as the way he closed his eyes and took several deep breaths. He pressed fingers against his wrist as if checking his pulse. When he opened his eyes, he had a wary smile on his face.

"You gave me quite a fright," he said, picking up the paint can and starting toward her. "Looks like I startled you as well."

"That's all right," Kat found herself saying. "I'm guessing you don't get a lot of visitors around here."

The man picked up the paint can, shifted it into the hand holding the plastic bag, and put his free hand out to shake.

"Elliot Bonner," he said. "And that's one way of putting it. If you came down King's Hollow, I'd guess you know we haven't exactly laid out the welcome mat."

Kat shook his rough hand and introduced herself. She stood five foot nine, taller than the average woman, but Bonner was half a foot taller. Another day, somewhere else, she suspected she would have found him quite attractive, but something about the set of his eyes made her uneasy. Elliot Bonner looked worried.

"Sorry," she said. "I'm looking for someone and I guess I was too focused on that to pay much attention."

"Not too late to turn around," Bonner said quietly. "Not yet."

Kat frowned. "Are you being funny? Cuz I've come a long way and maybe I'm too tired to get the joke."

The man laughed nervously. "Just joshing ya. Who are you looking for? Might be I can help."

"His name's Ray Lambeau. We served together in Iraq. We've been keeping in touch the old-fashioned way for a while, writing letters. Ray said there was no internet and not much phone service up here. But I haven't heard from him in six months or so and that didn't seem right. So here I am."

"Ray," Bonner said, as if the name tasted like shit in his mouth. He sighed, and his smile vanished. "Listen, miss—"

"Kat," she said. "Or Sergeant Nellis."

Bonner narrowed his eyes. Looked her up and down like he was sizing her up, wondering if he could take her in a fight. Kat had seen that look a hundred times before.

"I'm gonna make a suggestion, Sergeant," Bonner said, and he pointed to a split rail fence on the other side of the road. "If you go and sit there and wait for me, I'll run over to the diner up the street and get you something to eat, packed up all nice for your trip back to the main road. On me. Trust me when I say that accepting my hospitality and my advice would be the smartest decision you ever make."

Something in Bonner's eyes, a frightened animal skittishness, reminded Kat of Iraq in the worst way. The guy felt to her like an IED packed into a broken down truck on the side of the road, ready to explode if you nudged him wrong.

"I guess I'll find Ray myself," she said, and strode toward the village green.

The diner seemed like the most obvious place to start. This late in the morning there wouldn't be many customers, but there had to be at least one server and a cook. In a tiny community like this, odds were good they would know pretty much everyone in the village.

Bonner caught up with her as she stepped onto the green, still carrying his purchases from the hardware store.

"Hold up, Sergeant," he said tersely. "You need to listen."

"I don't think so."

An elderly woman came out of some kind of clothing shop a couple of doors up from the diner. She had a fall knit scarf around her neck and when she spotted Kat and Bonner she clasped it to her chest like a church lady clutching her pearls. As Kat started to cross the street, she could see the old woman's lips moving in a silent mutter. Fearful, the woman pushed her way back into the shop and Kat heard her calling out to someone inside.

"Damn it," Bonner murmured as he caught her arm from behind.

Kat spun, tore her arm free, and stood ready for a fight. "You want to keep your hands off me."

Bonner held up his hands and exhaled, uttering a small laugh. "I don't want trouble—"

"I didn't come here to make any," Kat said, studying his face. "I'm just looking for my friend."

Bonner's mouth pinched up like he'd been sucking a lemon. He exhaled loudly. "I know how crazy this must seem, but you have to leave right now. For your own safety."

It was Kat's turn to laugh. "Are you threatening me?"

"Please calm down—"

"I'm plenty calm," she said, and meant it. In combat, she'd earned a reputation as an ice queen. "When I'm not calm, you'll know it."

"Lot of that going around," Bonner said.

Kat cocked her head in confusion. Then she heard voices behind her and turned back toward the diner. A waitress in an apron had come outside with a silver-haired man in a brown suit. Other people had come onto the street and as she glanced around she noticed a pair of teenagers crossing the village green in her direction. They paused at the bandstand and draped themselves over its railings in classic American teenager poses. Studying her, like there was a show about to start.

"Get her out of here, Elliot," the waitress called from in front of the diner.

Kat could only laugh. What was wrong with these people?

"Look!" she snapped. "I'm trying to find Ray Lambeau. If he's here, I just want to talk to him. If you hate outsiders so much, I'm happy to be on my way as soon as I've talked to Ray."

Bonner grabbed her by the backpack and shoulder, turning her toward the road out of town. "I'm sorry, but you just need to—"

Kat twisted and pulled him toward her even as she hammered him a fist into his face. Bonner staggered backward, arms flailing, and went down on his ass.

"I told you not to put your hands on me," she said, a trickle of ice along her spine.

Bonner's lips curled back in anger as he scrambled to his feet. "You little bitch," he said, stalking toward her, fists raised, "all I wanted to do was—"

She stepped in close and hit him with a quick shot to the gut, followed up with a left to the temple, and then a knee in the balls. Bonner roared as he went down.

"Kat, no!" a voice cried out.

She turned to see Ray Lambeau running across the green. Her first thought was that he looked like shit, pale and too thin and with dark circles under his eyes.

"Sarge, please," Ray said, rushing up to her and grabbing her arm. "You don't know what you're doing. You can't be here."

He started hustling her away from Bonner and she let him, startled and hurt by his reaction to her arrival. Her backpack felt much heavier all of a sudden and she looked over at the hardware store and the beginning of King's Hollow Road and realized that Ray was propelling her back the way she'd come, just the way Bonner had. Corporal Ray Lambeau wanted her out of his hometown.

Behind her, Kat heard cussing and shouts of alarm.

"Kat—" Ray began, his breath warm at her ear.

She shook loose and turned to stare at him, saw the fear in his eyes. "You're all insane..."

"Go," he pleaded with her, shaking his head in frustration as he glanced toward the village green. "Please, just go."

More shouts came from that direction, but she kept her gaze fixed on Ray. His eyes had begun to moisten and he seemed to realize it the same moment she did. Letting out a breath, he struggled to keep his emotions in check the same way Bonner had. Then they both heard a clanking of something metal, followed by the unmistakable sound of someone cocking a rifle.

Ray lowered his head. "Kat, *please*..."

She'd been so wrapped up in her hurt and irritation that she had focused entirely on him. Now she turned toward the spectators again and saw that they had lost all interest in the spectacle of her little drama with Ray. They had surrounded Bonner. The man hunched over and a keening wail began to issue from his lips. He dragged his fingers through his hair and tugged at his beard and bent over further, arms folding inward.

One of the spectators stepped forward, a rifle hung in his arms.

"Jesus," Kat whispered.

The teenagers who'd been loitering by the bandstand dragged a net across the grass, its edges weighted with cast-iron pans and an array of other metal objects.

All these people had wanted her to leave. For the first time, she wished she had.

"Ray?" Kat said, taking several steps back onto the village green.

People were talking to Bonner the way they would talk to a toddler holding a gun or a loose dog with a penchant for biting. Nobody wanted to go near him, but the guy with the rifle took a bead and then nudged the teenagers forward.

"Listen—" Kat said.

At the sound of her voice, Bonner whipped around to snarl at her.

She froze, mind trying to make sense of what she saw. Bonner's mouth opened impossibly wide. Rows of needle-sharp, black teeth glistened in the morning light, viscous saliva drooling onto his beard. His skin had turned a bruise-yellow leather, run through with thick crevices and dry cracks in the flesh. His eyes were a sickly orange and they fixed on her as he opened those deadly jaws and hissed wetly.

Jaw slack, body numb, Kat flinched and reached for her hip, where she would've had a gun if she were still in the army. Her fingers closed on empty air and she blinked, understanding that all of this was real.

As Bonner took a step toward her, Kat stumbled back.

"Ray," she mumbled, "what the fuck is that?"

Bonner leaped at her. Kat twisted out of the way, let

him sail right by, and punched him in the back of the head. As people shouted, she followed through with a blow to the kidneys. Ray called to her to get back, but she kicked the back of Bonner's leg and his knee buckled. She felt the familiar sensation of ice sliding into her veins, the calm that always came over her on the battlefield.

She drove a fist down at Bonner's skull, then pistoned her arm back for another blow. He turned on one knee and lunged, tackled her around the waist, and drove her to the grass. Kat hit hard, all the air bursting from her lungs. Bonner threw back his head and roared in savage triumph and she saw those black teeth again. Pink spittle hung in webs from his jaws and dripped onto her face. Kat bucked against him, kidney-punched him again, but Bonner slapped her arms away.

The crack of a rifle shot echoed across the village green and off the main street façades. Bonner jerked. Blood sprayed as the bullet punched through his right side and kept going. Enraged and off balance, the berserker turned toward the man with the rifle. Kat bucked harder, reached up and threw him off, scrambling away as Bonner roared again, trying to recover.

The teenage boys were there with the net. They threw it over him and Kat wanted to shout at them, thinking no way could a simple net hold a man so monstrously strong, even with the metal weights tied around its circumference. But Bonner cried out and smacked against the ground. He thrashed once and then was still, wide-eyed and panting like a dog, as if something about the cast-iron pans and other weights caused him pain.

A second passed as they all stared.

Kat turned on Ray. “What the *fuck*? Shit like this does not happen in the real world.”

Ray put his hands out. “Kat, calm down...”

“Don’t tell me to calm down! Talk to me about this!” She gestured toward Bonner, netted and moaning on the grass. “This isn’t just a freak out. Look at the guy’s face! Look at his skin!”

In combat, her ability to remain calm could be eerie. But with the fight over and the reality of what she’d just seen sinking in, panic began to unravel her. Kat could practically feel her self-control shattering.

Ray approached her, hands still up. “Kat, stop. Just breathe, and listen to my voice—“

“I’m listening!”

She looked over at Bonner again, glanced at the bloody fissures in his leathery skin and saw the murder in his eyes, trying to match this visage up with the man who had walked out of the hardware store with a can of paint.

Ray put his hands on her arms. “Kat—“

She recoiled from his touch. “What is he? What is...”

Kat felt it, then. Panic, fear, and anger had all been roiling inside her, and now the anger surged upward in a wave of malice. She snapped around to glare at Ray and her lips peeled back in a snarl. His eyes widened in alarm and he stepped backward but she pursued him, swinging a fist. Ray tried to block, but too slow. She struck him in the cheek and heard the bone crack, then followed up with a left to the gut that sent him reeling across the grass.

She ran her tongue over her teeth and felt their

sharpness...and their number. Horror seized her. Thick drool ran out over her bottom lip and dribbled down her chin. Raising her hands to lunge at him, she saw that her skin had darkened and split, and she understood, but Kat could do nothing to stop herself. She grabbed a fistful of Ray's hair and she laughed as she dragged one yellow fingernail across his cheek, opening up a bloody furrow.

When the gunshot rang out and the bullet punched through her back, she felt only relief.

Kat woke with a groan. Her throat felt parched and she ached all over. When she shifted on the hard cot, bright pain seared a place on her back just below her left shoulder blade. She rolled onto her side and opened her eyes to see metal bars and flickering fluorescent lights.

A jail cell.

She shifted on the cot and saw Ray leaning against a desk out in the room beyond her cell. *Village jail,* she thought. *Police chief's office, one cell. Fucking Mayberry.* Sitting up, she felt like she might pass out again, but she forced herself to sit there and she stared at Ray...at this man who had been her friend under fire. More than a friend.

"It started in Iraq," he said quietly.

"Say again?"

Ray gestured toward the door and whatever lay beyond it.

"That. Out there," he said. "It started in Iraq. Since then I've done some research. Different stories come from different parts of the world, Greece in particular, but the name translates pretty much the same in Arabic as in Greek. Both call in 'the Bad Hour.'"

Kat tried to clear her head. "Are you making zero sense or am I just not—"

"You remember the day I lost it?"

She stared at him, a ball of ice in her gut. Images slid through her mind of a shattered door and a dead family, a grandmother with her head caved in, two little bloodstained boys full of bullet holes, and a grief-mad mama shot for trying to take revenge. Kat had seen worse in her time in Iraq, but not at the hands of a friend, someone she trusted. After that day it had been weeks before she had let Ray touch her again.

"I remember."

"That wasn't the only time something like that happened. Just the only time you were there to see it." His voice was a guilty rasp. "A couple of days before the incident you remember, Harrison picked me for a squad to search a little enclave on the outskirts of Haditha for insurgents. Local informants told us the place was off limits—nobody ever went there and nobody ever left. Merchants brought supplies up from the city and left them at a drop point. People from the enclave came out to get them after the delivery men had gone."

Kat blinked, alert now, remembering her walk into Chesbro and the sign she'd encountered at the roadblock. The parallel was not lost on her.

"I don't know if we got intel that insurgents were hiding there or if we just figured what better place for them to hide than somewhere considered off-limits, but we went in hard," he continued.

Ray stared at her, his eyes so damn sorry. She remembered those eyes well, even that look, and she hated him for making her remember how she'd felt on those dark nights in the desert.

"What you saw out there with Bonner?" he said. "We saw it with everyone in the enclave. Killed every last one of them because once they went rabid like that, killing them was the only way we could stop them. When it was over, Harrison told us the rest of what the locals had fed him, the story about the enclave and the Bad Hour. It's like an infection. You let yourself get too angry or too emotional in general, and it just...takes over. The people around Haditha said the Bad Hour was a demon, that once it touched you it stayed with you always, ready to take over if you couldn't control yourself."

"Bullshit," she whispered, the weight of the story crushing her. If she had heard about it before coming here, she'd never have believed it. But now?

"They also said it was contagious," Ray went on. He closed his eyes and breathed evenly, and she recognized the effort he made to stay calm. Remembered him doing the same earlier, and Bonner as well.

The ice in her gut grew heavier. Kat stood and grabbed the bars of her cell. "Let me out of here, Ray."

"In a while."

She smashed an open palm against a bar. "Let me out, asshole. I can't stay here!"

Ray pushed away from the desk and walked toward the cell. He stopped a few feet from the bars and studied her with those I'm-sorry eyes.

"You can't leave, Kat. We'll let you out in a little while, but the Bad Hour's in you now. Harrison's squad killed everyone in that enclave but we brought it out with us. Some of the guys in that squad are dead. Others are probably out there infecting people the way I did in Chesbro. I didn't mean to. Even after the times I lost it in Iraq, I chalked it up to the war. PTSD, maybe. But once I came home...once I was in one place long enough...I started to see it happen to other people."

Kat remembered Bonner's face, the way he'd changed, and the strength and rage that had filled her when she had turned on Ray. Then she remembered the day she had seen him go berserk, the day he'd killed that family.

"When you lost it, you didn't look like Bonner," she said. "Yeah, you were a fucking lunatic, but—"

"At first none of us looked any different when it came on. The way I've got it figured, once the Bad Hour takes root in a place, it gets stronger. The people in the enclave looked like Bonner when they went rabid—"

"But I...this *just* happened to me. If you don't look like that at first..."

Ray grabbed one of the bars. "I'm explaining this badly. It's the Bad Hour that's getting stronger, taking root. Maybe it's one demon or maybe it's a bunch of little ones, like parasites, but it gets stronger. Doesn't matter if it's your first time giving in to it...it's the strength of the Hour that matters. Not always an hour, either. The stronger it gets, the longer it can hold on to you."

Kat laughed softly, but it wasn't really a laugh at all.

She rested her forehead against the bars. Impossible. All of this was simply insanity. For a moment she wondered if she had fallen asleep on that northbound bus and still sat there, dreaming with her skull resting against the window. But that was mere fantasy.

"What you're talking about...it can't be," she said softly.

Ray wrapped his fingers around hers, him on one side of those bars and her on the other. "I've seen the way you can rein in your fear, Kat. You can do this. You have to."

Kat began to tremble. She pressed her lips together, trying to stay in control, but tears well in her eyes.

"You don't know what you're saying. I have to..."

Ray squeezed her hand sharply and she snapped her head up and stared at him.

"Stop. You know what will happen," he said. "*Calm down.*"

Kat pulled her hand away and wiped at her eyes. She nodded, took a shuddery breath, and straightened her spine. Another deep breath. Terrified of the Hour taking her over again, that madness...she didn't want to believe, but she could not erase from her mind the things she had seen. The things she had felt.

"I'm all right," she told him firmly. "But you can't keep me here. I have to go home, Ray."

"Kat—"

"I have a daughter."

He frowned, staring at her.

Kat inhaled. Exhaled. Felt that familiar battlefield chill spread through her. This was an altogether different sort of combat.

"I have to leave," she said, "but I get it, Ray. And I'll come back."

Ray held onto the bars from the outside as if worried he might fall over if he let go. "How old is she? Your girl?"

Kat embraced the combat chill in her bones. Met his gaze. "She's four."

"Four," he said, a dull echo.

"I wanted to raise her myself," Kat said. "You were my friend, but I'd seen what kind of man you could be. What kind of father you might be. I thought it would be better—"

"You started writing to me," Ray said, gaze pinning her to the floor inside her cell. "Then when I stopped replying, you came looking. If you didn't want me to know—"

Kat approached the bars again. This time, it was she who put her hands over his.

"At first I just wanted to reconnect. I guess I figured someday I'd tell you. Then later...I needed to talk to you," Kat said. Breathing evenly. "Her baby teeth started falling out at the beginning of this year. That's early. *Really* early. The new ones have been growing in ever since..."

She breathed. Steadied herself.

"Tell me," Ray said through gritted teeth, and she saw that he was doing it, too. The both of them just breathing. Slow and steady. In control.

But they couldn't stay in control every second of every day. Not forever.

Nobody could do that. Especially not a toddler.

"The new teeth are coming in and she has too many of them, Ray. They're tiny things, sharp and black, and there are too many—"

"Kat, no."

She let the cold fill her, stared into his eyes.

"And, Ray," Kat said. "Your little girl has such a temper."

PIPERS

~1~

Ezekiel Prater drove his ancient Ford pickup along Doffin Road, enjoying the cool night air that streamed through the open windows. His daughter, Savannah, had never understood why he had spent the time and money to restore a sixty-year-old vehicle, but she sure liked riding in it.

"Turn it up, Daddy," she pleaded from the passenger seat, barely turning from her open window. "I love this song!"

He smiled and obliged her, though it was one of those bubble-gum pretty boy songs all the young girls seemed to love and anyone over the age of sixteen wanted to scrub from their brains. Zeke felt eighty years old when such thoughts entered his head, but he couldn't help himself. Savannah's preferred entertainment might have rhythm, but it didn't sound much like music to him.

"So, who's going to be there tonight?" he asked.

The wind blew through the cab of the old pickup and carried his voice away. Savannah put her head back against the seat and closed her eyes, letting the breeze whip her hair across her face. His heart melted just looking at her. Savannah had gotten her big blue eyes and the spray of freckles across the bridge of her nose from him, but the copper skin and dark brown hair and lovely, sculpted features had all come from her mother, Anarosa, who'd found the lump in her left breast too late.

Zeke felt the familiar pinch of grief, but by now it had become his bittersweet friend, his reassurance that he had found love in his life. Seven years had passed since Anarosa's death and he still missed her constantly. Once in a great while he would find himself realizing that he had gone an entire day without thinking of her and the guilt would nearly suffocate him. Savannah always saved him with some bit of prattle about her day, a fight she was having with a girlfriend or a boy who had paid her some special attention.

He turned down the music.

"Hey, bud," he said, when she shot him her patented, irritated teenager look. "Who's going to this thing, tonight?"

"Most everyone, I guess. We talked about this already."

"Refresh my memory. Terri, Vanessa, Abby...?"

"Abby can't make it," Savannah said, twisting slightly in her seat to face him, the seatbelt fighting her. "She went to Austin to visit her brother."

Zeke flexed his fingers on the steering wheel. "Her parents are okay with her sleeping in her brother's college dorm room? She's thirteen!"

"She's fourteen."

"Oh, well, that's so much better."

He laughed and shook his head, watching the road ahead for the potholes that had played hell on his gorgeous whitewalls a few months before. The October moon was so bright that it suffused the ranchland that rolled away on all sides with a golden glow. Zeke had known people from up north who believed they had a claim on autumn, and on October in particular, because they believed folks down south never had a proper autumn. But the moonlight in south Texas this time of year had a certain quality to it—a kind of soft, tender magic—that made the world seem a kinder place, rich with possibility. Nights like this made the threats of an uncertain economy and the dangers of living so close to the border seem far away indeed.

"Daddy, please. You know Daniel. It's not like he'd let anything happen to his little sister." She rolled her eyes with a huff.

"I just don't want you gettin' ideas in your head, is all. You're not sleeping in any boy's dorm room, even when you get to college!"

She smirked and cast him a sidelong glance. "And how will you know if I do?"

"Twenty-four-hour surveillance, kid," he joked. "Three hundred and sixty-five days a year."

"Better be careful, Daddy. One of these days you're liable to see something you don't want to see." She waggled her eyebrows in a way that seemed goofy rather than suggestive, and that silly, innocent part of her warmed his heart. "Besides, one of these days you're going to want grandchildren. You can't keep me away from boys forever."

"Slow down there, girl. I'm not halfway old enough to be a grandfather."

"Oh, don't have a heart attack. I'm not in any hurry." Her voice grew quieter, though he could still hear her over the wind. "You've got nothing to worry about, anyway. The boys I like never like me back, and the ones who do make my skin crawl."

Zeke swallowed hard. Nothing pained him more than hearing the hurt in her voice.

"I'm sure that ain't true, Savannah. Maybe it seems that way—"

"It seems that way because it *is* that way, Daddy. I know it won't always be, but for now, that's my life."

"What about that Marco boy? I know he's been flirting with you. He texts you often enough."

"Oh, he likes me all right. He just likes Kasey Mason more."

Zeke scowled. "That'll pass, honey. A boy that age, why he's just mesmerized by how much faster Kasey's filling out her bra. The rest of you girls will get there."

Savannah gave him an amused look, one corner of her mouth lifted in her trademark smirk.

"Well, there you go," she said. "Right there is a stretch of conversational road I hope we never traverse again."

"What's the matter, bud? You uncomfortable talking about bras with the guy who pays for yours?" he teased. "Or is it just me talking about Kasey getting boobs that—"

"Ding ding ding! We have a winner! Daddy, *please*—"

"Boobs. Breasts. Knockers—"

"'Knockers?' Wow, you're old."

"—Titties—"

"Ugh. Now you're just gross."

"Next I'll start talking about nipples or pubic hair or—"

"Okay, Daddy, okay!" Savannah cried, her whole body cringing as she covered her ears. "Enough enough. I surrender!"

They shared a laugh and Zeke couldn't wipe the grin off his face. Embarrassing his daughter always felt like a triumph. Slowly, though, his smile slid away.

"Listen, honey, I know you don't like talkin' about this stuff, but—"

"Daddy," Savannah said sharply, her tone turning serious. "I know, okay? We went through this when I was ten, and again when I got my period, and again and again. Without Mom around, you had to step up and have some talks that most fathers probably avoid like the plague. And you did great. I'm not kidding. Sure, sometimes it got weird, but I don't know...I feel kind of lucky to have a father I can talk to about anything."

"You can, y'know?"

"I know. Really, I do." She took a deep breath. "But I'm thirteen, now—"

"And you've acquired the wisdom of the ancients."

"No!" she snapped. "I'm not saying that!"

They fell silent for a moment, cast adrift on a sea of shared awkwardness.

Then Zeke let out a breath, all trace of amusement gone. "Sorry, honey. I really do understand. And I trust you. Hell, I wish I'd been half as smart and savvy as you when I was thirteen. It's just that you not needing me so much is gonna take some getting used to."

"Don't worry, Daddy," she said. "I'm always gonna need you. I'm sure some boy or other is gonna break my heart soon enough—"

"Well, it *has* been at least a couple of weeks."

Savannah smacked his leg. "—And I'm gonna need a shoulder to cry on."

"Well, I'm good for that much, at least."

"Always," she promised.

Savannah turned the music back up and Zeke smiled and sat up straighter behind the wheel, a sly smile on his lips. His daughter was growing up to be one hell of a young woman.

He studied the road ahead, enjoying the rattle of the ancient Ford and the thrum of the wheel in his hands. His day-to-day truck was less than a year old, a red beauty he used both on the ranch and on longer drives. But on a lovely fall night when the temperature had fallen to the mid-sixties and they could have the window open to let in a breeze that was actually chilly for once, he hadn't been able to resist the F1. He'd done most of the restoration himself, including repairing a sizeable dent in the clunky, metal grill, which he'd painted white to match the whitewall tires. The rest of the truck was a crayon-box blue that had just seemed right. Bright enough to satisfy the little boy in him, who had thrilled at the idea of restoring his grandfather's old pickup when he'd rescued it from the crumbling ruin of the ranch's original barn, and yet manly enough not to draw ridicule from his friends, who'd been envious as hell once all his hard work had paid off.

"Daddy?" Savannah ventured.

Zeke glanced at her. "Bud?"

"I just want you to know that I'm okay," she said. "I wish Momma had been here for all of this. But even if she had, I'd be saying the same things to her now. I'm almost fourteen. I know about sex and I know boys are pretty much like puppies who'll piss everywhere and hump your leg unless they're properly housebroken."

A wonderful pride swelled Zeke Prater's heart, and yet it was also melancholy. An end-of-an-era sort of pride.

"You've got that right," he said.

His little girl smiled and reached over to take his right hand off of the steering wheel. He squeezed her hand and she held on tight for a minute, and then they were approaching the turn onto Hidalgo County Road and he wanted both hands on the wheel.

He slowed at the corner, waited for two cars to pass—high traffic for the area—and then turned right, traveling parallel to the new fence Bill Cassaday had put up along the eastern edges of his ranch property. A couple of horses grazed in a pasture and Zeke frowned at the foolishness of leaving the animals out this far from the barn after dark. They were two miles from the Rio Grande here—two miles from the Mexican border—and while old-time horse thievery was a thing of the past, there was never any telling what might happen to people, property, or livestock. That was the whole reason the Texas Border

Volunteers had been formed—Zeke and Cassaday and Alan Vickers and a bunch of others taking it upon themselves to improve the policing of the border, at least in Hidalgo County. They'd installed lights and hidden cameras and had been reporting drug and human trafficking activities to the government for half a year, leading to a flurry of deportations and drug seizures. Just five nights ago, they'd caught a trio of hikers coming through the well-trodden paths at the back of Vickers' acreage, each carrying a hundred pounds of cocaine from the Matamoros cartel. They'd come across the river on a raft and would have been long gone if the Volunteers hadn't picked them up on video and reported them. The Border Patrol had caught them before they'd made it to the highway.

It was hard on the younger folks, living out here. Their elders all knew it, and over the past few years had been dreaming up one program after another to give them alternatives to sneaking off into the fields to drink beers or have sex. Dances and clubs and outdoor movies projected on the back of the Praters' barn. Tonight was the best of all, the First Annual Lansdale Music Festival. People had laughed at first, mocking the idea that a town as tiny as Lansdale, Texas, could draw enough people to warrant such an event, but every roadhouse in the state had a band or two dreaming of bigger things, and right there in Lansdale they had Annie Rojas and Jesse McCaffrey, both of whom were gifted musicians and had lovely voices.

Lansdale had been founded in 1912 and only then because of the five huge, sprawling ranches that surrounded it—thousands and thousands of acres. The ranch families had wanted a post office closer than the one in Hidalgo and then it had seemed only natural for a grocery and a hardware store and a gas station and soon enough Jesse McCaffrey's grandmother had opened a dress shop and the saddlery had been replaced by an auto mechanic's shop and someone had the bright idea to open a bookshop. Decades had passed, and there still wasn't much more to Lansdale than that. They'd never had a movie theatre or anything as precious as a florist; the grocery had rented videos when such things were still of interest, and the hardware store had a garden center these days. Not long before the 20th century gave up the ghost, a medical equipment company with its factory in Hidalgo had moved its home office to Lansdale, bringing an influx of out-of-towners. Half a dozen Border Patrol officers called it home, as well. There were only a few hundred houses, but the ranch owners and workers and their families were all a part of the Lansdale community, swelling its ranks.

When Zeke was growing up, it had been a nice little town.

Now it lay squarely in the path of drug smugglers and the coyotes who guided illegal immigrants across the border, and Zeke Prater wore a gun belt that made him feel like as idiot, as if he were some kid playing cowboys. Tonight he had left the gun belt and his Smith & Wesson

1911 back at the ranch...but he had a high-powered rifle in the back seat of the rattling old pickup, just in case.

Around his daughter, Zeke wore a mask of confidence, doing everything he could to cast an illusion, but he kept vigilant at all times in order to assure her safety, and the safety of all of the people who worked on his ranch.

He glanced over at Savannah just as she pushed her hair away from her eyes, and the gesture caused his heart to stumble. *God, she's so beautiful,* he thought. *Too beautiful.* He knew that all fathers must have similar fears, but he worried about his daughter not only because she was pretty, but because she looked older than her age. She often drew the attention of older boys and even young men who misjudged her years, and like most girls, she relished the attention. Young girls were apt to be persuaded to do almost anything to maintain a constant stream of such affections.

Not Savannah, he told himself. You've always been blunt with her, always open and fair. She's too smart.

But Zeke figured lots of fathers told themselves the same things about their daughters, and ended up being dead wrong.

"I assume Ben Trevino's going to be there," he said, keeping his eyes on the road. He had attempted to keep his tone neutral and hoped that he'd succeeded. Savannah was in the eighth grade, but she liked the older boys just as much as they liked her; the Trevino boy was a sophomore at the high school in Hidalgo.

"I assume Skyler's going to be there," Savannah said.

Zeke shook his head. "Touché, kid. Touché." He'd been on half a dozen dates with a waitress at a diner in Lansdale called the Magic Wagon, and Savannah knew that he'd fallen hard for her.

Rounding a corner, they came in view of the lights of Lansdale and Savannah sat up straighter. Zeke smiled as he took in the multi-colored bulbs that had been strewn from lamppost to lamppost, like Christmas had come early. With the windows open, they could hear the discordant jangle of instruments tuning up.

"Wow, this is going to be loud," Zeke said.

"You really are getting old," Savannah replied.

He couldn't argue. Forty-one didn't feel old, but if his first reaction to the volume of the speakers set up for the music festival was something other than excitement, maybe he truly had gotten ancient before his time.

They found a parking space behind the post office and Zeke locked up the pickup, hoping he didn't regret having brought the antique to town. He patted his pockets to make sure he had his wallet and phone and keys and then they set off, walking out to the main street and joining the flow of people moving toward the park in front of the town hall, where a stage had been erected just for the event. Zeke glanced around, admiring the size of the gathering even as he searched the crowd for Skyler, who'd told him that she'd be wearing a yellow hat.

Beside him, Savannah bumped into a thirtyish woman Zeke didn't recognize, and he realized that she'd been looking down at her phone, texting someone.

"Hey, bud, pay attention," he said, gently pushing her arm down. "Why not put the phone away."

"Terri just texted me. She's here. I'm just trying to figure out where."

Zeke took a breath and decided not to fight her. They weren't used to having this many people downtown at once, and it *would* be hard for Savannah to find her friends in this throng without texting them.

"Just watch where you're going," he said.

They were half a block from the town hall when the first band began to play. People howled and applauded and groups of young people put their arms around each other and swayed together. Zeke figured there must be six or seven hundred people—not exactly throngs, but a massive gathering for Lansdale. Glancing around, he saw faces and the backs of heads, sweatshirts and t-shirts and jackets and then a quick flash of yellow glimpsed between moving bodies.

Skyler?

"Daddy, I see Vanessa!" Savannah said, tugging his arm. "Can I go hang with those guys?"

"Just a second," he said, rising to the tips of his toes and moving around, trying to get another glimpse of that yellow flash, hoping to find that it had been Skyler's hat.

"They're just over there in front of the bookshop," Savannah said. "I have my phone. Can I just catch up with you in a bit?"

There! Another glimpse of yellow.

He hesitated, turning toward Savannah and then glancing over at the little bookshop across the street, its windows dark, the CLOSED sign on the door. A group of kids clustered on the sidewalk there and he thought he did recognize Vanessa amongst them.

"All right," he said. "But don't leave this block. I'll text you in—"

"Thanks, Daddy!" Savannah cried in triumph, waving at him as she pushed away through the crowd.

The band's first song ended. In the moment between the last chord that rolled out of the speaker system and the beginning of the audience's applause, Zeke heard the roar of car engines coming fast.

He turned and saw the headlights, frowned as he saw the pair of dust-coated, jacked-up pickup trucks with their blacked out windows—

—began to shout as he saw the figures that crouched in the beds of the pickup trucks and the guns they held in their hands, a rainbow of multi-colored festival lights gleaming off of the barrels and the truck hoods and the windshields.

The band charged into their second song, a country-rock anthem everyone in the crowd knew by heart, but people had already begun to shout, and when the first gunshot split the night and echoed off of the storefront windows, they began to scream.

"Savannah," Zeke barely whispered. And then he shouted her name.

Hurling himself through the crowd, shoving people aside, he caught sight of her at the edge of the lawn, nearly to the sidewalk. She'd raised her hand in a wave to her friends across the street, but stood frozen there as she turned toward the roaring engines and the gunfire that erupted in the very same moment, silencing the music but not the screams.

Zeke had his arm outstretched, reaching for her, no more than five feet away when the bullet punched a hole through her chest. Her white denim jacket puffed out behind her, the fabric tugged by the exiting bullet.

Savannah staggered several steps backward but remained standing for a second or two, a sad, mystified expression on her face as a crimson stain began to soak into the pale blue cotton of her top.

He froze, fingers still outstretched, still reaching for her as she lifted her gaze to focus on him. Zeke was sure of that. Savannah *saw* him.

And then she crumpled to the street, bleeding, her mouth opening and closing as if she desperately wanted to speak, until at last her chest ceased its rise and fall and Savannah lay still.

By then the gunfire had stopped and the sound of engines had faded, but the screaming went on and on.

~2~

On a Monday morning, the first week of February, Zeke Prater stood in his east pasture and stared at a job only halfway done. He'd gotten the gate off of its hinges and scraped the hell out of his knuckles in the process. The top hinge had rusted nearly all the way through, and over the weekend it had finally given way, the weight of it twisting the bottom hinge and wreaking havoc on the spring mechanism that swung the gate closed automatically. Of all of the hardware bolted into the wood, only the lock seemed in good working order.

"Son of a bitch," Zeke sighed, stepping back and wiping the sweat from his forehead.

The dark red cotton sweater he'd worn this morning lay hanging over the pasture fence. Winter mornings had a special chill, even all the way down in Hidalgo County, but it had warmed up nicely. He'd worked at the hinges for half an hour before he'd managed to get the gate off. Now he had to remove the twisted hardware before he could install the new hinge set, and then he would see if the spring could be salvaged.

He turned and walked to his truck. His toolbox lay open in the flatbed of the F150 and he tossed the screwdriver into it. The drill case sat beside the toolbox, along with the new set of hinges. Zeke reached for the drill but paused as he noticed the blood dripping from his knuckles, surprised he had not felt it.

Swearing under his breath, he grabbed a rag from the toolbox and wrapped it around his right hand. As he leaned against the tailgate, he took a deep breath, trying to enjoy the feeling of the sun on his skin and the cool winter morning air. But he couldn't help glancing down at the rag, noticing the thirsty way the cloth absorbed his blood. He got lost in that moment, thinking of blood and fabric.

When he heard the sound of an engine he snapped his head up as if awoken from a trance, dropping his right hand—rag and all—to the butt of the pistol hanging at his hip. A plume of dust rose from the road to the west, and he recognized the battered old Jeep coming his way. Even so, it took a few seconds for him to move his hand away from the gun.

The Jeep skidded to a halt in the dirt a dozen feet from his truck and the driver climbed out, smile beaming beneath the shadow of his wide-brimmed hat. Lester Keegan had put fifty in his rearview mirror a couple of years past and never looked back. Wiry and tan, in his daily uniform of tan work pants and blue cotton button-down shirt, he'd have looked every inch the working cowboy if not for the hat. Zeke had an eye for hats and he knew a custom job when he saw one. Lester might own the smallest of the five ranches surrounding Lansdale, but he had the most money and the expensive tastes to match. Oil had done that, two generations back, and the Keegans had never squandered their windfall.

"I'm assuming there are still folks around here somewhere that you pay good money to do things like fix pasture gates," Lester said, surveying the scene with an eyebrow cocked.

"Sometimes a fella likes to get his hands dirty," Zeke replied, checking his knuckles, satisfied to see that the bleeding had stopped.

"Seems to me I recall you saying you were too old for this sort of thing."

Zeke narrowed his eyes. Something in Lester's tone troubled him. They were in the habit of paying each other a visit now and then, sharing a beer or a coffee. Lester's wife, Anita, had taken an interest in Zeke's widower status years ago and had determined to do something about it. The Keegans had reached out to him many times in the past four months—since the night of the music festival—but he'd driven them away just as bluntly as he had everyone else, even though their own son, Josh, had been among the dead.

"If you're not too old to ride or to sink a fence post now and again, I guess I'm not too old to fix a damn gate. I just turned forty-two, Lester. That don't make me old; it makes me lazy."

Lester took off his hat and ran his fingers around the soft brim. "Well, now—"

"What brings you out?" Zeke asked.

Lester's smile slipped away and suddenly he looked his age. "Didn't have much choice. You're not answering your cell and you haven't returned my calls from yesterday."

Zeke wiped the back of his hand across his brow. "This doesn't sound like a lunch invitation from Anita."

"No," Lester agreed. "You're right about that. I need you to come with me, Zeke. We've got an appointment in town. Vickers said someone's gotta be there to represent everyone we lost, and Savannah doesn't have anyone but you to stand for her."

Zeke felt a trickle of ice along his spine. He stared at the ground, at a blade of grass growing up through the dirt road.

"This some insurance thing?" he asked without lifting his gaze.

"I asked Vickers the same question. He says no."

"Then what is it?"

"Asked him that, too. He says 'revenge.'"

Zeke stood a little straighter. Doubt and suspicion flooded him, but logic prevailed. Vickers had lost his wife, Martha, that terrible night. The cartel had killed twenty-three people in all, with Savannah the youngest of them. As much as the Keegans and some of Zeke's other friends might want to see him leave the ranch for some human interaction, even just for a few hours, none of them would stoop so low as to hold out the possibility of revenge for bait.

"Feds say they're working on it," Zeke noted. "We get directly involved, more of our people are gonna die. Leave it to them, they say."

Lester's blue eyes narrowed, the edges crinkling, and suddenly he looked older than ever.

"Leave it to them? We've tried that before and it didn't work. Hell, that's why we formed the Volunteers, ain't it? The Mexican government is too damned disorganized and too corrupt, top to bottom, to stop the drug war and all the killing that goes on around it. If you could call this an act of terrorism, maybe you'd get the funding it would take to launch an all out war on the cartels, and to hell with Mexican sovereignty. But the Feds know it's all drug-related, so what do we get? Exactly what we got the last time the media got up in arms about killings along the border: another fifteen hundred National Guard troops for additional patrols and promises from the FBI that they're infiltrating the cartels, working to dismantle them from within, 'cause they've had so much success in the past. Now even the media's forgotten about us, not that they were much help. All the spectacle they put on, all that mock horror, only lasts until the next tragedy comes along. That school shooting in Rhode Island knocked us right out of the news cycle."

Lester gave a slow nod, as if to affirm everything he'd just said. He glanced up at Zeke.

"They can send all the National Guardsmen they want, but if there's revenge to be had, nobody's going to go out and get it for us. Hell, I didn't get to be my age without learning at least that much, and neither did you."

Zeke felt an all-too familiar rage burning in his chest. It had been there ever since that October night.

"You don't have to preach to me, Lester," he said. "I'm living this, too, remember?"

Lester pushed his shaggy hair away from his eyes and slid his hat back on.

"I haven't forgotten," he said, and glanced away from Zeke, up toward the main house.

Zeke averted his eyes, not wanting to see his vacant windows for fear that his voice might betray him and he might speak aloud the question that concerned him the most. Did he even belong out here anymore? Without a wife or a child, with his sister up in Virginia and their parents dead in the ground, what was the point of this life, holding every breath an extra beat just in case the bullets started flying?

Zeke had spent four months trying to come up with a reason to stay. The only one he'd found was the promise he'd made to himself—the promise that he wouldn't leave until he knew the men with Savannah's blood on their hands had paid the price, in full.

He slid the toolbox and the drill kit off the tailgate and onto the truck bed, then slammed the tailgate.

"You drive."

As they made their way into town, Zeke spotted small clusters of people gathered near parked cars or milling about in front of shops. Victoria Jessup was in front of the post office with her two younger boys, and she looked to Zeke as if she were holding her breath. Sarah Jane Trevino, little sister to Ben, sat on the hood of his mother's Ford. Some of the people in Lansdale that day watched Lester Keegan's Jeep as it rolled through town and pulled into a spot across from the hardware store, but most of them ignored the new arrivals. They were all watching the front door of the Magic Wagon.

"What the hell's going on here, Lester?" Zeke asked as they left the Jeep and started across the street toward the diner.

"Your guess is as good as mine, *amigo*."

Bells jangled overhead as they entered the Magic Wagon. All around the diner, familiar faces turned toward them. Victoria Jessup's eldest boy was there, along with Ben Trevino's mother, Linda, and the pretty young wife of Tim Hawkins, the sheriff's deputy who'd been shot through the throat. Mrs. Hawkins looked about five months along with her pregnancy, now, and as sorrowful as her loss had been, Zeke couldn't help thinking how lucky she was to have her new baby to remember Big Tim by. Now that he and Lester had arrived, there were more than two-dozen people gathered in the diner, all but three of whom he knew had lost someone to the cartel's bloodlust back in October. Two of the three were employees of the Magic Wagon, a waitress named Deena Green...and Skyler Holt.

It shamed Zeke to see Skyler, though he'd suspected she would be there. She smiled tentatively at him and he could muster only a nod in return. She'd gotten blond highlights in her hair and the look suited her. Curvy and bright and charismatic, Skyler was ten years his junior and the first woman he'd met in his life as a widower who had brought a lightness to his heart. She had called a dozen times after Savannah's murder, but he had returned not a single one and had avoided her when he'd seen her in town. This was the first time he'd set foot in the Magic Wagon since October.

She nodded back, just a little tilt of the head. He would have liked to talk to her—had thought all along how nice it would be to see her smile again and hear her laugh—but he had nothing to offer in return. No joy to give.

Of all the faces that'd turned toward him and Lester as they'd entered, only one was entirely unfamiliar to Zeke. A stranger. The little man with the brown skin might have been thirty-five or fifty-five, depending on how many years he'd spent working in the sun. Perhaps five-feet-three-inches tall and tipping the scales at a mighty one-hundred-and-twenty-pounds or so, he ought to have gone almost unnoticed in the room, but Zeke could feel an aura of intensity around him, as if he had everyone's attention though everyone studiously avoided looking directly at him. He wore loose black cotton pants and a white shirt that made his sun-darkened skin stand out even more starkly, and his eyes were wide and round...the eyes, Zeke immediately thought, of a man who sat in the last row on a bus, talking to people nobody else could see.

His eyes were unnerving, and Zeke lowered his gaze, discomfited by his regard.

Alan Vickers stood up from the stool where he'd been perched.

"Zeke, welcome," the white-bearded rancher said. "I'm glad Lester could persuade you to join us."

Zeke glanced again at the little man, and again he looked away.

"Well...yeah, I'm here, Alan. But I've got work to do, as I'm sure we all do, so why not say your piece, whatever it is."

"Of course," Vickers replied. He glanced around the diner. "Deena? Skyler? If you ladies would step out for a time, maybe go on down to the park, I'll send someone to fetch you when we're done. And thank Agnes for the use of the place."

Zeke watched curiously as the two waitresses took off their aprons, said quiet good-byes to several of those gathered, and then departed. Skyler walked within five feet of him and barely glanced up as she passed. For the first time, he noticed that the people in the Magic Wagon all seemed to have coffee or some other beverage, but not a single plate of food had been set before them. None of them had come here to eat. Whatever Vickers had in mind, the whole diner had been put at his disposal.

And why not? Zeke thought. He's the landlord.

Vickers wore the smile of a heartbroken man trying his best. Zeke figured his own smile must look like that and vowed to himself to try and avoid smiling ever again. It was a wretched, pitiful expression, but Vickers cast it about with the confused air of excitement and apology found in men who'd sought truths better left unspoken.

"I want to thank you all for coming," he said, his face reddening. "I'm not going to waste your time. I know most of you don't want to be here. Hell, looking around at each other, knowing there's only one thing everyone in this room has in common…it makes me want to scream."

Vickers paused and took a breath. To Zeke's surprise, nobody called out for him to get to the point. *Maybe because they recognize the pain in his eyes from the mirror*, Zeke thought.

"I could give you a whole long build up, folks," Vickers went on. "But I'd lose you halfway through because no matter how long you've known me, you're gonna have a hard time believing a damn word I say. So here's the only preamble I'm gonna give you. Reality is a consensus. It is what we agree it is, and by 'we' I don't just mean the people in this room, I mean society. We all grow up with an idea of what's possible and what's impossible. Most of you folks believe in God, or you did, once upon a time. We spend…"

His voice broke, thick with emotion, and then he smiled that painful smile again and forged on.

"We spend our lives building up these walls between what we believe in and what we don't believe in, and it's never easy when one of them gets broken down."

Vickers gestured to the little man seated on a counter stool just beside him. The stranger had been sitting as still and silent as a monk in meditation, but now he blinked as if coming awake and glanced around at the mourners. His face held no expression and his storm-gray eyes were cold.

"This fella here is Enoch Stroud. His daughter, Lena, dated a small-time drug dealer out of Houston by the name of—well, his name doesn't matter, really—point is, he stole from the Matamoros cartel. They could've just killed this kid, but there's always some fool who thinks he's smarter, thinks he can get away with something, and the cartel wanted to teach a different kind of lesson. They took Enoch's daughter—"

The little man interrupted with a choking laugh that gave Zeke chills.

"Took 'er," Enoch said, glaring at the gathered mourners one by one, as if accusing them of the crime. "Raped 'er. Left pieces of her for the boyfriend to find, wrapped up like birthday gifts and set on his bed or in the back seat of his car. Hands. Feet. Teeth. Breasts. Then her head, just to make sure we knew she was dead."

"Oh, sweet Jesus," Alma Hawkins said, covering her eyes so nobody would see her cry.

Tommy Jessup swore under his breath, but in the silence between Enoch's words, they all heard it.

"It was after we got her head that we buried her," Enoch went on. "Oh, we waited a week or so, but then we understood that the message had been sent and that we wouldn't be getting any more of Lena back."

Vickers had turned away from the man, and for the first time Zeke noticed that he was fiddling with something in his right-hand pocket, clutching it like it was some sort of talisman. For some reason it unnerved Zeke, as if he'd peered inside the man's secret sorrow. He'd known Alan Vickers for most of his life but they'd never been friends, never had much in common besides geography. Now they had pain.

Zeke shifted his gaze. He wanted to bolt from the diner, from Lansdale, from fucking Texas, and go somewhere he could watch the snow fall and sit by a fire and feel like a stranger to the world. Because something was coming; he felt that very powerfully. This moment was building up to something that clearly frightened Vickers. And Zeke would have run from it, would have gone north until there were only white mountains and warm hearths, except for the single word he'd heard out of anybody's mouth today that had tantalized him. The word Lester had used as bait to get him here.

"You want revenge," he said, surprising even himself by speaking aloud.

Every pair of eyes in the diner shifted toward him, but Zeke kept his focus on Enoch.

The little man did not smile. He nodded, just once. "Yes, Mr. Prater. It is Mr. Prater?"

"I'm Zeke Prater," he confirmed. Though how you knew that, I'd like to know.

"Here it is, then, Mr. Prater," Enoch said, then took in the others with a sweeping glance. "I know a way to have my revenge on the Matamoros cartel and if you will all cooperate, you can have your revenge as well. Revenge and more."

"What do you mean, 'more'?" Lester asked, arms crossed.

A chair squeaked across the floor as Arturo Sanchez shifted to look at Enoch directly. "The Lord has a poor opinion of revenge, Mr. Stroud."

"Not in the Old Testament he don't," Linda Trevino said. "Go on, Mr. Stroud. If there's a way to fix these sons of bitches, we're all ears. It won't bring my son back, but it'll ease my soul when I go to bed at night."

Enoch looked at her, head bowed slightly, dark shadows beneath his eyes. "Interesting that you should put it that way, Mrs. Trevino."

"What way?" she asked, and Zeke could see she was unsettled. "And how do you know my—"

Enoch clapped his hands on his thighs, still seated on the stool by the counter—so tiny in comparison to Vickers and yet somehow the focus of all attention.

"That's enough of what Mr. Vickers called 'preamble,' don't you think?" Enoch said, nodding as if in conversation with himself. "I think so. There's only one way you folks are going to listen to the rest of what I've got to say without laughing me out of town or maybe stoning me in front of the town hall, and that's if you see what I can give you with your own eyes."

Zeke frowned. His skin prickled with a dark sort of anticipation that he didn't like one bit. Whoever Enoch Stroud was, he didn't want anything to do with the man. But when Enoch nodded to Vickers and Vickers produced the object he'd been fiddling with from his pocket, Zeke couldn't turn away. Several people muttered and Zeke saw the same unease he felt ripple through the diner.

"What the hell's that supposed to be, some kind of tin whistle?" Lester asked.

"I don't—" Vickers started, a strange combination of apology and relief flooding his face.

"Just play the tune, Mr. Vickers," Enoch said. "Just play the tune."

With a hitching breath, Vickers put the yellowed instrument to his lips and blew into it, one finger shifting across a trio of small holes on top. It was a kind of flute, strangely carved and with little streaks of dark brown along its shaft like war paint. The sound it emitted could not rightly be called music, but Vickers managed a sequence of discordant notes that had a certain melody when he repeated them a second and third time. It was one of the strangest displays of incongruity Zeke had ever seen, but something about the tune tugged at the base of his skull as if part of him remembered it, down in what Lester always called his lizard brain—the part that hadn't changed in people since cave days.

"This is stupid," Big Tim Hawkins' widow said. "What is this supposed to—"

The swinging door at the back of the dining room squeaked open, and Martha Vickers walked in from the kitchen, wearing the same dress she'd been buried in.

The bullet hole in her right bicep was still open, a dark, winking wound. Above her left eye, the missing part of her skull—the part blown out by the cartel gunman's kill shot—had been covered by a thin membrane of skin like a birth caul. Even from across the room, Zeke could see the pulsing beneath it.

Screams filled the Magic Wagon.

Alan Vickers kept playing the flute, tears streaming down his face. He would not look at his wife. His dead wife, now up and walking, pale and sickly and shuffling but alive, a slow, uncertain smile making her lips tremble.

Zeke felt sick.

"Stop!" Lester shouted, storming across the room to knock the flute from Vickers' hands. "*Stop it!*"

The bone pipe—for it was bone, Zeke could see that clearly now—skittered across the floor. Vickers shoved Lester away and lumbered after it, shifting a table out of the way to retrieve it while his dead wife swayed in place, waiting for another note.

"What the hell is this?!" Lester demanded, rounding on Enoch.

The little man had still not risen from the stool.

"It's exactly what it looks like," Enoch said, not smiling, his lip curling with hate. "Resurrection. Mrs. Vickers has been up and around for three days. Another week or so and she'll be good as new, if I let her stay above ground that long."

"What the hell do you mean if *you* let her?" Zeke snarled, feeling his own hate—and his own hope—rising like a cobra.

"It's all or none," Enoch said. "I can give this gift to all of you, bring back all of the folks the Matamoros cartel murdered back on October twelfth. If you want it. If you all agree. In exchange, you—and the dead ones, the ones you lost—will help me get my revenge. We will *all* have our revenge, as long as you all are in agreement."

Enoch rose and glanced around.

"I'll expect your answer by noon tomorrow."

"But what do we have to do for you?" Linda Trevino asked. "What do *they*—"

Enoch had started to move toward the door, but he paused and turned toward her. Zeke thought he caught a glimpse of the real pain inside the man, the loss and ruin.

"Does it matter?" Enoch asked.

When no one seemed to have an answer, he continued to the exit, people moving aside to let him out.

In his absence, the mourners could only stare at the resurrected Martha Vickers and her strange, lost smile, until her husband collected her and led her back out through the diner's kitchen.

~3~

Lester drove Zeke home in stony silence. The radio whispered, volume turned down so far that the music was barely audible. The sun had moved almost directly overhead and it felt too warm for February, even in south

Texas. Zeke sat in the passenger seat and watched the fields rolling by, his heart numb and growing more so by the moment. He felt sick and hollow at the same time. Empty, as if he were the one who had died—and wasn't that the truth, in a way? Savannah had died just once, and he had spent the past four months doing the same, a little bit every day.

The thought made him cringe with self-loathing. Fuck, listen to yourself. You get to watch the wind move the trees and the sun rise over the ranch. You get to breathe.

If a small cry came from his throat in that moment, as he turned fully away so that his friend could not see his face, Lester had the decency not to remark upon it. His own son, Josh, had been thirty years old, married and with his first child—Lester's first grandchild—on the way. Grief had become like a secret they shared.

"Son of a bitch," Zeke whispered, pressing the heels of his hands against his eyes, as if he could drive the image of dead Martha Vickers from his memory.

He couldn't, and neither could he stop himself from imagining Savannah standing there in the diner in Martha's place, alive but not quite alive, the bullet wounds she'd sustained beginning to heal.

How is it possible? he asked himself. How in the name of God...?

An icy knot formed in his gut. Maybe it wasn't in the name of God at all.

The big question was whether or not that even mattered. If Enoch had only been able to raise the dead, had them shuffling around looking the same way they had when they'd been buried, or worse, decaying...that would have been easier. Zeke would never have wanted Savannah to live that way, no matter how much the pain of her death gnawed at his insides. But if she could be fully alive again—really alive, restored to her true self—what then?

He'd never have believed it if he hadn't seen it with his own eyes.

Lester turned in through the gates of the Riverbend, which was the name Zeke's grandfather had given the Prater ranch in 1927, and drove back out to the pasture where they had left Zeke's truck ninety minutes and a lifetime before. When he skidded to a stop, clouds of dust rose up from the dirt road and swirled around them.

"What are we gonna do, Zeke?" Lester asked in a strangled voice. He looked pale and drawn, as if he'd aged twenty years in the past hour.

Zeke opened his door and put one boot on the running board. "What do you think we're gonna do? If there's even a chance, what else *can* we do? Go home and call Vickers, Lester, and tell him we're both on board."

Lester gripped the steering wheel, staring out the windshield as if the dusty ranch beyond the glass was the starry nighttime sky and he sought the answers to every question he had ever been afraid to ask.

"It's unholy, Zeke. It must be. One of these days, we're gonna come face to face with the Lord. What do I say to Him on that day if we do this now?"

Zeke turned to stare at him, unable to keep the snarl from his voice. "You say, 'Where the fuck were you on

October the twelfth, you son of a bitch'. How does that sound?"

The main house was so quiet at night that Zeke felt like a ghost haunting his own home, but if he sat on the porch with a beer and listened to the wind, it brought him the sounds of laughter and camaraderie from the bunkhouse. Sometimes he welcomed those noises, but more often they pained him.

After Savannah's murder, the ranch hands had quieted down for a time out of respect. Most of them had been in Lansdale the night of the festival and somehow they had all come home unharmed, just as Zeke had. They had loved Savannah and doted on her like extended family and her death left a wound in all of them, but in the end they weren't her family. Not really. They could move on and heal and Zeke could not, though he never blamed them for it.

When he heard a car door slam out in front of the house, he imagined it must be one of the hands getting up the nerve to approach the house to ask for an advance on his pay. Zeke tried to be as flexible as he could, as long as he didn't think the money was going to drugs or gambling and none of the hands borrowed too much up front. A couple of times it had bitten him in the ass with guys who'd taken off for greener pastures still owing him days or weeks of work, but for the most part, he had found honest men for the ranch.

Zeke didn't answer the knock at the door. He didn't feel capable of holding a conversation tonight. How could he pretend there was anything else that mattered to him beyond what he had seen at the Magic Wagon that morning? He remained in the easy chair in his living room, an ancient Cary Grant movie flickering on the television. He had barely paid attention to a moment of the film, but it was a balm to his soul, allowing him to travel back to a simpler, gentler time.

The knocking ceased for only a moment before his visitor began to rap again, harder this time. Zeke stayed in his chair, admiring the stern lines of Myrna Loy's pretty face. As a boy, he had found a genuine comfort in classic cinema, inheriting the love of old films from his parents. Savannah had never understood his interest and had teased him about his boring taste in movies, but she had been sucked in the night he'd watched *Rear Window* while she did her homework on the living room floor, and Zeke had hoped to introduce her to other Hitchcock films, and then to Bogart, who'd always been his favorite. He had hoped to share so many things with her, to watch her grow and learn and turn into a young woman and maybe a mother someday.

Despite the terrifying, monstrous miracle he'd seen today, he dared not allow himself to hope for those things again.

His cell phone buzzed once, a text coming in. Exhaling, he shifted in the chair and tugged the phone from his pocket to discover that the message was from Skyler.

Open the damn door.

Zeke almost didn't get up. He had never wanted to hurt Skyler, but since Savannah's murder t the idea of loving *anyone* made him want to lock himself in the cellar and never come out. Love meant pain and loss; better to be alone.

But he had known Skyler a long time before they had begun dating, and he knew she would not go away just because he ignored her—seeing her earlier today at the Magic Wagon confirmed that. She had come out here with some purpose in mind and as long as she believed he was at home—and his car out in the driveway had already given him away—she would see it through.

"Shit," he muttered, rising from his chair.

When he opened the door, Skyler barged in without an invitation. She had made no effort to pretty herself up for the visit; her hair was in a ponytail and the only make up he could see was mascara. Her hooded burgundy sweater fit her tightly enough to show off her curves but it was frayed at the cuffs and the laces of her boots were untied, as if she'd made the decision to come abruptly and hadn't paused even to tie them.

"Come in, I guess," he said, letting the irony into his voice.

Skyler spun on him, there in the foyer, stammering nonsense for several seconds, the words crowding each other to get out. She paused and took a breath, so furious with him...and she was so beautiful that it made him want to shove her back out the door. He loved the fire in her, the passion, but he did not want to love her.

"You guess...? That's the greeting I get after you ignore me?" She looked as if she didn't know whether to cry or slug him. "I've given you all the space you could ever have asked for, Ezekiel. I've respected your desire to be alone even though I think it's the opposite of what you need. But I come and bang on your door and you *ignore* me—"

"I didn't know it was you banging, Skyler."

"—hush, now, I'm yelling at you!" she said, waving a finger, blue eyes alight with righteous fury.

Zeke couldn't help smiling. "I can see that."

Skyler faltered, the corners of her mouth turning upward, tempting a grin. Instead she punched him in the shoulder.

"Ow!"

"Don't try to make light," she said grimly, searching his eyes. She tucked a stray lock of hair behind her ear. "I figure you know why I'm here."

Zeke glanced out the still-open door, then slid it slowly shut.

"I'm guessing it's to do with the meeting at the Magic Wagon today."

"You know it is."

He narrowed his eyes, turning to look at her. "That doesn't concern you, Skyler. You didn't lose anyone that night—"

"I lost *you*," she said softly. Angrily. "If you think I'm overstepping, well, I don't know why I should care. You've already put me out of your life. But I care for you, Zeke, and that's not going to change. You're a good man. Don't let yourself be talked into this."

"Too late."

Zeke walked into the living room with Skyler trailing behind him.

"It's not too late," she insisted. "Nobody's done anything yet that they can't take back except for Alan Vickers and his little hoodoo conjuror, or whatever the hell that Enoch fellow is."

He sat on the arm of the sofa with his arms crossed, staring at the knots in his pine floorboards.

"This about God?" he asked, not looking up.

"Partly, I guess. But it's more just about what's right. Up until today, I never gave a second thought to the rules I always thought the world worked by. Dead was dead. Maybe that's not so. Unless it's some kind of trick—"

"It wasn't a trick. It was Martha Vickers in there, I'd swear to it."

"Trick or not, it isn't natural, Zeke. You know that. Even if you can bring Savannah back, you'll never erase the truth from your mind."

"If she can come back, the truth'll be that she's alive," he said.

"The truth will be that you saw her get shot and you held her while her body went cold and she was dead, and the dead are not supposed to come back to us. You look inside your heart and you won't be able to run away from the fact that you're doing this for yourself, not for Savannah. You have no way of knowing what it means to come back from the dead, what she'll remember, or if she'll even be whole. All you have is this creepy little fella's word. Don't do this, Zeke. It's abominable. And if you bring her back, she'll *be* an abomination."

For a moment he could not breathe. He closed his eyes and ran a thumb over a spot on his temple that had begun to throb. Skyler only wanted the best for him; he knew that. And, in quiet moments, he had allowed himself to imagine a future with her. But how could she not understand?

She has no children, he thought. *She can't feel what you feel.* Skyler would never know the silent screaming that went on inside his heart, day and night. His wife, Anarosa, had been a God-fearing woman, but he had no doubt what she would have done if she were still alive. Hell, he figured if he gave up this chance, Anarosa would find some way to come back and haunt him, but Skyler would never understand.

To have lost his daughter, seen her die in front of him, and now to have a chance at restoring not only her life, but her lifetime—all the days the future still held in store for her—he would do anything. No matter how noble her intentions, Skyler wanted to rob him of that. For a moment, Zeke hated her for that.

He looked up at her. "You need to leave."

Skyler flinched. "Please, Zeke—"

"You announced that you'd be overstepping, and by God, you kept your word. Now you need to go, Sky."

"Ezekiel—"

"I don't want you here!" he roared, pushing away from the sofa, crowding her backward into the hallway. "*Get out of my damn house!*"

Skyler's hands were shaking and her chest rose and fell in short little breaths as she glared at him.

"You don't get to..." she began, tears welling in her eyes. "I only wanted to—"

His face a mask, Zeke stared at her. "Go. *Now.*"

Skyler nodded slowly, wiping at her tears, and then turned and left, slamming the door behind her. Zeke went to the door and laid his hand on the wood, listening to the growl of her engine starting up. The ice in his gut—in his heart—was the only thing protecting him, and he invited it deeper inside him, wanting to be cold. To be frozen.

He could hear her tires on the driveway as she turned the car around and he wanted to go after her, to kiss her and let her cry with him. But if he went after her, then he would have to admit that she was right, and then where would he be?

~4~

The following night, Enoch passed out the pipes.

Each of the bereaved who had gathered in the Magic Wagon—one mourner for each of the twenty-three people murdered on October the twelfth—received one; none had declined Enoch's offer. They gathered in a haphazardly formed circle on a gravel path that ran through what was called the New Field, the modern part of the cemetery where the recently dead had been buried. Enoch moved wordlessly amongst them, reaching into a burlap sack and producing yellowed bone pipes similar to the one that Vickers had played in the diner the day before.

Vickers stood at the edge of the road, not far from the crypt where his wife had been buried, but she wasn't inside that marble tomb any longer. Martha now stood with her husband, clad in a flowery dress and a light green sweater and wearing a wide-brimmed hat that hid much of her face from view. Somewhere between dead and alive, it was as if she were ashamed of herself, but she held her husband's hand and though Zeke knew it might be the moonlight, he thought that her skin looked less pale than it had the day before, as if some of the pink health had returned to it.

Enoch paused in front of Zeke and rooted in the burlap sack, which made a rasping noise as he drew out the next pipe. Zeke hesitated before accepting the instrument, but Enoch narrowed his eyes in suspicion until he took it. The pipe might have been human bone, but it had been carved and shaped so that it was difficult to know for certain, and Zeke chose not to examine it too closely. It had three holes in the top and otherwise had no markings.

Clutching the pipe in his hand, nursing the icy numbness inside him for his own sake, Zeke glanced around at the others—friends and neighbors and near strangers—and found that most of them wore expressions as blank as his own to mask their grief and hope and doubt.

Several yards away, Aaron Monteforte leaned against the trunk of a massive, dying oak tree with his arms crossed and an almost petulant air about him, as if he thought no one could understand his grief. With twenty-three dead in a small town, everyone in Lansdale had lost a friend or family member in that massacre. There was nothing special about Aaron's grief and, Zeke knew, nothing special about his own...except that it was *his*. His pain. His rage. His loss. His daughter, goddamn it.

Aaron tended bar at the Blue Moon but looked more like he ought to have been the bouncer, with a weightlifter's build and reaper and angel tattoos on his thick biceps, brown hair to his shoulders and a perpetual scruff that couldn't rightly be called a beard. Several years before, Aaron had spent the summer as a hand on the ranch and Zeke knew he ought to go over and say something. But what could he say that he hadn't already said four months ago to Aaron and everyone else who'd lost someone that night? That he was sorry? They were all fucking sorry.

Still, he managed to catch Aaron's eye for a moment and gave a solemn nod, just to say, *hey, man, you're not alone.* After a second of recognition, Aaron returned the gesture. The kid had lost his sister, Trish, who'd been twenty-five and unmarried, and he had chosen to be her proxy. That was how Vickers had referred to them all, "proxies," just folks stepping in to do a deed on behalf of those who couldn't do it themselves.

When Enoch reached Aaron, the big man with the tattoos and the muscles took the pipe and knelt to pray with it clasped in his hands. When Enoch held a pipe out to Linda Trevino, she backed away, shaking her head.

"I can't," she said. "No, Jesus, I can't."

Lester strode over to her, took her firmly by the arm, and brought her to Enoch. "You will," he said. "You already agreed. It's all of us or none of us. Are you going to take this chance away from everyone because you're afraid?"

She spun on him, stared into his weathered face. "Aren't you?"

Only the wind spoke. Otherwise the cemetery was silent.

"We all are," Zeke said at last, quietly but clearly.

Linda stared at him with wild eyes. "But he won't even tell us—"

"Take it, damn you!" Mrs. Hawkins snapped. "Just take it or you might as well be killing them all again!"

Linda sucked in a breath as if she'd been punched in the gut. Shaking, she took the carved length of bone from Enoch, who moved on to young Tommy Jessup and then Arturo Sanchez and to a man Zeke knew only as Mooney, a salesman from the medical supplies company who had brought his new bride to the music festival and then lost her to a bullet only a week-and-a-half after they'd been wed.

The last two pipes in the sack went to Lester and to Harry Boyd, the owner of the oldest of the five ranches that surrounded Lansdale. His boy, Charlie, had been twenty-one and the spitting image of his father, with ginger hair and a freckled face and a lanky, awkward build. Harry looked as if he might be sick when Enoch offered him the pipe, and the gathered mourners held their collective breath until he accepted it.

They had all agreed before, but this was the moment when it felt to Zeke that a bargain had truly been struck. The air around them turned cold and when a gust of wind rustled the branches of the trees in the cemetery, he shivered.

I'm here, bud, he thought. And I'm not running.

It had almost been a prayer, and he wondered if Savannah could hear it, or if she felt the love he had for her.

Enoch moved to the center of their ragged human circle, ignoring those who wept or who had gone so pale that Zeke feared they might faint. The little man—*hoodoo conjuror,* Skyler had called him—glanced around the circle and then reached into his pocket, taking out a small metal tin, which he opened to reveal the glitter of metal and then passed on to Zeke.

"These are pins. Take one and pass them along until everyone has one."

Zeke did as he'd been told, giving the tin to Lester before looking at Enoch. "What now?"

"Now you stick yourself with the pin," Enoch said, his eyes a stormy gray. "Don't be gentle. When you're bleeding well enough, you can toss the pins aside, and then write the name of the one you've lost on the pipe in your own blood. It's got to be the name you called them, the name in your heart, not the name they were born with."

"Blood ritual," Arturo Sanchez muttered. "Blasphemy."

"What did you expect, Artie?" someone said.

Zeke glared at Sanchez. "Blasphemy is murdering twenty-three people, not loving them so hard you'll do anything to have them back."

Zeke tucked the pipe into his pocket and then thrust the pin into the index finger of his right hand, jabbing hard and giving the pin a little jerk to make sure the tiny wound would not seal itself up too quickly. When he'd dropped the pin, he took out the pipe with his left and scrawled small, crude letters onto the bone in bright crimson, turning it in his hand so that her name encircled the pipe and so that he could fit all of the letters.

Savannah.

He had a dozen nicknames for her, but her name was beautiful. In his heart, that was who she'd always been.

"I will show you the notes to play, the notes they'll hear," Enoch said. "I'll play my own, tool, and the notes will weave together and call to them, and they will rise."

Zeke closed his eyes, feeling the trickle of his own blood along his fingers. Hope and horror were at war within him and he could not allow either to triumph, because either would defeat him. He thought of Anarosa, and how beautiful she'd looked the first time she'd held Savannah in her arms. Anarosa had left this world behind, but it might just be that the daughter they had both cherished was not yet out of reach. Holding the pipe with two fingers so his blood would dry, Zeke listened to Enoch go on.

"It'll take 'em eight or nine days to heal...to come back to themselves," the hoodoo man went on. "They won't know you at first, but in time they'll start to recognize their surroundings and your faces. Till then, they'll follow your commands completely, as long as you play that pipe."

The words chilled Zeke. The dead of October the twelfth would be like puppets until they began the final stage of transition from living to dead.

"What is it you're going to ask us to do, exactly?" Harry Boyd demanded. "How the hell is my son supposed to help you get your revenge?"

Enoch shot him an angry glance. "Not only my revenge, but his own, Mr. Boyd. And I'll explain my price in due time. For the moment, just ask yourself this—is any price too dear? "

Boyd didn't look satisfied, and neither was Zeke, but they were in no position to argue—not if they wanted what Enoch had to offer.

"Now," Enoch said, "be careful not to smear the blood but put the pipes to your lips. Here are the notes you need to play."

The little man's fingers moved smoothly over the pipe, covering and uncovering holes. The tune was simple but it took Zeke more than ten minutes to master it, and others took even longer, muttering in frustration as they fumbled with the pipes. As Zeke played the tune over and over, perfecting it, Harry Boyd's question echoed inside his mind, followed by one of his own.

Enoch stood by Mrs. Hawkins, showing her the notes more slowly until she seemed to have the tune.

"It can't really be this simple, bringing them back," Mrs. Hawkins said.

"There is nothing simple about it," Enoch replied. "Now, all of you—play."

One by one, the pipers began. The music was strange and discordant and haunting, lifted up by the strangely chilly breeze and spread throughout the cemetery. The branches of the trees trembled, and when Zeke shifted his stance, the scrape of gravel underfoot was impossibly loud.

"What's to stop us from not keeping up our end of the deal?" he asked, raising his voice to be heard over the pipers.

Lester stood next to him, already playing, and he shot Zeke a glance that seemed to take him to task, not for the question but for its timing. Zeke knew he ought to have waited, that only an idiot would telegraph a double-cross before they had what they wanted. But he wasn't going to gamble with Savannah's second chance.

Enoch did not reply. Instead he produced another pipe, this one from inside his jacket and twice the length of the others and streaked with dried blood stains, turned to look at Vickers and his dead wife, and played.

Half a dozen notes, and Martha Vickers dropped abruptly to the ground. Her hat fell off and tumbled off along the gravel path in the breeze. The pipers all halted their haunting music as her husband cried out in anguish and knelt beside her, her hat forgotten as he cradled her head in his lap and turned a rage-filled gaze not upon Enoch, but Zeke.

"Always the smart one, Prater. Always the one who can't just go along, you arrogant son of a bitch," he snarled. "This here...this is a miracle. You don't question it. And whatever we have to do in return, it's goddamned worth it."

Vickers twisted around to glare at Enoch.

"Now give her back, you bastard. Give her back to me!"

Enoch turned a questioning gaze upon Zeke, as if to say, *Is that enough for you?* Zeke nodded his assent. He would ask no more questions. A fist of anguish clenched around his heart. They had come too far along this damning path to turn away now. Enoch had them at his mercy, for no one would refuse him, now. Not when they had seen the consequences. Whatever darkness might be hiding inside it, he would accept the miracle...and whatever it cost him.

"Play," Enoch said, and the chorus of pipes began again.

This time, Zeke played with them, and so did Vickers.

Martha, who lay on the gravel path beside him, was the first to rise.

She staggered to her feet and studied her husband for a moment, and then dusted herself off as if vaguely embarrassed...as if she had done nothing more than trip, rather than dying again and being resurrected in front of them all in the space of a minute.

Big Tim Hawkins was next. He'd been buried only a dozen feet from the path in a plot that the Hawkins family had been using for years. His father had been laid there a decade ago and there were spots for Tim's mother and siblings and their spouses. A family grave.

The hands that punched up through the soil were huge and fish-belly white, nails torn and one finger broken from smashing through the top of the coffin and digging his way up through the dirt. Zeke shuddered at the sight, and the thought of the inhuman strength required for such a feat. Whatever power Enoch had called upon, it had instilled within October's dead more than just a renewed spark of life.

There were screams and Mrs. Hawkins nearly fainted, one hand on her pregnant belly as Aaron Monteforte caught her.

"Play, damn you!" Enoch cried shrilly before going back to his own pipe, his notes different from the others, weaving in and out of the discord and creating an unnerving sort of order.

They played, and some of the dead rose. Some, but not all.

Five minutes passed, no more. Zeke could not look at their faces but he knew them. Ben Trevino was there, standing near his mother like a sleepwalker as she wept and kept playing the same, ugly, maddening notes. The funeral home had done an excellent job with the bullet hole in his neck.

Enoch stopped, lowering his pipe.

"That's enough," he said.

"But..." Lester said, looking around. "Where are the others? I count nine."

Enoch slipped his pipe inside his brown wool coat. "The others are buried in metal coffins. They're going to need your help. Mr. Vickers has shovels in the back of his truck."

Arturo Sanchez made the sign of the cross.

"Dig them up," Enoch said, his stormy eyes alight with golden sparks as whatever magic he'd wielded began to burn off.

As he turned, Zeke strode up and grabbed his arm. "The cost, damn it. What's the price?"

Enoch glanced at the lumbering, shuffling dead who were even now being embraced by the living who had summoned them.

"Tomorrow night I'm going across the border," Enoch said. "There's a compound, a house where the cartel lieutenant who oversees all their local business lives and works. The drugs. The murder. His name is Carlos Aguilar, and I intend to kill him and everyone who tries to stop me. Your people—he gave the orders to the men who killed them—your people, they'll come with me and help me do this, and so will you."

Mrs. Hawkins began to shake her head, covering her mouth as she cried.

Zeke thought of Savannah facing down cartel enforcers with guns, hardened killers. He steeled himself, knowing the bargain had been struck, the gift Enoch offered and the consequences of refusing.

"You need us to control them," Zeke said. "Pull their strings."

"That's right, Mr. Prater. And you'll be happy to know that no more harm will come to them. Right now they're dead, more or less. They're...recovering. Another bullet hole or a knife wound will add to their recovery time, but it won't hurt them."

"What about us?" Linda Trevino asked, horrified.

Enoch's gaze was hard as flint. "I suppose you'll just have to be careful."

Zeke went to get a shovel.

~5~

Late the next morning, Zeke stood on the scattering of hay and dusty horseshit that carpeted the floor of his stable, wondering if he had run out of tears. His eyes burned and he knew it was partly from the lack of sleep—he'd surprised himself by dropping off for a couple of hours just as the sun came up—but he thought the sandpaper feeling came from the unfulfilled need to cry. He felt empty in so many ways; the inability to summon tears was just one more.

"Come on, bud," he rasped. "Say hello to Jester. He missed you."

His voice cracked on that last bit, but Savannah didn't notice. She stood in front of the stall where her horse, Jester, snorted and chuffed and turned his back to her. From the moment Zeke had led Savannah into the stable, playing the ugly tune on his pipe—which still had the coppery scent of his blood on it—Jester had done his best to stay as close to the back wall of the stall as possible.

Zeke clutched the pipe in his hand, forcing himself to loosen his grip, afraid he might break it or rub off some vital part of its magic.

Ain't magic, he thought. It's a curse.

What could it be but a curse that let him see his daughter like this? Savannah still wore the rose-hued dress she'd been buried in, a lovely thing she had persuaded him to buy her for the fall dance at her school and that had garnered far too much attention from the boys than he would have liked. The funeral director had gently implied that the color might be too red, that it might trouble him to see such a red on her, there in her casket at the wake, but Zeke had insisted, remembering the smile on her face when she'd worn it.

Now it seemed obscene. A party dress on a corpse.

He stared at her pale skin and noticed the way the warm breeze through the barn stirred her limp, dead hair, and bile burned up the back of his throat. He turned away, dropping to his knees as his stomach revolted and he vomited in the sawdust and hay. On his knees, trying to breathe, waiting for his stomach to calm, he thought sure he would weep then, but still his eyes were dry.

After a few seconds, he rose shakily to his feet and looked at her.

There were bruise-dark circles under her eyes and she had the tallow complexion of old candle wax. Her blue eyes had paled, faded like their color had been nothing but paint, left in the sun too long. In the warm, late morning light coming through the open doors at the far end of the stable, the shadows around her had acquired a gold hue. In that golden darkness it would almost have been possible to believe she was merely ill, were it not for those eyes, staring into a null middle distance, as if she could still see back into the land of the dead.

"Come on, honey," he breathed. "Do it for Daddy. Say hello to Jester. You love your Jessie-boy, don't you? He's right here."

It felt to Zeke as if something at the core of him was collapsing inward, a little black hole growing in his gut. An invisible fist clenched at his heart.

"Hey. I'm here, bud."

Something darted along the left side of his peripheral vision and he turned to see a furry orange tail vanishing into an empty stall. Tony was a marmalade cat who had been born in the stable. His mother had been a stray who had taken up residence there, and Zeke had never tried to drive her away because he believed that every stable and barn needed at least one cat to catch the mice who would invariably find their way in. The rest of the litter had been given away, but Savannah had kept the orange marmalade and named him after Tony the Tiger, the mascot of her favorite cereal.

The memory struck him hard—seven-year-old Savannah sitting on the floor of the stable, holding Tony and stroking him and giving him his name. She'd put a little bow in her hair that morning that nearly matched the color of Tony's fur, her way of making the moment into a sort of ceremony. The image led to a rush of others. Zeke closed his eyes and let them come, a sad smile on his face as he recalled nine-year-old Savannah's first ride on horseback, and the squeals of delight a year later when he brought Jester home and told her the new horse was hers and hers alone.

Mine forever? she'd asked.

He could still hear the little girl voice in his head.

"Oh, Jesus," he whispered, though not in prayer.

Or maybe it is a prayer, he thought. Maybe it always is.

"Come on, Savannah," he said, slapping his hands together and moving to stand only a foot away from her, face to face. "Come on, bud!"

His hands were empty. Frowning, he turned to search for the pipe. When he'd thrown up, he must have tossed it aside. *No, no. Where the fuck are you?* he thought as he scanned the floor until he located it. He'd worried that he might have broken it, but the pipe seemed intact. He stared at it, turning it over in his hands.

The night before, he had begun to experiment with the tune that Enoch had taught them. Lester had suggested that they work together, that he bring his son, Josh, over to Zeke's ranch and they practice how to influence their children with Enoch's pipes. Zeke had refused. What they were doing was both a miracle and an obscenity, and either way it was too intimate to share.

His hands and arms and back still hurt from digging up Savannah's grave. His muscles had burned as he'd thrown himself into the work, numbing his mind and heart so he would not let horror stop him, knowing she must have awakened down there in the cold ground along with the others. But he hadn't really believed it until he had used the shovel to smash the casket's lock and then pried open the lid and seen her moving, milky eyes staring blindly through the webbing of thread that had been used to sew her eyes shut. The thread had torn loose, her ripped eyelids almost instantly healing. A corpse, to be sure—she already looked so much better than she had last night—but a corpse resurrected.

Zeke had screamed, then, but not in fear or horror. He'd screamed out the pain and grief of her death and dragged her up into his arms and sat there cradling her inside her grave, whispering to her, promising her that he would do anything to bring her back to him, all the way back to him. She had been the light in his life, the sun around which his heart and soul revolved.

He would do anything.

Once he had more or less mastered the notes Enoch had taught them to play, he had put her into his truck and brought her home, cleaning her hands and face and feet, but not willing to change her clothes. Eventually he would take off her dress and put her in a pair of jeans and a sweatshirt and boots, but not yet, because he didn't want to see the wounds on her chest and back where the bullet had entered and left her body. They'd have been sewn up, but he didn't want to see. Enoch said the wounds would heal, and so he wanted to give her a little more time.

"Time," he whispered now, standing in the stable. Zeke took a breath. Time was really the only thing of value in the world; time to live, time to be with the ones you love.

Stuffing the pipe into his pocket, he turned away from Savannah's catatonia and went to the vacant horse stall into which he'd seen the cat disappear. Zeke unlatched the door and dragged it open. Tony had curled into a pad of hay in one corner and jumped up as he entered. As Zeke approached, the mouser tried to bolt past him, but Zeke had been wrangling cats in the ranch's old buildings since he could walk, and snatched Tony up before he could escape.

The cat struggled, but Zeke carried him out of the stall and over to Savannah. He knew that he was supposed to use the pipe. Enoch had made it clear to all of them that it would be days before any of the dead could think clearly enough to direct their own actions. Their brains were not working properly. The ritual Enoch had taught them made it possible for others to give them direction, as if the notes the pipers played turned on some kind of motor inside them and the words of the pipers were their navigation.

Zeke wanted to believe it. He needed to believe that there was a happy ending, because having Savannah back like this was worse than having her dead. Anarosa would have cursed him for it. He could endure it if he could accept Enoch's promises, but in order for him to have that kind of faith, he needed just one glimpse of the future, one hint of awareness in Savannah's eyes to prove that she was still in there.

"Look, bud," he said. "It's Tony the Tiger. Remember him? Remember when Ginger had her kittens? She hid under the stable but you heard the mewling and you were the one who found them. You were such a big girl and when I told you that you could have one you knew right away it had to be Tony the Tiger. Remember the bows you wore when you—"

Zeke took a step closer to Savannah. The cat hissed and clawed his arms and he swore and dropped the beast. It raced the length of the stable and out the door, a rare excursion. *It knows*, Zeke thought, his stomach dropping. *Even the damn cat can see this is unnatural. It's wrong.*

"God, what have I done?" he whispered, hanging his head in the shadows.

The noise might have been the creak of a beam or the shifting of one of the other horses, but it sounded to him like a soft moan, deep in his daughter's throat. He whipped his head around and stared at her, catching his breath as an impossible hope emerged like sunrise within him.

Savannah had not moved. Her gaze remained vacant and distant.

But there were tears on her face, streaking the dry, waxy skin of her cheeks.

"Bud?" he ventured.

Nothing. No reaction. But the tears were hope enough.

"All right," he said, nodding firmly. "All right."

He dug out the pipe and began to play.

~6~

It was late the following afternoon when they boarded a school bus Lester had arranged to borrow from the city of Hidalgo. Faded yellow, with no working heat or air and windows that didn't close all the way, the bus seemed the relic of another era, but it would serve their purposes. They gathered at the Vickers ranch, dust rising from the cars and trucks that made their way up the road. People parked in a fallow field, lining up their vehicles the way they would for the state fair.

The sun beat down as if it were early summer instead of the dregs of a haunted Texas winter. Zeke sat in the fifth row on the driver's side. He'd taken the aisle and given Savannah the window, but she made no effort to look out through the glass or turn away from the glare of the setting sun. He had changed her into blue jeans and high-top sneakers and a thick cotton t-shirt that hung loosely on her so as not to draw attention to the hole in her chest. The shirt had a sparkly design on it and he thought she might have borrowed it from her friend Imogene, who'd loved such things but hadn't laid claim to it after Savannah's death, either because she didn't know how to ask or because she thought it might carry some of Savannah's bad luck.

As he had undressed her, Zeke had kept expecting to feel embarrassed. His little girl had been evolving into a young woman and had all the hallmarks of that transition, and fathers weren't supposed to see their girls unclothed past a certain age. But fathers weren't supposed to see their little girls dead, either. Instead of making him blush, her nudity only made him want to weep at her fragility. Without him blowing notes on the pipe, Savannah lay there and let him do all of the work, but he didn't mind. He had changed her and bathed her and held her when fever and sickness had seized her. This was his daughter, and he would walk through the fires of hell for her.

As the last of the pipers arrived, the bus remained eerily silent. The dead did not speak and the living had nothing to say. Like Zeke, either from fear or shame, they barely made eye contact with one another. Linda Trevino sat several rows ahead of him, keeping up a constant stream of whispered endearments to her dead son. Zeke could barely breathe, watching her. Waiting for Ben to move. To reply.

"Okay, bud," Zeke whispered, turning to look at Savannah. He touched her chin and turned her to face him, noting a momentary alertness in her eyes. She had focused on him. Just for a moment, but he would take it. "We're just going for a little ride."

Enoch stood out in the road, a little man who somehow managed to look smaller with every glance. He carried a small leather bag that hung from his shoulder as if he were a college professor instead of some kind of hoodoo man, and Zeke knew that his own pipe must be inside that bag. Aaron Monteforte moved toward the bus, playing those now familiar discordant notes on his pipe, walking with his sister, Trish. Like Savannah's, Trish's death wounds were hidden by her clothing. If not for her complexion and the utter lack of expression, she might have been alive—just another twentysomething south Texas girl waiting for her life to really begin.

Zeke took Savannah's hand and tried not to be disheartened by the lack of any confirming squeeze from her. *Time,* he thought. *Give it time.*

People began to shift in their seats, some craning around to look out the windows of one final vehicle coming down the long, dusty drive. Zeke had been counting and knew there were forty-two people already on the bus, twenty-one dead, and an equal number of those who had followed Enoch's ritual to resurrect them—the ones Zeke thought of as pipers and Vickers called proxies.

Music drifted to them, a thumping, crashing rhythm that started low and grew louder as the car approached. In the front seat, Vickers moved his considerable bulk and leaned over Martha—whose dented forehead throbbed like a newborn's fontanelle—to look out at the car roaring up his driveway.

The music blared from the open windows of Alma Hawkins' little Volkswagen as it pulled to a stop forty feet from the bus. Big Tim looked absurd sitting in the passenger seat, jammed in and hunched over. Zeke recognized the music only because the deputy had tried to convert the whole town over to his love for the Dropkick Murphys. It wasn't the sort of thing Zeke could ever have enjoyed—headache-inducing stuff—but he figured if anything would get through the fog that clouded the minds of the returned dead, it would be that kind of jarring noise.

Big Tim didn't seem to notice. His wife came around the passenger side of her VW and opened the door. Her pregnant belly hung low as she bent to coax him from the car. Alma Hawkins looked pale, almost corpse-like herself. Big Tim had a chunk missing out of the side of his face, but a kind of dry crust that was more like papier-mache than flesh had begun to fill in the hole.

"Thank God," someone said, a few rows behind Zeke.

In the second row, just behind Vickers, Arturo Sanchez turned to stare into the back, looking just as pale as the revived dead.

"Please…" he said. "I beg you, let that be the last time any of us mentions God tonight."

No one spoke. *What could we say?* Zeke thought.

With Monteforte and Alma Hawkins playing their pipes, they directed their beloved dead onto the bus and arranged them in the remaining seats. Enoch was the last to board. When he did, Vickers rose and offered up his place, which Enoch took while he dropped his considerable bulk into the driver's seat.

"You all know the plan," Vickers said. "We're only going to get one chance."

The bus choked and then roared as he started it, coughing gray smoke out of the exhaust. Vickers drove the bus out to the gates of his ranch and turned south.

Out on the road, beyond the fence that lined his property, a couple of dozen cars were parked on either side and fifty or sixty people had gathered to watch them go. Enoch would allow the dead only one proxy a piece, but many had other family members who would have gladly taken the job.

Dressed in mourning clothes, they stood along the road and prayed, some with rosary beads and others hand-in-hand. Some held up photographs of the dead, back in their living years, and Zeke did not allow himself to focus on those pictures. He did not want to compare them to the pale, withered creatures riding on the bus with him.

Gazing out the window, he saw Skyler near the end of the line. She had swept her hair into a ponytail and wore a plain black dress. Her eyes searched the windows of the bus but Zeke could tell that she hadn't spotted him yet. In her hands she held a small cardboard sign upon which she'd written two words in large black letters.

COME BACK

Throat dry, he forced himself to turn away. If she saw him then, at least she would not see the doubt in his eyes.

Grinding noises came from the engine as Vickers shifted into higher gear. The bus lurched forward and then they were speeding west, toward sunset, with a cargo of breathless fears and unlikely hopes.

The McAllen-Hidalgo-Reynosa International Bridge spans the Rio Grande and connects the United States to Mexico. Though it passed through Hidalgo on the U.S. side, the bridge began in McAllen, Texas. Zeke held Savannah's hand as the bus rattled through miles of ranch and farmland all the way to Route 241, which Vickers followed straight through Hidalgo. In summertime, the sunlight seemed to linger forever, but in winter the night came on quickly, and by the time they were rolling along the bridge toward the checkpoint, it was full dark. Bright lights illuminated the short span and the four lanes going either direction. A high fence and a stretch of plain concrete separated the two, and with the towering light posts, it reminded Zeke of the time he'd gone as a boy to visit his uncle Frank in the state prison up in Houston.

"All right," Vickers called from the front. "We're almost there."

Zeke took a breath and dug out the bone pipe that had been sitting heavily in his pocket, jabbing into his thigh. He hesitated, but others didn't, and soon the whole bus was filled with a chorus of ugly notes, just a brief flurry of cluttered music that ended as abruptly as it had begun. He was one of the last to play, and once he had sounded the notes, he turned to Savannah.

"Close your eyes, kiddo. Pretend you're sleeping."

As the bus juddered and then surged forward, Vickers shifting gears, Zeke discovered he was praying. His entreaties amounted to little more than *Please, Lord, let us both come back alive*, but it surprised him to find himself on speaking terms with God again. After Savannah's death, he had all but given up prayer. Now he lowered his head and reached out with his heart, hoping to be heard, and that what they had done was not the abomination he feared it must be. *She's my baby girl, Lord*, he thought. *What else was I to do*?

And then, grimly, feeling the weight of his own guilt: You brought your own son back to life. Can you blame me for following your lead?

Though the air had cooled and the breeze that blew in through the partly open windows circulated well, he felt a damp sheen of sweat under his arms and down his back. It might have been his imagination, but even Savannah's hand seemed warm and clammy to the touch. He tried to take that as a good sign.

The bus idled in line for a few minutes, but it was a weekday evening and they were coming from the American side into Mexico, so the wait wasn't long. On the other side, Zeke could see headlights stretching back into the distance. Some of those people, he knew, would be waiting for an hour or two to cross the border into the States.

Vickers parked the bus and then worked the handle that rattled open the doors. Most cars were waved through, but with a bus like this, the Mexican border guards almost had no choice but to at least ask them what they were up to. The woman who stepped onto the bus wore her uniform proudly. In the dim orange glow from the tiny light above the door, Zeke could see the frown that creased her forehead.

"Some tired people," the guard said.

"We were up very early this morning," Vickers said. "I have all of the passports right here."

He offered her a small plastic container that held forty-seven passports and the guard frowned at the box, obviously not inclined to examine them.

"Where are you going?" she asked.

"Voices of Faith conference in San Fernando," Vickers said. "This is the St. Matthews Family Choir."

There were a dozen obvious questions the guard could have asked, beginning with why they didn't have any suitcases on board. Instead she frowned at them for a few seconds longer and then looked at Vickers.

"Your passport?"

He set the plastic box on his lap and handed her a single passport, which she gave only a cursory glance before returning.

"Good luck."

"Thanks so much!" Vickers said brightly. "God bless you."

The guard muttered something as she climbed off of the bus—perhaps returning the wish for the Lord's blessings—but Zeke couldn't make out the words. Then Vickers put the bus in drive, gears grinding, and they were rumbling over the bridge into Mexico.

"You said you'd made a deal with the border patrol," teenage Tommy Jessup said from the back of the bus. "Was that a part of it?"

Vickers' face was visible in the huge rearview mirror, bathed in yellow light from the dashboard. "No. That was just them not caring. Not a lot of people sneak *into* Mexico. The deal we've got is with the U.S. Border Patrol, and we're going to need it to get home."

The salesman, Mooney, spoke up from two rows behind Zeke. "Let's just hope the ones you bribed keep their word."

"Yes," Linda Trevino said. "Because people who take bribes are usually so honest."

"Linda, for once please shut your fucking mouth."

It took Zeke a moment to realize that those words had come from his own lips, and then he smiled in the dark, happy to have told her off. It made him feel more alive. On a bus full of people coming back from the dead, it had begun to seem as if their presence was dragging him in the other direction.

He turned and looked at Savannah, marveling at her beauty as he always did, and he longed for morning to come, for all of this to be behind them and Enoch out of their lives forever.

The bloodstained pipe felt heavy in his hand.

And the bus rolled on.

~7~

Twenty minutes past the border, Enoch finally spoke up. It was strange the way he seemed to vanish when he did not want their attention, as if they had all somehow managed to forget he was among them. Zeke doubted that the Mexican border guard had even glanced at him, though he'd been right there in the front row, a little man sitting with his hands in his lap, quiet and still as a meditating monk.

"Get off here," he said. "On the left."

Vickers did not argue. Many eyes glanced out into the darkness, but no one questioned Enoch. The bus shook as they traveled along a rutted, narrow road through a small town that seemed to be nothing more than graffiti-covered shacks and a boarded-up gas station. Four or five miles further, Enoch told Vickers to turn left again, but this time there was no road at all, only a rough dirt path that deteriorated until it vanished completely.

Moments later, Enoch said, "Okay, stop here," and the bus groaned to a halt. Zeke stood in the aisle and looked out the window on the right side. An ominous black SUV sat in the darkness, moonlight glinting off of its surfaces. As Zeke watched, all four doors opened and a quartet of grim-faced men climbed out.

Vickers opened the door of the bus and Enoch rose, turning toward them.

"Stay here," Enoch instructed. "Not a word."

Two rows up and across the aisle, Aaron Monteforte buried his face in his hands. "Jesus Christ."

Zeke took a deep breath, waited for Enoch to step off the bus, and crouched in the aisle beside Aaron. He put a hand on the young man's arm.

"Hey, brother. Take a breath."

Aaron glanced at him, swallowed hard, and nodded. "I'm trying, Mr. Prater."

Beside him, up against the window, his dead sister had left a streak of drool on the glass. Zeke had to fight to keep from recoiling at the sight, telling himself that it was good, that body fluids meant life, but his stomach roiled in disgust.

"Zeke," he managed. "Call me Zeke."

Through the window beyond Trish Monteforte's drool, he saw Enoch talking with one of the men as the others unloaded two heavy gray plastic boxes from the back of the SUV. Enoch reached inside his jacket and handed over a thick envelope that Zeke realized must be cash, and then two of the men carried the plastic boxes on board the bus. Neither of the men, both young and dark-eyed Mexicans, so much as glanced up at the passengers as they set the boxes down in the aisle.

And then they were gone.

Enoch climbed back onto the bus as the SUV tore away across the ragged, dusty plain, headlights popping on, brake lights like devil's eyes in the dark.

Zeke took his seat as Vickers first closed the bus door and then rose to help Enoch open the crates. Enoch had told them what would be expected of them, so Zeke knew what was to come—they all did—but the sight of moonlight glinting off gun barrels still made him catch his breath. He'd been trained to use a gun since childhood and knew the same would be true of nearly everyone on board the bus, but these were no hunting rifles or protective sidearms. The guns in the cases were Herstals, Belgian-made pistols that fired armor-piercing rounds, so popular with the cartels that they were more commonly known by their street name, *Mata Policias*. Cop Killers.

Either Enoch had just bought guns from the same people who supplied the Matamoros cartel, or he'd bought guns from the cartel itself. The little man had told them as part of the plan that they'd be picking up weapons on the Mexican side of the border—trying to sneak them across would be idiotic—but the presence of the Mata Policias on the bus gave the moment a terrible, weighty reality.

"You'll each take one of these," Enoch said, a golden glow in his eyes that could not be attributed to the moonlight. When he spoke, his upper lip curled back like a wolf's. "We'll wait until it's time for us to abandon the bus, and then you'll take one gun and give it to the person you came here for. Remember why you're here and you won't hesitate. There are enough guns that you can also take one for yourself, but if you do as I ask, there should be no reason for it. Once you've played your pipes and given instructions, you'll just wait for it all to be over."

Lester cleared his throat, sitting up a little straighter in his seat, trying to regain some of the dignity stolen by riding in a school bus.

"What happens if one of them doesn't come back?" he asked. "If I send my boy in there and they shoot him full of holes—"

"I told you, he'll heal. Whatever damage they do—"

"—heals eventually," Lester interrupted. "But what about tonight? If he's too damaged to come back to where we're waiting?"

Enoch stared at him, the glow in his eyes seeming to brighten. Zeke knew that there must be others on the bus who had questions, but Lester was the only one who had dared to ask. This close to satiating his thirst for revenge, Enoch did not want to deal with their trifling doubts and fears, that much was clear.

"Then you go in and get him," the little man said. "The cartel members inside the compound will already be dead."

Lester started to speak again, but Enoch ignored him, turning to Vickers. "Drive."

As they started moving again, bumping across hard terrain, Zeke turned to check on Savannah, whose condition seemed unchanged. He decided that was for the best. If she started to get her mind back now...he didn't even want to think about it.

Glancing back toward the front of the bus, the desert moon casting the interior of the bus in a pale, ghostly light, he saw Aaron Monteforte shifting uncomfortably in his seat and caught a glimpse of the reason—a pistol jutting from Aaron's rear waistband. Zeke frowned, wondering what the hell Aaron was thinking. Bringing his own weapon could have blown the whole operation if the border guards had been more vigilant.

He opened his mouth to speak, but Aaron beat him to it.

"Turn the bus around, Mr. Vickers," he called, head bowed so that his voice was slightly muffled.

"Oh God, Aaron, don't," Linda Trevino said.

Enoch turned to glare at the young man.

"Fuck you and your spooky eyes, man," Aaron said, growing more agitated. He shook his head and turned to look at his resurrected sister, reached out to touch her cheek, and then shot a hard look at Enoch. "We can't do this. You've got to turn this fucking thing around."

"Shut your mouth, son," Lester growled.

Enoch stood but made no move toward the back of the bus. He seemed to ride the juddering rumble of the bus without needing to steady himself. In the moonlight, his eyes began to turn oil-black, gleaming with a terrible, deep malignance, as if the night itself began to glow from within him.

"You agreed to this," Enoch said. "You bled for this. The bond has been forged. You can't break it now."

"Bullshit!" Aaron barked, jumping to his feet, one hand clamped on the back of the seat in front of him. "There's no way a bunch of half-dead zombies are going to kill this fucking Carlos Aguilar. He'll have a couple of dozen guys with guns around him. My sister can't even speak! She can barely make eye contact, and she's supposed to—"

Enoch spoke. *"Sit down, boy."* Three words, but they reverberated through the bus as if the metal itself had spoken, the windows rattling with the power of his voice.

In that moment he did not seem like a little man at all.

"Sit down, or I will cut your sister into pieces the way they did my daughter."

Aaron sat.

No one spoke.

Enoch's chest rose and fell with barely contained fury, but at last he sat as well, turning to stare straight out the windshield. In the driver's seat, Vickers' hands gripped the steering wheel tightly. The bus's headlights showed nothing ahead but scrub brush and desert but Vickers kept driving, with Enoch quietly urging him onward.

The bus shook mercilessly, and once Savannah struck her head on the window. Zeke saw her wince and his chest ached with cruel hope. If she had felt that—if it bothered her—then surely she must be getting better. Such thoughts were the only things that kept him from screaming.

Vickers had driven through rough no-man's-land for nearly half an hour when, at last, Enoch commanded him to bring the bus to a creaking stop. When he killed the engine and turned off the headlights, their eyes quickly adjusted to the moonlight. Zeke blinked and rubbed at the bridge of his nose and when he looked up, Enoch had stood again.

"The compound is three miles due south, on foot. If we get any closer, they'll see the headlights," he said. "So we walk from here."

Again, this was nothing they hadn't been warned about, but even if any of the proxies wanted to complain, none of them would dare. Not now. One by one, they took out their pipes and began to play, breaking off only to issue instructions to their broken loved ones, who staggered to their feet and shuffled off the bus, trapped halfway between the living world and the land of the dead. Vickers had gotten Martha off first and Enoch had put the gun crates on their seat, so that the proxies could each take a weapon as they climbed out into the cool night.

Zeke took one of the Mata Policias and stuck it into his waistband. He took a second gun, intending to keep the first for himself, and then blew a few extra notes on the pipe, just to make sure that he had Savannah's attention and that she wouldn't fall on the steps. For a moment, his mind went back to the hour of their departure, when he'd seen Skyler standing by the roadside with her hopeful, handmade sign. COME HOME, she'd written. But out there in the Mexican desert, home had never felt so far away. The future he hoped for, days of peace and laughter for himself and Savannah, seemed little more than a dream.

Out in the middle of nowhere, the day's heat quickly vanished. Zeke saw many people shivering with the chill and it took him a moment to realize Martha Vickers was one of them. He exhaled a quiet thank-you to whatever powers might be watching over them—if she could feel cold, maybe she really was creeping nearer to being fully alive again.

Savannah's hand brushed his. Zeke turned toward her, heart pounding. She had been standing next to him, but had she touched him on purpose? He stared at her for several seconds as more people climbed off of the bus, guns stuck in pockets or carried in hand, aimed at the ground. It struck him that he had left her sweatshirt on the bus and he started back toward it, frustrated that he had to wait for the rest to get off and not wanting to leave Savannah alone for too long. Again, he thought of Skyler and her sign. COME BACK. Zeke stood at the bus door as Arturo Sanchez climbed off. The man stroked his graying mustache and played several notes on his blood-smeared pipe, and then Zeke found himself face-to-face with the resurrected corpse of Arturo's mother. Her glazed eyes blinked and then narrowed, focusing on him, and Zeke found himself smiling at the dead woman. She'd seen him. Was aware of him. Another hopeful sign.

He had turned to say that to Arturo when the night erupted with the roar of multiple engines. Bright lights bathed the pitiful school bus from all sides.

"Mother of God," Arturo whispered, turning and trying to push his mother back onto the bus.

Zeke tightened his grip on his second gun—the one intended for Savannah. He spun and ran toward her, instinct kicking in, knowing the thunder of those engines could only mean danger and he would not allow her to die a second time. People were screaming around him, some picking up the barely alive and struggling to carry or drag them back toward the bus while others drew guns and aimed at oncoming headlights.

"What the hell is this?!" Lester shouted at Vickers.

But Vickers' eyes had gone wide like an animal's and he drew Martha to him and began to cry, surrender etched deeply into his face.

Zeke reached Savannah. He stared into her eyes for a second. He knew she was in there, fanning the spark of life back into a flame, if only he could give her the time. He kissed her forehead, put one arm around her, and waited, gun ready.

"Enoch!" Lester shouted, rushing at the little man whose eyes were once again alight with a golden glow. "What's going on?!"

"Are you blind, Mr. Keegan?" Enoch said, his words dripping with venom. "It's an ambush."

"No," Lester said, shaking his head as he backed away, running to his son but twisting around as the five raised pickup trucks charged toward them. "This ain't happening!"

"Lester!" Zeke shouted. "Get your shit together!"

He saw Lester freeze, nod, and then raise his pistol.

"All of you!" Lester shouted. "Guns up. Shoot the first son of a bitch who—"

A bullet blew out his left temple, spraying brain and bone shards onto his dead son. The gunshot echoed across the desert as Zeke screamed his friend's name and turned to see that Aaron Monteforte had fired the shot, using the gun that had been tucked into his waistband. Sweating, eyes frantic, Aaron took aim at Zeke.

"Guns down, Mr. Prater," Aaron said. "I don't want to have to kill you."

"Aaron," Zeke said. "What—?"

One by one, the pickups skidded to a halt, caging them all in a lattice of headlight beams. The men who jumped out of the backs of the trucks and climbed from the cabs carried assault rifles instead of pistols.

Zeke had watched his daughter die once, and he'd die himself before he would witness her murder again.

He raised his gun and pulled the trigger.

Nothing happened.

Around him, others had done the same. Arturo Sanchez ejected the magazine, trying to figure out what the hell went wrong, but it was too late. If there had been a moment when Zeke could have punished Aaron Monteforte for his betrayal, it had already passed.

The cartel gunmen surrounded them, gun barrels taking aim, promising death.

Zeke moved himself in front of Savannah. He could feel her reedy breath against the back of his neck and prepared to die for her.

~8~

Don't be a hero, Zeke told himself, thinking only of Savannah. But as they were all herded together at gunpoint, their weapons torn violently from their hands, he realized that there would be no heroes that night.

The cartel gunmen stared at the resurrected dead amongst them and he caught several of the hardened killers crossing themselves and muttering quiet prayers. A few others laughed in amazement. One poked a finger through the bullet hole in Big Tim Hawkins' neck and Alma shoved him away, leading to amazed chatter among the gunmen.

"Hold up, *amigo,*" Aaron Monteforte said, trying to extricate himself from the other pipers, all muscle and scruff and just enough bravado to veil his terror.

Aaron held his gun with the barrel aimed at Linda Trevino, who hugged her undead son, Ben—Ben, who Savannah had once had such a crush on—and shielded him with her body. Tears streamed down Linda's face, but she did not beg to be left alone. She was smart enough to know there was little chance of that at this point.

"Put it down, asshole," one of the gunmen said to Aaron, the moonlight making the jagged scar on his left cheek look like mother of pearl.

"Whoa," Aaron said. "I'm with you guys."

Zeke felt bile burning up the back of his throat and his fingers flexed, either wishing for another weapon or wanting to be wrapped around Aaron Monteforte's throat, or both.

The man with the gleaming scar raised his assault rifle, braced it against his shoulder, and took aim. "Gun on the ground, *chingado*. Now."

Aaron held up his left hand and gently lowered his weapon to the dirt. "Okay, all right. But take a breath, man. I'm with you, I said. All this shit wouldn't be happening if it wasn't for me. Ask Carlos—"

A cluster of cartel thugs scattered, parting like the Red Sea as a tall man strode amongst them.

Unlike the rest, the newcomer carried no gun, only a hunting knife sheathed at his hip. His white cotton shirt and brown dress pants had clearly been tailored to fit his slim, powerful physique and seemed out of place amongst the denim and leather of the others. The shoes on his feet were of a soft leather than must have cost a fortune. With his thick mane of hair slicked back, curling at the ends, and his beard trimmed to a stylish severity, he looked as if he had just walked out of a business meeting and into a nightclub.

"Ask Carlos what?" the man inquired.

Aaron exhaled. "Carlos…Mr. Aguilar…tell 'em, please. Tell 'em I helped you."

Aguilar nodded emphatically, spreading his arms wide as if in a spirit of generosity.

"Did he help me?" Aguilar said, turning a radiant smile on his prisoners, both living and not quite.

"Absolutely, he helped me. You should *all* know that. Your friend, here...he's been working for me for more than a year."

"*You son of a bitch!*" Alma Hawkins cried, pushing forward to loose a wad of spittle that did not reach its target. She had one hand on her roundly pregnant belly as if she could protect the baby inside...just as Linda Trevino held Ben and Zeke stood in front of Savannah. Behind her, Big Tim Hawkins stood numbly, his gaze following her the way it might a hypnotist's pocket watch.

Aguilar gestured the scarred man away from Aaron, walked over and picked up Aaron's gun from the ground.

"I agree with you, lady," Aguilar said, nodding again. "He is indeed a son of a bitch. Running drugs through your town. Selling to kids. Giving up the names of the motherfuckers on the Texas Border Volunteers, the guys putting my business on video for the Border Patrol...it's just un-American."

The cartel enforcer tried to keep a straight face but couldn't manage it, and his men all laughed along with him. Looks of hatred and despair appeared on the faces of the herded pipers who were clustered together with the resurrected.

"Look at that, *hermanos*. It's true." Aguilar turned to grin at his men. "I see dead people."

More laughter raced around the circle of killers. Aguilar's eyes lit up with dark intelligence and unsettling hunger.

"I mean, I've heard of this kind of shit, but never thought I'd see it," he said.

Zeke felt the others closing in around him and Savannah, everyone wanting to move as far away from the guns as they could, and he pushed back, trying to keep her safe. He glanced up and caught Tommy Jessup gazing at him with desperate eyes, silently imploring him to do something. Zeke turned away; there was nothing to be done except ride it out.

"Mr. Vickers, please," he heard someone say, but when Zeke glanced at Vickers, he saw that the man still hugged Martha close, his eyes as dead as his wife's.

Zeke glanced around and saw red-headed Harry Boyd holding the hand of his grown son, Charlie, the way he must have done when Charlie was a boy. His expression was stern, his eyes steel, just waiting. Zeke pushed past the Jessup kid and guided Savannah toward Boyd.

"Look after her, Harry," he said, giving her a last shove. Savannah shuffled enough to get to Boyd and Zeke kissed her temple without looking at her face. If he had, he knew he wouldn't have had the courage to turn away.

"We'll make a deal!" Zeke called out, pushing his way through the herd.

Half a dozen weapons swung toward him, the dark holes of their barrels almost seeming to dare him to take another step.

"What are you doing?" Arturo Sanchez hissed.

But standing out there, outside the circle of his friends and neighbors and the risen dead who comprised all the hope they had ever mustered, he could see the corpse of Lester Keegan lying in the dirt. Lester had been his best friend—he had come out here to save his son and been murdered for his trouble.

But we can bring him back, Zeke thought, feeling the pipe in his pocket digging into his hip. *If we're still alive to do it.*

Aguilar stroked his narrow beard, smiling beatifically. "Well, well. Which one are you?"

"Ezekiel Prater." He kept his chin up and his eyes locked on Aguilar's when he said it.

The devil arched an eyebrow. "One of the ranchers."

"That's me. One of the Border Volunteers, too. Aaron just killed Lester Keegan. Vickers and Boyd are here, too. Cassaday didn't lose anyone back in October, but we can speak for him."

Aguilar glanced at his men and then at Aaron before turning back to Zeke.

"All right, Ezekiel. Speak."

"We never wanted to come here," Zeke said, heart pounding, trying to hide his hatred of this man and his comrades. "We knew it was crazy—suicide—but we had no choice."

"Your friend, Aaron, told us all about it," Aguilar said, waving Aaron's gun around. "We knew you were coming, *Ese*. Knew about the guns you were buying."

"Which is why the first couple of bullets in every magazine are dummies," the scarred gunman said, grinning. "Click click. *Nada*."

Aguilar laughed softly. "Yeah, that was Guillermo's idea. Pretty funny, actually. And it helped get you all the way out here."

Zeke felt like throwing up.

"The school bus was a nice touch, though," Aguilar said appreciatively.

"Please, just let us go," Linda Trevino begged.

Aguilar shot her a hard look, so Zeke shifted to block his view of the woman.

"Hold on, here's my offer," Zeke said. "Full access to all four ranches. We'll cover for you with the Border Patrol, make it a hell of a lot easier for you to get whatever you want across the river. Guns. Drugs. People. Anything."

"Really...?" Aguilar said, eyes widening, impressed. "And what about the rest of your people? They're all going to go along with this?"

Zeke glanced around at the others, waiting for an argument, but nobody dared to say a word.

"They are," he said firmly.

"Well. This I've gotta think about," Aguilar replied, a jaunty sort of amusement coming into his eyes.

He turned and shot Aaron Monteforte in the head with his own gun.

Screams burst from the herded pipers as Aaron crumpled to the ground. Zeke flinched, but somehow he found it within himself not to cry out or run back into the cluster of familiar faces. Unlike his father and grandfather, he'd never been to war, but those men had taught him a thing or two about fear and cowardice. Fear was the real enemy, the one foe that had to be defeated. For himself—for his own safety—Zeke could do that.

It was his fear for Savannah that he could not overcome.

"Ah, dammit," Aguilar said, looking down in dismay at the spots of blood on his expensive white shirt. "Messy. But...if we're going to make some kind of deal, we couldn't have him around. A man who will betray his friends cannot be trusted. His sister died that night in your town, you know? She wasn't supposed to be there. He thought she had gone to Hidalgo to visit friends. My men murdered his sister, and he *still* called to tell me what you were all planning. What a pal."

Aguilar spit on Aaron's ruined face, the second time he'd been spit on in mere minutes. Zeke saw that Aaron had fallen on his left side, baring the Reaper tattoo on his right bicep and burying the angel on his left, and that seemed only right.

"He used to work on my ranch," Zeke said, gazed fixed on Aguilar. "I was fond of him back then, but as of this moment, I can't say as I'm sorry the son of a bitch is dead."

Aguilar began to walk, gun pointed at the ground as he circled the cluster of prisoners. There were more than forty of them and half that number of cartel killers, but the gunmen were ranged about them in a circle like a pack of wolves. Aguilar moved through the open space that separated the wolves from their prey.

"I'm not going to lie to you, Ezekiel," Aguilar said, his voice carried on the desert wind though Zeke couldn't see him from the other side of the circle. "I've just been having a little fun with you. We spent so much time on business that when we get an opportunity to play, it's hard to resist. You of course know that if word got out that we let even one of you live—"

Prayers went up from the group, and curses followed in equal measure.

"Listen to me, Carlos," Zeke said. "If you're worried about how it'll look, what kind of message you'd be sending, think about how it will look when word gets out that you've staked a claim in Hidalgo County, that you've got an open pipeline into the U.S. Or how it'll look that you turned such a thing down."

Aguilar had made it three quarters of the way around the circle and come back into view. Zeke glanced at the faces of his friends and neighbors and the vacant gazes of the dead and he held his breath.

"It would be an interesting experiment," Aguilar admitted. Zeke exhaled, glanced over in search of Savannah's face and did not see her. "But if we were to negotiate, there is only one place to start."

"Where's that?"

Aguilar's smile vanished and the amusement bled from his eyes, revealing only ice beneath. He turned to his prisoners with a snarl.

"Which one of you is Enoch Stroud?"

Zeke blinked several times and shook his head. It felt as if he'd just woken up from a dream in which Enoch had never existed. Until the moment Aguilar had mentioned his name, he had forgotten all about the little hoodoo man. Enoch had come to them, had raised their dead and dragged them all down here to Mexico, and yet for a few minutes it was as if he had been erased from Zeke's mind.

A ripple of confusion went through the pipers and they began to shuffle aside, expanding the circle, nudging and guiding the blank-faced undead until a path had formed among them leading to a circle within the circle. At its center, alone, Enoch stood staring at Carlos Aguilar with murder in his eyes.

"How the hell—?" Harry Boyd said.

Aguilar aimed his gun at Enoch and the pipers and their dead scuttled further away. The cartel killers raised the barrels of their weapons and barked orders in English and Spanish, making sure no one tried to make a run for it.

"You?" Aguilar scoffed. "You're the great brujo? El Nigromante?"

Enoch said nothing, but Aguilar walked toward him, pausing to look more closely at the resurrected dead. He glanced at Charlie Boyd and Big Tim, but when he got to Martha Vickers, he reached out and ran a finger over the strange new fontanelle skin growing over her head wound.

"Oh, you're going to teach me how to do this," Aguilar said, turning to stare at Enoch. "Whatever it is, I want to learn. When one of my people is killed, I want to be able to bring them back."

Enoch's gaze glimmered with a familiar yellow light, but it was as if an eclipse were taking place in his eyes. They turned black and the little man seemed to darken, as if the moonlight could no longer find him.

"*Chingate*," Enoch muttered.

Aguilar sneered, pointing the gun at Enoch's forehead. "Fuck *my*self? Fuck you, *chilito*. You want revenge because I killed your daughter? Big deal. I killed a lot of people's daughters, and their sons, too. That's what we *do*, asshole. You get in the way and you get *dead*."

He gestured toward the people gathered around them.

"Maybe you got some black magic in you, brought these people back to life. But now you got a chance to keep them alive...them and the rest of the idiots you brought down here with you. You've got five seconds, man. You gonna teach me, or am I going to put a bullet in your heart?"

Zeke caught a glimpse of Savannah, standing behind Harry and Charlie Boyd. He mentally urged her to retreat, to hide herself more deeply among the others. For a second, he thought she had seen him, that she had returned his gaze, but then Aguilar started marching back and forth in the gap, counting.

"One. Two. Three."

Aguilar glanced over at Zeke and shrugged as if to say he was trying his best here.

"Enoch!" Zeke shouted. "For God's sake—"

"Four!" Aguilar barked, turning on Enoch with a venomous glare. Then he sniffed, as if he couldn't quite summon a laugh, and shook his head. "Ah, fuck it."

He shot Enoch twice in the chest.

"*No!*" Zeke roared, rushing toward the widening gap between the two frantic groups of prisoners and then staggering to a halt, staring in astonishment.

Enoch had barely flinched. Blood began to soak through his shirt.

"You want to talk about making deals?" Enoch said, eyes so black they made the night seem bright. "I made a lot of them, Carlos—deals with every devil who would listen. You cut my daughter into pieces and I'm going to do the same to you, first here, and then down in hell, for every minute of eternity."

Aguilar shot Enoch twice more in the chest and then once in the forehead. The force of the gunshots knocked Enoch down, blood flying, as Aguilar rapidly pulled the trigger on an empty chamber.

Enoch lay on the ground, half-curled into fetal position, chuffing with laughter as blood drooled from his lips.

"*Guillermo!*" Aguilar shouted, and the scarred man rushed over to hand him an assault rifle.

He turned the gun on Enoch, bullets erupting from the barrel, blowing holes in the little conjuror at close range, turning his body to bloody wreckage. When the gunfire stopped, it echoed out across the desert and the smell of oil and cordite floated on the air. The good citizens of Lansdale, Texas, now so very far from home, wept and prayed, and Alma Hawkins fell to her knees and sobbed loudly, cradling her belly in both arms.

Zeke felt tethered to Savannah by some invisible umbilical. Carefully, not wanting to spook Aguilar or draw attention to his daughter, he started moving toward her. Harry Boyd stood by Savannah with his son, visibly struggling against the urge to fight back.

No, Harry. No, don't do it please don't do it, Zeke thought.

"Damn. That's too bad," Aguilar said, scanning the faces of his prisoners and then looking beyond them, to his men. "It would've been pretty useful, being able to bring you sad *culeros* back from the dead if necessary, but I guess we'll have to make use of the dead folks we've got right here."

Ice ran through Zeke's veins. He couldn't breathe, could only stare at Aguilar's grinning face.

"Nothing like slave labor," Aguilar said, admiring the size of Big Tim Hawkins. "Especially when the rest of the world thinks they're dead anyway and nobody's gonna come looking for them."

Aguilar's grin turned sly. He approached Harry and Charlie Boyd and Zeke froze, trying to will the killer away, wishing him upon anyone else, damning any of the others to whatever suffering might be in store as long as Savannah could live.

Not again.

But Aguilar waved Harry aside with the assault rifle and—eyes downcast with shame—Harry gave Charlie a shove and let the devil pass.

"Beautiful," Aguilar said. "Some of them might be more useful than others." He reached out with his left hand to caress Savannah's brown cheek, tracing a finger along the freckles on the bridge of her nose.

Zeke was sure he saw her wince. It felt like a trigger in his heart.

"Don't you fucking touch her, you son of a bitch!" he roared, rushing at Aguilar. "You killed her once! Isn't that enough?!"

A big hand grabbed his arm, holding him back, and Zeke whipped around to see that Vickers had finally woken from the fog of his grief. Vickers shook his head, eyes pleading with Zeke to say nothing more. But Zeke knew nothing he did would make a difference in the end.

"Enough?" Aguilar said. "I guess not."

Zeke screamed as Aguilar shot Savannah in the chest and belly.

As she crumpled to the ground, he tore free of Vickers' grasp and lunged. Aguilar turned and the gun barked again, three or four rounds stitching across Zeke's chest; the pain searing through him was nothing compared to the anguish in his soul.

He fell face first, kicking up dust as he skidded in the dirt on his stomach. The smell of his own blood filled his nostrils, his vision already dimming.

Unable to do more than twitch and loll his head to one side, he watched as Aguilar backed out of the gap among his prisoners. The rest of the cartel killers tightened the circle, wolves finally drawing near at the scent of blood.

"Fuck it," Aguilar said. "Kill them all."

The gunfire seemed almost quiet compared to the screams.

~9~

Zeke drew a long, gasping breath, eyelids dragging open. He could feel the chilly night air on his face but nothing else, save for a dreadful heaviness, as if his body had been submerged in fresh cement. His breaths came at long intervals, wet and ragged, each of them a chore. His mouth opened and closed and he forced himself to take a single breath through his nose.

The copper stink of blood filled his head and he squeezed his eyes shut, trying to clear his vision, only to discover that the blurriness and the blackness that seeped in at the corners of his eyes would not go away. The stars above him were dimming, the moonlight fading. A rush of sound filled his ears and he felt himself flinch, but when he took another breath, he realized the barrage of thunder was nothing but the memory of gunfire, that the bullets were now only ghosts, their voices echoing across the desert.

Dying, he thought, the cold weight on his chest heavier. Zeke strained to move and succeeded in shifting his body just enough to feel things tearing inside him. He didn't have the strength to scream.

Savannah, he thought. My baby girl. I'm sorry. I hope you're with your mother now.

The cold weight of his flesh began to lift and he felt a lightness spread through him. His head lolled to one side, the shadows that veiled his eyes deepening. Yet he saw the bodies that lay around him and recognized the long bone pipe clutched in one ruined hand. The blood smears originally painted onto the pipe had been obscured by a new flow of blood, and the hand-carved pipe seemed to soak it in.

So much for the hoodoo man.

But then the bloody hand twitched. Enoch had been torn apart by bullets, body a blood-soaked mess, but now his fingers gripped the pipe and he sat up. Through darkening vision, Zeke watched Enoch bring the pipe to his lips. A portion of the little man's skull had been obliterated, but his eyes glowed with bright golden light as he began to play a variation on those same, ugly, powerful notes.

Zeke felt nothing.

He forgot to breathe.

He did not close his eyes, but they went dark, nevertheless.

~10~

When his eyes open, his first reaction is relief. The ceiling overhead is the ceiling of his bedroom, with the frosted glass dome light fixture that Anarosa had chosen for the room. He closes his eyes again, just for a moment, and lets out a wheezy breath of gratitude before opening them again.

Not dead.

But then he tries to move and cannot manage it. Not a twitch. Fear floods through him and he thinks about where the bullets struck and realizes that he is paralyzed, that one of them must have severed his spine.

Someone moves off to the left of his bed. He hears a soft female sigh and thinks for just a moment that it must be Skyler...and then she moves toward him, standing beside the bed, filling his field of vision, and he sees that it is not.

It's Savannah, whole and beautiful, alive and well. Her hair is tied back tightly and she wears no makeup, but she is so pretty that it fills his heart just to see her. His baby girl. Tears spill from her eyes as she gazes down at him and he wants to take her hand, to hold her and speak a father's love for his daughter, but he is frozen.

"Oh, Daddy, I'm sorry," she says, voice breaking. "It was the only way."

Only when she lifts it to her lips does he see the small bone pipe in her hand, his name scrawled upon it in her blood.

A figure moves to the foot of the bed and he realizes that it is Enoch, also whole and healed.

And Savannah begins to play.

STORY NOTES

THE ABDUCTION DOOR

Writer and editor Mark Morris has been one of the champions of the non-themed anthology for years now. As an editor of anthologies myself, I know how difficult it has become to persuade a publisher to take a change on any anthology, and non-themed anthologies are even harder to sell. Mark has been persistent and skilled enough to become a regular purveyor of such treasures, and when an opportunity comes along to write for a non-themed anthology, it's wise not to pass it up. For *New Fears* (2017), Mark Morris asked contributors for their best, and I like to think I gave him what he asked for. This is among my favorites of all the stories I've written. I remember the rush I felt as I wrote it and the satisfaction I felt upon completion. It's so rare that I've written anything at all that leaves me with that feeling. I loved it, and I hope you did, too.

As for where it came from—who knows? I've seen those little doors in elevator walls from time to time, certainly some kind of access hatch for repairs or something. But I remember talking to someone, possibly Tom Sniegoski or Jim Moore, about that little door and saying "You know what that is? That's the Abduction Door," and the whole story just popped into my head. My family will tell you I've a bad habit of taking any mundane thing and twisting it by adding "And then (insert horrible thing here)." This is probably the best example of that bad habit, and it makes me very happy.

WENDY, DARLING

In 2014, Jonathan Maberry's anthology OUT OF TUNE presented an array of very dark stories inspired by folk ballads. I chose a particularly nasty one entitled "The Cruel Mother," about a woman who covers up her indiscretions by murdering her own children. The story combines elements of the story at the heart of the folk song and merges it with a new take on the characters and story in J.M. Barrie's *Peter Pan*, a story also at the heart of my early novel, *Straight on 'til Morning*. I read this one aloud at Boskone a few years ago with Joe Hill in the audience. Afterward, Joe complimented the story and there was something about the way he delivered it that suggested to me that he felt maybe I was better at this writing thing than he'd previously thought. If my interpretation of that exchange is wrong, I hope he never tells me, because it was a nice moment.

IT'S A WONDERFUL KNIFE

I'm being as open as I can be in this little write-ups, so here's a confession. Years ago, when Tom Sniegoski was writing his Remy Chandler urban fantasy series, I suggested he do one set at Christmas and call it *Hark!*

The Herald Angels Scream. Our dear friend and editor Ginjer Buchanan dismissed the idea and the title with typical razor-sharp derision, but I never stopped loving the title. So many of my projects have been born from offhand comments and jokes. Years later, Tom and I were on the phone and he just tossed out the suggestion that I take the title and edit a Christmas horror anthology and let him write a story for it. I loved the idea and immediately ran with it, and I think it even have been on that same phone call that I joked that I would write a story for the anthology called "It's a Wonderful Knife." (For the handful of you who may not realize it, this is a reference to the James Stewart-starring classic Christmas film *It's a Wonderful Life*.)

I'd written a story years before called "The Hiss of Escaping Air," which appeared as a chapbook from PS Publishing, timed with my appearance as a Guest of Honor at FantasyCon in the U.K. That story had its roots in a true experience, a meeting that Mike Mignola and I had in the Hollywood hills. My manager drove us up to the mansion of a legendary film producer whose self-absorption and bizarre behavior made him impossible to forget. He became my model for James Massarsky, the producer in these stories, who has a museum-worthy collection of Hollywood oddities and memorabilia, including some items with occult or supernatural folk tales around them. As soon as I came up with the title "It's a Wonderful Knife," this story—the second about The Massarsky Collection—practically wrote itself.

WHAT HAPPENS WHEN THE HEART JUST STOPS

Jonathan Maberry had struck a deal with the Horror Writers Association for him to edit a Young Adult horror anthology, SCARY OUT THERE (2016), and he'd invited me to contribute. It had been a good few years since the last time I wrote YA, but I'd been toying with something for a while—a story about a dark future where the separations in our society had become even more explicit, where if you were one of the privileged you didn't have to worry about your health at all, but if you were without that privilege, a simple heart attack would be a death sentence. But I'd also had this idea about a different sort of vampire, a monster I could see when I closed my eyes. I called them "Cloaks," and I've been wanting to do something more with this story and with these monsters ever since. Maybe someday.

THE REVELERS

I start out this story with something like "We've all had that friend," but maybe we haven't. Maybe you're lucky enough that you haven't, but I'll say it plainly—I sure as hell have. Up until the moment it turns really weird, supernaturally weird, "The Revelers" is more or less a true story. Most of us will have someone in our lives at some point or another who we really ought to leave behind. Like the theme of this collection's title, there are people and places and imagined obligations that haunt us, too, and we've got to find the strength to leave those ghosts behind. It can be agonizingly difficult to break away from someone who claims to be your friend, even when they've proven again and again that they have zero idea what friendship means. But becoming a healthy, mature adult includes having the spin to set firm boundaries and to stop rewarding bad behavior with your attention. Sometimes you just have to leave the party. I tend to frown on editors who include their own stories in anthologies they're editing. The second time I did it was so that I could write a story called "It's a Wonderful Knife," and that was a massive self-indulgence. With "The Revelers," I had sold an anthology called DARK CITIES (2017) to Titan Books, and the publisher made it a condition of the deal that I write a new story for the book. I'm glad they did.

A HOLE IN THE WORLD

Australian horror publisher Geoff Brown has been putting together his SNAFU anthologies for years. They're all military horror stories and can best be summed up by writing out the meaning of SNAFU—"situation normal, all fucked up." Geoff had approached both Tim Lebbon and myself to write a story for his upcoming SNAFU anthology, UNNATURAL SELECTION (2016). Tim and I had already collaborated many times, and we decided to ask Geoff if we could join forces for this one and produce a novelette instead of two separate short stories. Geoff readily agreed, and Tim and

I quickly brainstormed "A Hole in the World," exactly the kind of creepy action horror story we'd be first in line to see if somebody made it a film. I love the monsters in this one and still think they'd look fantastic onscreen. I generally pick one collaboration to include in my solo collections, and as much as I love the friend and collaborators I've worked with on other such stories (most of them collected in my book *Don't Go Alone*), there was no doubt in my mind that this would be the one to include here. It's just so damn much fun!

THE CURIOUS ALLURE OF THE SEA

I've been fishing, but I'm not a fisherman. I've been on plenty of boats, but I don't know how to sail. Even so, I feel connected to the ocean in a way that's difficult to put into words. Just the sight of the waves will bring me a wonderful peace. I enjoy walking along the ocean in midwinter as much as—sometimes even more than—sitting on the beach and reading a book. Aside from an interest in erasing the toll the passing years have taken, if I could go back to my youth again one of the few things I would do differently is spend more time by the ocean, or at sea. In high school, I briefly considered joining the navy, but that lasted only a couple of hours before I remembered how I tend to respond to authority. If you've read more than a couple of my books or stories, you're likely to have come across at least one that focuses on the mystery, danger, and fascination of the ocean. So when Ellen Datlow asked me to write a story for her anthology

THE DEVIL AND THE DEEP, I jumped at the chance. "The Curious Allure of the Sea" takes the phenomenon implied by the title to a more extreme level. The story also features a tattoo with its own mysterious power, and not long after the story I went and got my first tattoo, which resembles the one in the story.

THE FACE IS A MASK

The third story about The Massarsky Collection, "The Face is a Mask" is the most straightforward of the three. It's an homage to precisely the kinds of horror movies described in the story, and to various 1970's films you'll likely find on Shudder, including many Italian giallo horrors by the likes of Mario Bava, Lucio Fulci, and Dario Argento. In retrospect, I should have injected a more direct giallo influence and Italian origin to the film we're revisiting in the story, but alas it's too late for that.

While I was putting together the anthology *Hark! The Herald Angels Scream*, I attended World Fantasy Convention in Columbus, Ohio. One afternoon, having coffee with Ellen Datlow, I told her about that anthology and when I grinned and revealed the title, she groaned. Her facial expression was half scowl and half grin. "Oh, no. That's awful!" she said. My response: "Wait until I tell you the name of the story I wrote for it!" The bad Christmas horror puns caused Ellen physical pain, but we were both laughing. You'd better believe that when I wrote this story for Ellen's anthology FINAL CUTS (2020), I struggled to find the right title. I didn't want to hurt her with any more bad puns. Fortunately, she liked both the title and the story of this one to include it in that anthology.

THE OPEN WINDOW

Jonathan Maberry put out a call for stories for an anthology that would eventually be called DON'T TURN OUT THE LIGHTS. While Jonathan's book is an homage to the famous SCARY STORIES TO TELL IN THE DARK books of horror stories for kids, I'd like to think "The Open Window" is scary for all ages. It's one of the shortest stories I've ever written and also one of my absolute favorites. I'm not usually a "happy" writer, by which I mean that some writers really enjoy the process and others still love doing it but find it more like real work. I'm one of the latter, but not with this story. As with "The Abduction Door," I loved every second of writing this story. I felt deliciously malevolent, thinking of the little kids I hoped to frighten with the story. If it creeps out grownups, too, all the better.

THE BAD HOUR

I wrote a great deal about "The Bad Hour" in my introduction to this book, so I won't go into too much detail, but I should say something about the concept. I've always loved mythology and folklore and that love is woven all through the books and comics and stories I've written over the past three decades. While I'm doing research for one project, I'll invariably stumble on a dozen other things that intrigue me enough to want to work them into something else down the line. I have printed articles in a pile on my desk, story concepts and idea bulbs in files on my computer. Books and books of folklore and monsters. The result of this is that I'm never at a loss for story ideas or at least for fascinating prompts that might become an interesting story if I can do something fun with it. The concept behind "The Bad Hour" is an existing bit of folklore, but the fun part is finding out just how devious you can be when you twist it for your own purposes.

PIPERS

I'm an excitable human. My bibliography is full of things that started with a conversation that included "wouldn't it be cool if...." PIPERS had its origin in a chat I was having with Jonathan Maberry at one convention or another. I suspect it was at Necon, but I can't be sure. We were discussing how frequently writers landed on the same themes or even basic plots, and how often we'd been working on something only to see a movie trailer or a book announcement for something similar. It's easy to get discouraged when such a thing happens, but writers must remember that it's your story, it's you who is going to make the difference. Chances are that your spin on any basic concept is going to be vastly different from whatever else is out there—at least if you're using your imagination, it will be. At some point, intrigued by the topic, I suggested an experiment—four writers would take the same basic concept, a single line, and write an original horror novella. We wanted it to be a familiar trope, all the better to explore. A stranger comes to town and offers to raise the townspeople's dead loved ones from the grave—for a price. Jonathan and I enlisted Kelley Armstrong and David Liss and sold the book to Gallery, an imprint of Simon & Schuster, as *Four Summoner's Tales*. For my story, I focused not on the how of the resurrections, but on the why. If you had the opportunity to bring a lost loved one back from the dead in exchange for the resurrectionist "borrowing" that person for a single task—after which it would be as if they'd never died—would you do it? I'm not going to lie, I'd do it in a heartbeat. I love a good pulpy tale of supernatural vengeance. Hopefully PIPERS fits the bill.

CPSIA information can be obtained
at www.ICGtesting.com
Printed in the USA
LVHW081912180322
713806LV00015B/323/J

9 781949 140286